GONE DOG

Carol Angel

This is a work of fiction. Names, places, characters and incidents are products of the author's imagination or, if real, are used fictitiously.

GONE DOG. Copyright © 2018 by Carol Angel

k edition 2018
ed States of America

ISBN 978-0-9996952-0-3

GONE DOG

Carol Angel

We tell ourselves stories in order to live.
Joan Didion

Things are not untrue
just because they never happened.
Dennis Hamley

There's no one thing that's true. It's all true.
Ernest Hemingway

PART ONE

Fact: *Life as a teen is a magical journey of
discovery and growth.*
Alternative Fact: *Life as a teen is a curse.*

PROLOGUE

BR (Before Ruby), I never paid much attention to
girls. I'd rather play ball or have a good wrestling match
with my best buddy, Oliver.

Ruby changed all that. She had long red hair and
glittery dark eyes, and she trash-talked me. Sweet.

But what really made her irresistible was that she
was wild. By that, I mean she did whatever she wanted,
anytime, anywhere.

At my house, I was expected to obey the rules, of
which there were too many. The idea of NO rules opened
up a whole new universe.

Naturally, I fell for Ruby big time. What happened
then shouldn't happen to a dog, but it did.

1

Call me Puppins. That's been my name ever since a
car ran over me in Seattle and wiped my brain as clean
as a whiteboard.

My nose got damaged, too. I don't need a nose job or
anything, but unlike most Labrador retrievers, I can't
smell a billion times better than a human can.

Other than that, I'm a pretty ordinary Lab, except for

a quirk or two that I'll confess later. Right now, I'm just going to reveal stuff on a "need-to-know" basis.

First Need-to-Know: I'll start my story with Ruby. She's an Irish setter. They're a great-looking breed, of course, but kind of stuck on themselves. Skittish, and not good at obedience. At least that's what Kristin says, and Ruby was a pretty good example of that.

Second Need-to Know: Kristin is my owner. Her mom is the veterinarian who saved my life after that car hit me. Dr. Holly couldn't find my owner, so she named me Puppins and shipped me to Los Angeles to live with Kristin.

Lucky dog, you're probably thinking. True. In L.A., unlike Seattle, the sun shines almost every day. There are some super beaches where a dog can run free without getting arrested. A lot of big movie stars live here too, like those Chihuahuas in Beverly Hills.

I like L.A., and Kristin gives me a good home. She does have too many rules, like I said, and some unfortunate character flaws (more on that later). But for the most part, she is okay.

Third Need-to-Know: At the time I met Ruby, I was bored with my life. Nothing much happened except eat, sleep, catch a ball, sleep, eat, walk, sleep, catch a ball, sleep, eat, sleep. You get the idea. Those are all good things, of course, but where's the adventure?

AR, action and drama filled my world. And isn't that how life in Los Angeles is supposed to be?

Sadly, I found out the hard way that drama has a definite downside. Almost getting killed *again,* for example. (The hit-and-run in Seattle was the first near-death experience.)

Cats may have nine lives, but how many lives does a dog get?

Fourth Need-to-Know: Like most Labs, I am friendly by nature. Still, some people are scared of me, just because I am the proverbial "big black dog" and I bark a lot.

Take our mailman. He stopped putting mail in the box on our porch just because I barked hello to him every day. Kristin had to move the mailbox up by the front gate, and she was not pleased.

Anyway, I am not at all fierce. In fact, according to Jodi (Kristin's best friend), I have a Velcro heart, which means it latches onto things and won't let go.

I guess that's what happened with Ruby. But Ruby was nonstick, like those pans Jodi bakes on. Cookies slide right off and sometimes drop on the floor, which pretty much makes my day.

Fifth Need-to-Know: There's a darker side to me: I'm a teenager. Kristin thinks I'm somewhere between 2 and 3 years old, which puts me in the danger zone in human years.

Apparently we teens have the occasional lapse in judgment, and make the odd bad choice. We also have a whipsaw of emotions, wagging our tails one minute, then snarling at our best buddy the next.

When Kristin and Jodi talk about their teen years (which evidently weren't that long ago), they say they were "ruled by hormones," and that's what made them do stupid stuff.

So it's possible that my teen hormones are what got me in trouble. Anyway, it's as good an excuse as any.

2

There's another thing you should know about me: I have some mysteries in my life. For example, because of that accident, I have no clue who I really am or who my first owner was.

I've come up with some possible scenarios. Maybe I belonged to an owner who couldn't deal with my puppy-ish ways. One dark night, she dumped me in another neighborhood. "Someone will take you in and you'll have a wonderful life," she told me, stripping off my collar and slamming the car door behind me. Then I got run over.

Or maybe my first owner was a gangster who made me wear a spiked collar and told me to "Kill!" when he gave the command. Instead, I jumped up on the target and licked his face. The gangster put me in a body bag and ditched me in a graveyard, where I got hit by a hearse.

I could go on, but you get the picture.

And here's another unsolved mystery: Why do scraps of books and poems sometimes pop up in my brain, like mutant kernels in a batch of microwave popcorn?

I don't say them out loud, so I guess that makes me a closet nerd. I'm not sure my friends could embrace dog nerdery.

Anyway, it doesn't take a genius to figure out that I must have heard this stuff before I got hurt, but who told it to me? I'm guessing it was not the gangster.

Getting these brain-bombs is strange, for sure. But

don't all Labrador retrievers have a few quirks?

For example, there's the tennis ball thing. Labs never get tired of retrieving tennis balls. Literally. We. Never. Get. Tired. I guess that's why we're called retrievers.

Anyway, I mention my weirdness because Mariah says it's important to be "authentic," even if you are a geek or a dork. Or a nerd.

Who is Mariah, you ask? Later.

***

Okay. On with my story. In the beginning of the Ruby era, Kristin and I lived in a little house she called The Cottage.

It was in a sketchy part of L.A. (which, by the way, is not just mansions and movie studios). Our neighborhood was what Kristin called "transitional," which meant that it used to be nice, and someday it might be nice again. Maybe.

Kristin told people that The Cottage was falling apart when she bought it, but it was all she could afford. She was determined to have her own home, even though she was just out of college and she works for a newspaper.

(Kristin says newspapers pay their writers peanuts and expect them to work like indentured elephants. Someday, she jokes, she'll be a famous author and sell her books to the movies, and we'll be rich. Ha. Hasn't happened yet.)

Anyway, it took a while, but Kristin managed to fix up that relic and give it a second life. You might say she rescued The Cottage, just like she (and her mom, the Seattle vet) rescued me.

Kristin is a good person, for sure. But she does have those flaws that I mentioned earlier.

For one, she is super rigid about my food. No doggy treats, no canned dog food, no people food. Just that tasteless dry kibble that veterinarians like to push. I know it's nutritious and all that, but do vets ever eat it? I rest my case.

Kristin has a lot of rules, like I said earlier. There's no getting on her bed. Or the sofa or the chairs. No chewing on things. No drinking out of the toilet. No begging, no stealing stuff off the table. No digging holes in the yard.

The list of no's goes on and on. It seems like no matter what I do, Kristin is right there, yelling, "Puppins! No!" It's depressing, and it gives me heartburn.

Another thing: She's a neat freak. I think a home should have a little clutter, a few dog toys and rawhides lying around. Crumbs to lick up, shoes to chew on. That kind of thing.

At our house, everything is picked up and in its proper place. That's unnatural, in my opinion.

Unbelievably, Kristin actually likes to vacuum. She says it helps her unwind after a long day at the newspaper.

I hate that beast. I hide under the bed when she turns it on, and I don't come out until she kills it and buries it back behind the washer.

Actually, the only thing that's messy about Kristin is her hair. Her friends call it tousled, which seems to be a compliment. But in my opinion, she looks like a blonde, blue-eyed, afghan hound that's been caught in a windstorm without a comb. I guess she doesn't like to be groomed.

***

Kristin has one more flaw, and it's her biggest: she is a workaholic. At the newspaper, it's dog-eat-dog (pardon the expression), and she has to work long hours so she can get a lot of bylines, whatever those are.

And when she's home, she's always cleaning or working on the house or digging in the garden. Not much time for her loyal dog, who pines to be petted and played with. Labs need a lot of attention.

She's actually somewhat better now, but at the time I'm telling about, it was really bad. I don't like to whine, but when you add on the "rules" thing and her other flaws, life for me was pretty grim.

One Last Need-to-Know: The whole reason I'm telling this embarrassing tale is because of Mariah. I mentioned her earlier. She's a greyhound runaway who heads up a secret hideout for strays.

Mariah wants me to be a storyteller like her. She believes that we animals should share our stories so we can learn from each other.

I don't know if anyone could learn anything worthwhile from all the trouble I got myself into, but I told Mariah I'd give it a try.

And that's what I'm doing. However, I don't think she'd like the way I'm doing it. She says stories should be told in a logical way, not by jumping all over the place like a crazed Jack Russell terrier.

So I guess I should start over. Maybe with why joining Ruby on the run was a really bad idea.

Still, if I hadn't gone off with her, I'd be clueless about a lot of things. Like how to survive on the backstreets of L.A. And how it feels to ditch all the rules and make out in the shadows with someone you're nuts about.

And, if not for Ruby, I'd never have met Mariah. Or Felicity. Or Loofah, or Mr. Pegasus or Oglalla Sue, or ...

Wait. I'm jumping ahead again.

"Down, boy!" I tell my inner Jack Russell. "Take a deep breath. Start over."

3

Okay. This time I'll begin with Jodi. As I said, Jodi is Kristin's best friend. If Jodi was a dog, I think she'd be a toy poodle. She's small, smart, has dark curly hair, dark skin and bright eyes, and she's usually the center of attention (in a good way).

Sometimes Jodi holds my face between her hands, looks deep into my eyes and says, "Puppins, there's nothing in that big head of yours, is there! You have no brain."

Harsh. Still, I know she loves me. She pets me a lot, and when Kristin isn't looking, she lets me jump up on the sofa beside her. Then she rubs my belly until Kristin makes me get down.

Now and then, Jodi even slips me one of those red licorice ropes she keeps in her bag. She says red ropes are her favorite forbidden treat. Mine, too.

It's possible that what Jodi says about my brain is true. Still, how do you explain that stuff from books and poems that sometimes pops into my head?

It doesn't happen a lot, but it did happen at Jodi's, the very first time I saw Ruby.

Jodi had called Kristin earlier with the news. Kristin, multitasking as usual, put Jodi on speakerphone and I heard every word.

"Kristin, you won't believe it! This gorgeous Irish setter just trotted up my steps today! She was hungry, so I gave her some leftovers. She's really incredible!"

"What are you going to do?" Kristin asked. "Have you called the Humane Shelter to see if she's been reported missing?"

"Yeah. No reports. And she's not wearing a collar. I think she's up for grabs. Listen, I need you and Puppins to go with me on a dog-outfitting expedition."

Kristin said okay and hung up.

I guess Jodi had a dog-sized hole in her heart just then, and Ruby seemed like a perfect fit: big, beautiful, just sitting on her doorstep.

As we say in L.A., it was karma.

**

Jodi lives in one of those tiny white houses that hang on the Los Angeles hills like decorations on a Christmas tree.

She likes to dramatize, so I was not expecting much. Then I saw this magnificent dog. She stood with Jodi at the bottom of the hill, a jump rope tied around her neck for a leash.

"This is Ruby," Jodi exclaimed. "Isn't she awesome?"

Awesome for sure! A weird sensation shot through me like that time I chewed on an electric cord. Only this time, Kristin didn't yell at me that I almost set the house on fire.

As I said earlier, girls didn't usually get my attention. But Ruby was different. Tall and proud like a show dog, her coat blazed in the setting sun, as red as the bougainvillea tumbling wild over Jodi's hillside.

Some words flashed across my brain: She will *burn, burn, burn like fabulous roman candles, exploding like spiders across the stars*.*

*Brain bomb citations: see pp 275-280.

9

I don't know where those words came from, but looking back, maybe they were a kind of warning: "She is hot, and you're going to get burned." So true.

Jodi climbed in the backseat of our car and pulled Ruby in after her.

"Ruby, this is Puppins," she said. "Puppins, Ruby. You two are going to be the best of friends."

Wow. I certainly hoped so.

***

As soon as Jodi and Kristin got out of the car at the pet store, I jumped into the backseat next to Ruby.

Jodi scolded me. "Puppins, what are you doing? Be nice. No fighting."

"Puppins fight?" Kristin laughed. "He's about as dangerous as a newborn kitten." Still, she made me get up front again, telling me to "stay."

After rolling the windows down a bit and locking the doors, she and Jodi disappeared inside the store.

I peered over the seat at Ruby.

"Do you live around here?" I asked.

Smooth opening, huh.

She ignored me, pacing back and forth across the seat. Then she stuck her nose through the cracked window, sniffing anxiously at the outside air.

"Is there any way to get out of here?" she growled in a low voice.

"No. Kristin always locks the car so no one can steal me."

She eyed me coldly. "Seriously?" she snapped. "Who would want to steal *you*?"

Ouch. That was harsh. But I wanted her to keep talking, even if it was trash talk. I forged ahead.

"Have you been to Jodi's before?" I asked.

"Don't be stupid. I never go to the same place twice."

Double ouch. She called me stupid. My pride took

another hit, but I couldn't stop myself from bumbling on.

"Where's your home?"

"Wherever. Stop. You ask too many questions." Collapsing on the seat, she put her head down on her paws and shut her eyes.

I kept quiet, hard as that was. But I could not help staring at her.

She was the most coolicious dog I ever saw. I don't know if that's a real word, but it says it all.

***

Kristin and Jodi returned, loaded down with bags. Jodi dumped them out on the back seat: blue leather leash and matching collar (blue went well with Ruby's red coat, Jodi explained). Bowls for food and water. Chewable vitamins, flea repellant, brush and comb. King-sized rawhide bones; toys, including a rolled-up rubber newspaper that squeaked when Jodi squeezed it. Dog treats, and *canned* food!

"I hope you'll like this stuff," said Jodi, patting Ruby's head fondly. Ruby turned away, resuming her vigil by the window.

When we got back to Jodi's, I stayed in the car while Kristin helped get Ruby and the provisions up the steep hillside steps.

"Let me know how her first night goes," Kristin called to Jodi as we drove away.

***

That night, I had trouble going to sleep. Maybe it was the delicious-looking bugs I'd foolishly devoured in the yard that morning, but I didn't think so. I was pretty sure it was those fireworks that Ruby set off in my brain.

4

"She tried to escape last night!" Jodi announced when she came over the next evening. "But I outsmarted her."

Ruby, sporting her blue collar and leash, trailed sulkily behind, not looking me in the eye.

"I guess she's not used to her new home yet," Jodi added.

"Maybe she misses her old one," Kristin commented drily. "Did you call the Humane Shelter again? Have you checked the online lost-and-found?"

"Yeah, yeah. I did all that. No one's looking for her. Probably some irresponsible creep dumped her in my neighborhood."

"Who would dump a beautiful dog like that?" Kristin asked.

"It happens more than you'd think," Jodi replied. "Someone can't keep a pet, and instead of finding it a new owner or taking it to a shelter, they drive to another neighborhood and turn it loose. They tell themselves it will find a new family. Wishful thinking, usually."

Wait. Wasn't that one of my scenarios for what happened to me in Seattle? Did Ruby and I share a common history? Just the thought of that possibility gave me a perverse kind of thrill.

Jodi went on. "Ruby wasn't wearing a collar when she showed up, right?"

"Right," Kristin admitted. "Anyway, what happened last night?"

"Well, it was hot when I went to bed, so I left my front door open a little. I woke up when I heard the floorboards creak. She was headed for the door, but I beat her to it."

I glanced at Ruby and saw a defiant gleam in those incredible eyes.

"How about today? How did she get along while you were at work?" Kristin asked.

Jodi hesitated, then told the sad tale. That morning, after brushing Ruby and giving her breakfast, Jodi locked her inside the house.

When she returned from work, all was chaos: chairs overturned, doors scratched, evidence of repeated escape attempts.

"Oh, my!" Kristin exclaimed. "What did you do?"

"I opened the door and sang 'Born Free!' I thought if she wanted to get out that much, I'd just let her go. But she didn't leave, so I'm taking that as a sign of commitment."

Kristin shook her head and laughed. "Maybe she was still hungry and saw those cans of dog food on the counter."

"That too," Jodi agreed reluctantly. "Anyway, she'll get acclimated. I don't think we'll have any more trouble."

I had my doubts. Still, I wondered: Why didn't she leave when Jodi gave her the chance?

***

Next evening, Kristin got a frantic call from Jodi. "I need your help! Ruby didn't escape, but she pretty much trashed the house again. Worse than yesterday."

"Oh, no! Do you want me to help clean up?"

"No, that's done. I want you to help me put up a fence."

"Tonight? Can't it wait until Saturday?"

"No. We've got to do it tonight. It won't take long. I'll get one of those prefab fencing kits." As I have long observed, if Jodi sets her mind on something, there's no talking her out of it.

She came over with Ruby in a borrowed truck. Ruby's face wore a dark expression, and she wouldn't look me in the eye.

We drove to LumberMaid and as soon as Kristin and Jodi went inside, I turned to Ruby.

"Why don't you like it at Jodi's? She bought you all that good stuff, and she'd never be mean to you. She's a little weird, but ..."

Ruby broke in. "I should have left when she gave me the chance, but I thought I'd have one more good meal. Anyway, I'm getting out of there as soon as I can."

"But where will you go?"

"Anywhere. What difference does it make?"

I had no answer. I didn't get it. But it was shaping up to be a continuous battle of wills, and I pinned my hopes on Jodi winning the war.

***

We went to Jodi's with the fencing stuff, and she and Kristin worked far into the night.

Jodi tied Ruby to the porch railing, and I stretched out as close to her as I dared.

I noticed that she made my skin itch. Not in a bad way, like fleas, but more like nerves.

While she and I watched the fence going up, I gave her the short version of my life history. The parts I remember, anyway.

She ignored me.

Finally, the fence was done. It was a good and sturdy one, and Jodi was pleased.

**

Next evening, Jodi called Kristin, shouting into the phone. "You'll never guess what happened today -- Ruby escaped from the yard!"

"No! How?"

"She squeezed under a gap in the fence. I can't believe we left a spot where she could do that! Anyway, I fixed it."

"What good is that, if she's gone?"

"I got her back. Some kids caught her and took her around the neighborhood to find her owner. It was so lucky that I was home when they came by!"

"Jodi, does it strike you that this dog may be impossible to keep?"

"She'll get used to being here. I know it. And I've been singing to her."

"What -- 'Born Free' again?"

"No, silly. You know, that country song: 'Ru-beeee, don't take your love to town!'"

**

The day after that, Ruby escaped again. Another undetected gap under the fence. This time, she was not captured by the neighborhood kids.

The Humane Shelter would not give out information over the phone.

"I have to go in and look at the dogs," Jodi told Kristin. "Will you come with me?"

The three of us drove to the shelter. I had to wait in the car, but the kennels were outdoors next to the parking lot, and I could see and hear the whole sad episode.

"Ruby? Ruby!!" Jodi called, as she and Kristin peered

into each kennel. A storm of barking marked their progress, as each lonely dog rushed up to its kennel door.

"Wait -- isn't that her?" Kristin called over the ruckus. She pointed to a large, mud-covered dog lying at the back of a pen, head turned away, nose tucked underneath its paws.

It was the only dog not barking at them, hoping to be freed. The only dog not looking for a home.

"That's not her," Jodi said confidently. "She'd be up here, trying to get to me."

"Was Ruby wearing her new collar?" asked Kristin.

"No, I gave her a bath last night and forgot to put it back on," Jodi admitted ruefully.

Kristin was insistent. "I think that's Ruby. Sing 'Born Free' or 'Rubeee' and see if it responds."

"Stop joking, Kristin. It's not Ruby. Look how beaten and grimy that dog is! Ruby is proud, and she was clean. I just gave her a bath, remember?"

I was pretty sure it *was* Ruby. I barked my head off to get its attention, but it didn't even raise its head.

Finally, Kristin and Jodi gave up, and we drove home in a sad kind of quiet.

***

When Jodi dropped us off, she slipped me a red licorice rope. Even though it's my favorite treat, all I could manage was a feeble wag of my tail before I choked it down.

Jodi stroked my head. "You're a good dog, Puppins. Not smart, but good. You'd never run away from a wonderful home, would you?"

Some words bombed my brain: *Neither have they hearts to stay, nor wit enough to run away.*

I guess Ruby didn't have the heart to stay, but she sure had the wit to run away.

5

After that, I obsessed about the shelter episode all the time. If that was Ruby, what would happen to her? And if it wasn't her, where was she?

Then something came along to distract my mind.

A cat.

She appeared one day in the backyard. I called out to her, but she raced away, a black-and-white streak that vanished under The Cottage.

I stuck my head underneath and gazed into the murky darkness. Finally I saw her, cowering in a corner that was draped with cobwebs.

"Hi," I said, in what I thought was a nonthreatening tone.

"Go away!" she hissed.

"Welcome to The Cottage," I continued. "I'm Puppins. Who are you?"

No answer.

"Kristin will be surprised to see you. You'll like her."

She hissed again.

I persevered. "I won't hurt you. Neither will Kristin. We're cool with cats, although both of us think dogs are better." Again, no reply.

Suddenly, something moved under her matted fur, and three tiny heads poked out, staring curiously at me.

"Kittens!" I exclaimed. "How old are they?"

She shoved them back underneath with a quick paw.

"I'm not sure," she replied in a timid voice.

"Were they born here?"

"Yes."

"How come I've never seen them?

"They can't come out. Too dangerous. Big dogs." She glared at me.

"I'm the only dog around, and I love kittens."

"I'm sure you do," she replied sarcastically.

I decided to change the subject. "Are you getting enough to eat? You're awfully thin. You can share my dog food if you want. It's dry, but Kristin says it's nutritious. You'll have to come inside The Cottage, though."

She shuddered. "No. I find things to eat."

I didn't want to think about what she found to eat, so I changed the subject again.

"Why did you come here to have your babies? Where's your home?"

"Go away! I don't feel like talking." Her voice was sharp again. She shut her eyes and hunched down over her kittens.

After a moment, one of them pushed out again. A miniature gray puffball with white markings. Not a bit afraid. Its mama quickly shoved it back out of sight.

I watched for a long time, hoping the kittens would get away from her. She seemed to sleep, but each time one of them ventured out, an eye flicked open and a paw pulled it back.

Suddenly, a stern, familiar voice rang out behind me: "Puppins! What are you doing?!"

Kristin, home from work. I scrambled up, barking wildly, then sent dirt flying with my front paws, hoping she would look under the house.

"Stop that!" she cried. "Have you cornered a skunk again? Don't you remember what happened last time?"

Yeah, I remembered. I thought it was a cat. When I trotted up to say hello, I got the surprise of my life.

Luckily, Kristin had a can of tomato juice on hand and washed me down with it. Disgusting, but it worked. Animal Control trapped the smelly creature and carted it off to the foothills where it belonged.

Good riddance. I was not that desperate for friends.

***

For the next few days, I stayed on the alert for the cat and her babies, but I only caught an occasional glimpse of the mama. I worried about her. Each day she seemed a little skinnier, and I wondered if she was able to give her kittens enough milk. How long could the little family last?

***

Kristin finally caught sight of the mother while working in the yard.

"A cat!" she exclaimed. "Puppins, look how thin it is!" She ran into the house and came back with a bowl that she set on the back steps.

I went over and sniffed. Tuna! I remembered a tuna sandwich I nabbed once off a picnic table; it tasted great.

I took a quick bite.

"Puppins! Leave that alone!" Kristin scolded, pulling me inside. We watched through the window, but I knew the bowl was too near the back door.

The next day Kristin put out a fresh bowl, this time setting it on the ledge. Sure enough, when the mother returned from her hunt, she stopped, peered around to make sure it was safe, then licked the bowl clean.

Kristin bought a bag of cat food (dry, of course) and put some on the ledge every day, along with a bowl of water. She named the mama Colette, which she told Jodi was the name of a famous French writer who loved cats.

Colette began to fill out, but I still had no luck

making friends with her. I wondered if she would ever get over her fear. Kristin said she was a feral cat, and feral cats are not social.

The kittens, on the other hand, got bolder by the day. Venturing out from under The Cottage, they soon were streaking across the yard, tumbling and scampering as fast as their furry little legs would go.

They discovered the tiny round berries that fell off the carob tree in our front yard. Bumping each other furiously, they batted the carobs around with their paws, like those soccer players I've seen on TV. Hilarious.

Those carobs were popular with our neighborhood birds, too. Especially the flock of wild parakeets. They swooped down every afternoon like a bright green cloud and gorged themselves on the berries.

Kristin says carobs taste kind of like chocolate, so I guess the parakeets had their own chocolate shop. Lucky birds! Their leader was Pepito, who always greeted me with loud squawks that were friendly but hurt my ears.

"Puppeens! Que pasa?"

"Hola!" I'd reply. I only knew a few words of parakeet talk, and that was one. When the parakeets had their fill of carobs, Pepito would screech, "Adios, amigo!" and I'd yell the same thing back at him.

Kristin and the neighbors didn't like the parakeets. Too noisy. But I was always glad to see them. They helped liven up the long hot days while Kristin was at work. The kittens were still shy with me, and I was lonely.

6

With the kittens darting all over the yard, it wasn't long before Kristin spotted them. She immediately called Jodi, who rushed right over.

They knew the kittens must live under the house. They crouched down, flashlights in hand, and did a visual sweep of the dark space.

I flattened myself down next to them. And there the kittens were, tiny fluffballs scampering fearlessly around their frantic mama.

"How precious! We must give them names!" cried Jodi.

"Yes. Umm, let's see. The gray one is ... Butch? No, that doesn't fit. Look at his white bib and spats. He looks like a miniature English gentleman. How about Cecil? Or, I know, Oliver!"

"Oliver. Good," Jodi agree. "And the yellow one with the eyelashes is ... Cleo. Like the goldfish in 'Pinocchio,'" Jodi proclaimed.

"Cool. How about the beautiful black one?"

"Uh... Beyonce? Aretha? Cleopatra? Wait. That's it! We'll call her Patra. Cleo and Patra. Get it?"

Kristin rolled her eyes. "Fine. But how do we know it's a girl?"

"I can just tell. Besides, how do we know Cleo's a girl, or that Oliver is a boy?"

21

"Good point. We'll change their names later if we have to," Kristin said. "Anyway, I guess I'm responsible for them, since they're under my house. I'll have to feed them and take them to the vet for shots, and get Colette spayed. Another litter would be the death of her."

"Yeah. We'll catch her and take her to the spay clinic," Jodi said.

"And when the kittens are old enough, we'll take them too. I especially like Oliver, don't you? He's so adorable. And look, he's coming over to us!"

Oliver was, for sure, creeping our way. He edged up to Kristin and Jodi and nudged their fingers with his little pink nose, inviting them to pet him.

Colette meowed piteously from her dark corner, but it was too late. Oliver had crossed the line.

***

I, the big black dog, was still off-limits to the cat family. But soon, I hoped, the kittens would be brave enough to play with me.

In the meantime, I was bored. While Kristin was at work, I stretched out under the shade of the carob tree and dozed.

When people happened to walk by, I rushed to the gate and barked hello. If they didn't seem afraid, I stuck my nose through to get a pat.

My favorite visitor was Dora, who lived across the street. She reminded me of a friendly Shar-Pei – chubby with a lot of wrinkles.

Dora worked nights at a hospital. During the day, when she saw me in the yard, she would trot over and give me an unauthorized treat.

She'd pat me on the head and say, "Puppins, you are so sweet. I had a sweet dog like you once, but he died." Then tears would spring into her eyes and I would be sad for her.

***

Colette began teaching the kittens how to hunt, and they trailed along on her expeditions like brave little warriors.

Kristin still put out cat chow, but now she placed the bowl on the back porch. It didn't take the kittens long to discover it, and they raced there every day to gobble down the food.

Colette would not venture that close to the backdoor, but Kristin and Jodi had a plan.

Sooner or later, they figured, the shy cat would come up on the porch to eat. Then they would capture her and take her to the vet.

***

It happened one evening. Colette crept up on the porch with the kittens and gulped down some kibble.

Kristin, watching with me through the window, gave me a hug.

"Puppins, we'll catch her soon," she whispered with satisfaction.

Each evening after that, Kristin moved the bowl a little closer to the backdoor, which she left open during feeding time.

Then she put the food just inside the house. Oliver was the first to come in, of course, and soon there was no stopping him.

Puffing out his little gray chest, he marched brazenly through all the rooms. He even sneaked up to me if I was napping and bumped my nose with his.

Cleo and Patra weren't so bold. They came in the house just far enough to eat, then ran quickly back outside.

As for Colette, she stared longingly at the bowl but would not go inside. That went on for several days.

Then once evening, she crossed the threshold and

joined the kittens, bolting down a few bites and then streaking back outdoors.

Kristin called Jodi. "She did it! Come over tomorrow and we'll set up the trap."

***

They called it "Catch Colette" day. Jodi, her eyes gleaming with excitement, lectured Kristin on how to capture wild animals.

"Never look them in the eye," she instructed. "Let yourself enter into their inner being. Be at one with them."

Kristin laughed. "Jodi, what does that mean?"

"I don't know. It's from 'Zen and the Art of Catching a Feral Cat.'"

"Yeah, right. Come on, let's get the trap set up."

She tied a rope to the back doorknob. Then, holding the other end, she crouched behind the doorway between the kitchen and the living room.

Jodi stood by with an old blanket in her arms; an open cardboard cat carrier stood ready on the floor.

I watched with interest, not sure what was going on. Then Kristin saw me and stuck me in her bedroom. Rats. I wanted to be in on the game, whatever it was.

As it turned out, I'm glad I wasn't. It was bad enough hearing things: the backdoor slam, thumps, bumps, bangs, ear-splitting human screams and truly appalling cat yowls.

Kristin: "She's climbing the walls! Throw the blanket over her!"

Jodi: "You do it! She's already scratched me! Look at my arms!"

Kristin: "We're scaring her to death! Throw it over her!"

More thuds, more screeches, more shrieks. It seemed to go on forever.

Finally, a triumphant yell from Jodi: "I've got her! Hold the carrier open while I put her in!"

Whew. It was over. Kristin opened the bedroom door and I rushed straight to the carrier. Pushing my face up against the air holes, I tried to calm Colette. She just mewed pitifully, too terrified to listen.

Jodi and Kristin, their faces grim and streaked with tears, carried her out to the car. I watched through the window as they put the carrier inside and drove off.

I collapsed and closed my eyes. My head ached, my stomach churned. Was Colette going to be okay?

***

When Kristin and Jodi returned, they huddled on the sofa and cried. Turns out the clinic people told them there's an easier way, using an outdoor "humane trap" such as the one that caught the skunk.

***

Kristin brought Collette home the next day. She kept her in the bathroom overnight, then brought the carrier outside and turned her loose. In a flash, she disappeared under the house.

Kristin put food and water for her on the ground next to the opening, then went back in The Cottage.

I stuck my nose underneath and scanned the dark space. The kittens were cuddled up to Colette in the far corner, licking her fur and trying to comfort her.

I knew they must have been really upset when their mama disappeared, and were so relieved to have her back. As for Collette, she already didn't trust people, and this encounter wasn't going to help.

But Kristin said taking her to be spayed and vaccinated was the right thing to do, and her mom's a vet so I guess she knows about such things.

I just wish Jodi had read a different book.

7

One afternoon a few days later, I stretched out on the cool dirt with my head sticking under the house.

I wanted to convince Colette that what happened to her was for her own good.

"I know it's scary going to the vet, and sometimes it hurts," I told her. "My whole body hurt when I woke up from surgery after that car hit me in Seattle. And those shots they gave me hurt too, a little. But Kristin says vets love animals and they do those things to help us."

"I don't see how hurting us could help us," moaned Colette.

"Kristin says those shots keep you from getting sick and maybe dying. And the spaying, well, that's harder to explain, but ...."

I could have gone on about how Kristin's mom told her that she'd neutered me when I was in the hospital, but that would be embarrassing. So I skipped that part.

"You don't want another batch of kittens, do you?" I asked. "Don't they just run off and leave you as soon as they're big enough?"

Harsh, but I had to make a point.

She sighed. "Yes. That's the way of the cat. But I've always been able to have another litter when the nest was empty. What will I do when these three little ones go out on their own?"

I gave this some thought.

"Well, you could become Kristin's pet. She likes cats. She says cats are less trouble and cleaner than dogs. I'm not saying that's true, but I know she would take good care of you. You could live in The Cottage and have a nice retirement."

"Oh no!" Colette cried. "I don't like people. They scare me."

I was puzzled. I only knew people who loved animals. Why was she so afraid?

"I think people are okay, Colette. You just have to trust."

"I can't," she replied, shuddering. She closed her eyes and said no more.

Some words shot through my brain: *I, a stranger and afraid, in a world I never made...*

I don't know where I heard those words, but they sure fit Colette.

***

A few days later, while Kristin was at work, I lay down by the front gate to watch the passing scene.

Nothing happening. Boring.

I was just about to doze off when a familiar shade of red suddenly flashed by.

I sprang up and stuck my nose through the gate.

Ruby!

"Hey, Ruby!" I yelled as loud as I could, but she was gone.

I hadn't seen her for weeks, but that empty space she left inside me was still there.

I had to see her. But how? Leap over the fence? Ha. Labs are not jumpers.

I stared at the gate. Maybe, if I pushed hard, I could make an opening big enough to squeeze through.

I knew it was wrong. I was not supposed to leave the yard. But what would it hurt?

I would just catch up to her, say hello, sniff her great-smelling butt (excuse the explicit description), then head right back home, no one the wiser.

I leaned against the gate and pushed as hard as I could. The gap got wider. Giving it my all, I sucked in my gut and shoved myself through.

Wow. For the first time since that car hit me in Seattle, I was on my own, a free dog.

Sprinting hard, I reached the corner and looked both ways. No Ruby. I kept going, up one street and down the next.

A chorus of barks followed me as I flew past envious, fenced-in dogs. Some kids tried to rein me in, but I dodged them.

I ran, and just kept on running.

The streets were familiar at first from my walks with Kristin. Then they weren't. Still, I didn't stop.

Ruby couldn't be that far away. Maybe just around the next corner.

I had a couple of near-misses, car brakes screeching, drivers yelling curse words at me. I barely noticed. I just ran and ran and ran.

Suddenly I realized I was running in circles. And just at that moment, a well-known blue car turned the corner in front of me. It braked with a loud squeal. The door flew open, and out shot Kristin.

"Puppins! What are you doing here?" she screamed. Grabbing my collar, she dragged me into the car.

She scorched me all the way home. "Shame on you! No walk for you today!"

Ouch. That hurt. But did I learn my lesson?

Are you kidding?

***

Kristin figured out how I escaped and tightened up the gate.

Fine. On to Plan B.

***

The next day, I nosed along the base of the fence until I found a place where the dirt was soft.

Digging furiously, I made a deep hole, crawled underneath and out to the sidewalk.

Free again!

This time, I paid more attention to where I was, and how long I was gone. I managed to get back in the yard just before Kristin got home.

She scrutinized me, shaking her head.

"Puppins, how did you get so dirty? Have you been playing under the house with the kittens?"

She hosed me down. I hardly noticed. My mind was fixated on Ruby.

Tomorrow I would try again. I would keep trying until I found her, no matter how long it took.

I guess that's when I realized that I was hooked.

Some words popped up in my brain, taunting me: *Love, nightmare-like, lies heavy on my chest.*

Sadly, those words felt true.

But wait. Is love supposed to be a nightmare?

***

After that, I became a serial escapee, scrunching myself under the fence day after day on my relentless search for Ruby.

Then one afternoon, as I dragged my sorry carcass back home after yet another failed outing, Dora, sitting on her porch, spotted me.

"Puppins! What are you doing out of the yard?" she cried.

Trotting across the street on her plump little legs, she took hold of my collar and pulled me inside our gate.

"Bad dog, bad dog!" she cried, still petting me like she always did.

Looking at her watch, she said, "Kristin will be home soon. Now you stay here like a nice dog!"

She slipped me a few M&Ms from her pocket, then went back across the street.

Staking herself out again on her porch, eating her M&Ms, Dora watched me like a hawk targeting a fugitive mouse. And when Kristin returned home, she hurried right over.

"Puppins got out of your yard," she announced, "but I caught him and put him back."

"Not again!" Kristin cried. "I wonder if he's been getting out a lot? He seems so tired lately."

"Could be," Dora replied. "Anyway, I'll keep an eye out for him when I'm home."

"Thanks, Dora. I'm going to see if I can figure out how he escaped this time."

Dora helped her, and it didn't take them long to find my lovely hole.

Kristin filled it in with some old bricks, but she was not reassured.

"Oh, Dora, what's to stop him from digging another hole? I don't know what's come over him." She shook her head, a sad look on her face. "I guess I'll have to keep him inside while I'm at work. He can't be trusted in the yard anymore."

Harsh, but true. I had to keep searching for Ruby. But if Kristin was going to pen me up in The Cottage, how was I going to do it?

8

Day One of Dog Detention. I tried to sleep the hours away. No use. I imagined the kittens were mewing at me to come out and play, which they had begun doing.

Then I heard Pepito and his band of wild parakeets, screeching from the carob tree: "Puppeens! Como esta?"

I stood in the window and barked a feeble reply. I could not explain in parakeet words how I'd been banished from the yard.

In frustration, I slunk into Kristin's bedroom to look for something to do. A dress she'd just bought, lying on a chair, caught my attention.

It was blue, like an Australian shepherd's eyes, the same color as hers. It smelled nice, like she does.

I pulled it down and laid my head on it, which made me feel close to her.

But I couldn't get comfortable. Something inside the dress was way too hard, so I thought I'd soften it a little.

After chewing on it for a while, I got rid of the stiffness. Kristin would be grateful. I went to sleep.

***

I woke up to one of the worst of sounds: Kristin yelling at me.

"Puppins! My new dress!" She picked it up and shook

it at me. "Look at this! There's dog hair all over it! And ... and you've shredded the shoulder pads! Bad dog!"

Day Two of DD: Being inside was, like the day before, frustrating. I decided to get the old sneaker Kristin gave me to chew on.

Then I remembered: I had buried it in the backyard, figuring it was dead. Bummer.

I surveyed her closet for a substitute. Hmm. A pair of white sneakers that I never saw before!

Kristin rarely buys shoes for herself; she says she's not a shoe person. I deducted, brilliantly, that these new ones must be for me, to replace the shoe that died.

I attacked one of the sneakers, then the other. New shoes don't taste as good as old ones; they need to be aged. But these were not bad. Not bad at all.

I dozed off. Kristin came home. I guess those sneakers weren't for me after all.

She was so upset that she didn't speak to me all evening, which was even worse than being yelled at.

I tried everything to get her to forgive me. Nothing worked. Not even the silly trick that Jodi had taught me, where I sit in front of her and fall backwards against her legs.

She just pushed me away with an unhappy look on her face.

Day Three: A book with a soft cover was on the coffee table. It appeared used, probably destined for the trash.

I got in trouble again. Need I say more?

Day Four: Kristin shut all the closet doors and dog-proofed the entire house.

"Now you be good!" she yelled as she left. I hate it

when she yells, but at least she was speaking to me.

As always, I had good intentions. But late in the day, I heard a dog barking outside. I imagined it to be Ruby. She was probably calling to me, but there was no way I could get out.

To relieve my anxiety, I checked around to see if Kristin left me a rawhide. She did, but I wolfed it down too quickly. No satisfaction.

Then I notices something in the corner of the living room. It appeared the day before, dropped off by a delivery guy in a brown suit.

Kristin phoned Jodi to tell her about it, calling it a spinning wheel. Jodi came over to see it.

She gave the wheel a few twirls, pressed her foot on something she called the treadle, and said it would be nice to know how to use it.

Kristin told her that her great-grandmother knew how. "Maybe I'll learn someday," she added.

That was it. No big deal.

I lay down and put my head on the treadle part. It had the smell of an ancient bone, like the one I dug up once in the yard, and a few chews revealed that it had the same comforting taste.

When Kristin came home, she cried. I felt like poop.

***

"I don't understand it. Why is Puppins behaving this way?" Kristin asked Jodi when she came over the next day. "He's always been so good."

"Maybe some kind of mid-life crisis. We don't know how old he is, do we?"

"Be serious, Jodi. He's young. He's not having a mid-life crisis."

"Well, maybe he has ADS."

"AIDS? What are you talking about? Dogs don't get AIDS."

"Not AIDS. ADS. Attention Deprivation Syndrome."

"You mean ADHD? Like kids who have short attention spans and can't sit still?"

"No, no. That's Attention Deficit. This is Attention *Deprivation*. It's a dog thing. A dog that's been deprived of attention in its formative stages has a compulsive need to be underfoot and to be constantly petted. That's Puppins, right?"

"Jodi, stop. There's no such syndrome."

"Well, maybe it was Abandoned Dog Syndrome. I forget the exact term. I heard it on that call-in radio show, 'Ask the Vet.'"

"Seriously?"

"Yes. When Dr. Dan described the symptoms, I said to myself, that sounds like Puppins! He was very young when he got hit by that car, right? And he probably had been abandoned. Now he craves a lot of attention. That's the primary symptom of ADS."

"But even if that's true," Kristin replied, "I can't stay home and shower attention on him all day, can I?"

"I think the person calling Dr. Dan had a similar situation. Dr. Dan's advice was to keep the dog in a small, quiet place where he can't get into trouble, and where he'll feel safe and secure. Too much freedom is contraindicated for dogs with ADS.'"

"Stop joking, Jodi."

"I'm not joking, Kristin. It's a good suggestion. Anyway, what do you have to lose? Try it."

"Try what?"

"Put him somewhere that's small, escape-proof and chew-proof."

"Like what?"

"Like ... like your bathroom."

"My bathroom? Get real. It's tiny. He's a big dog. I can't leave him in there all day."

"Why not? He'll be okay. Some dogs live their entire lives in a kennel. That's not a good thing, of course, but your bathroom is roomier than a kennel, right? Anyway, it's only while you're at work. It's better than you being mad at him all the time, isn't it?"

***

So, it was decided. I would stay in the bathroom all day. A few toys, a rawhide, and a bowl of water. That's it.

The next day, pacing round and round in the cramped space, I kept bumping into the cold bathtub and the hard toilet. (It was closed, so I couldn't even get a drink. Drinking out of toilets was traditionally forbidden, of course, but now and then I'd been able to do it.)

Having nothing else to do, I thought about what Jodi had said.

Apparently I was being punished because nobody cared about me or petted me when I was a pup. Is that fair? Is being deprived of affection any reason to deprive me of my freedom?

Some words passed through my brain: *Happiness to a dog is what lies on the other side of a door.*

So true. I've always been unhappy being shut out of the next room. And now, counting the front door, I was stuck all day behind *two* closed doors.

I heard with awful clarity the bark of every dog in the neighborhood. They might be fenced in, but compared to me, they were free.

Worst of all, Ruby might be running past my house at that very moment, looking for me. Little did she know that I was a prisoner for love.

***

Dog Detention went on, day after day. Then one evening, Dora knocked on the door.

I greeted her with leaps of joy and heaps of kisses;

35

she ruffled my ears and slipped me a melt-away wafer when Kristin wasn't looking.

"I never see Puppins in the yard anymore," she said to Kristin.

"I have to keep him inside now, remember?"

"Too bad. I miss coming over and petting him through the fence."

"I'm sure he misses you too, Dora. But he's gotten so bad," Kristin replied, shaking her head.

"You mean escaping from the yard? That's normal. Most dogs try to test their freedom now and then."

"Well, that's not all. He's started chewing up my things."

"That's just a sign of boredom," Dora said. "This sweet dog couldn't be bad."

"Whatever it's a sign of, I can't handle it," Kristin moaned. "The last straw was when he chewed on the spinning wheel my mother gave me. It belonged to my great-grandmother."

"Oh, dear. Did you put it away in a closet where he can't get at it again?"

"Yes, but it's ruined. And it's not the only thing he's chewed. I don't have that many closets! So now I ... I'm keeping him in the bathroom while I'm at work."

Dora's eyes opened wide in shock. "The bathroom? A big dog like Puppins in your little bathroom?"

Tears sprang into Kristin's blue eyes. "What else can I do, Dora? Have a dog that destroys everything I own? Or that runs away and gets lost, or gets hit by a car again?"

Dora didn't answer. Looking troubled, she said goodbye and left.

I felt like a criminal. Was I the proverbial BAD DOG? Was I sentenced to a lifetime of solitary confinement?

All signs pointed that way.

9

A few days later, Dora was back. After she and Kristin exchanged a few words, she said, "Did I ever tell you about my dogs, Skipper and Millie?"

"I didn't know you had dogs, Dora."

"I did. Millie died of old age a few years ago, so I got Skipper to fill the void. Both were special, but Skipper was the best little friend anyone ever had."

"What happened to him?"

"One night he just keeled over and died. The vet said his sweet little heart gave out. He was only 4 years old, so maybe something genetic. There's a lot of bad breeding that goes on, you know."

"Oh Dora, I'm so sorry. What an awful thing to happen!" Kristin gave her a hug.

"My heart was broken," she replied. "I cried for days. I still cry every time I think about it."

Her eyes brimmed with tears. It made me feel sad too. I wished that I could've known Skipper.

Dora wiped her eyes and continued, "I came over to ask you something, Kristin. Ever since you told me about locking Puppins in the bathroom all day, I've been sick about it."

"I feel awful too, Dora, but I don't know what else to do," Kristin replied, her voice filled with sadness.

"Well, I've been thinking. Maybe he could stay with me during the day. I get home from my night shift around 5 a.m. and sleep until noon. You could put him in my yard when you leave for work.

"It's very secure," she added. "My dogs never got out. Then when I get up, I'd bring him inside. He'd be good company for me. Please say yes, Kristin."

"But what if he chews your things?" Kristin asked.

"I don't have a stick of furniture that hasn't been chewed on at some point," said Dora. "I don't want to own another dog. Too much chance for heartache. But I miss having one around. This would be perfect for me."

"Dora, are you sure? I don't know ... I guess we could try it and see if it works. But if he causes any trouble ..."

"This darling dog? I'm not worried," she said, giving me a kiss on the muzzle.

Wow. Dora believed in me. That was a lot to live up to. And to be honest, I didn't know if I had it in me.

***

It turned out that Doggy Daycare with Dora was the complete opposite of Dog Detention.

She was home with me all day. When she had to go somewhere, she took me along. She let me stick my head out the car window, which Kristin didn't allow, saying a pebble might blow in my eye. I loved the wind on my face and whistling in my ears.

Dora was not supposed to feed me. I had my daily nutritious dry kibble at The Cottage, and Kristin told her the rules.

But one night when Kristin was late getting home, Dora gave me some canned dogfood. Wow.

"Please forgive me," Dora said to Kristin. "He seemed so hungry. I had some in my pantry, so I gave it to him.

Doggy Dinner, beef flavor. He loved it."

"I'm sure he did," Kristin said with a sigh. "Well, I guess it's okay this time."

I think she was so grateful to Dora for taking care of me that she didn't want to say much about food.

Anyway, after that I got canned food almost every day. Kristin worked late a lot, so Dora had a good excuse. Kristin brought over a bag of dry stuff, but Dora said it gave her pleasure to see me enjoy my meal.

Kristin shook her head and let it drop.

Then Dora began sharing her people food with me. Meatloaf, mashed potatoes, spaghetti. Chicken pot pie, tapioca pudding, carrot cake with cream cheese frosting.

Once in a while, she decided that we should have Snoopy the Dog's triathlon: pizza, donuts, and a hot fudge sundae. Dogs aren't supposed to eat chocolate, of course, so Dora didn't spoon syrup on my ice cream.

My food world exploded. Kristin eats like a rabbit, mostly greens and veggies. Dora, on the other hand, believed in the joy of food, and she wanted to share that joy with me.

With so much good stuff to eat, and so much loving attention, who needed to chew on the furniture? I guess Jodi was right. I had ADS, and Dora had the cure.

In fact, my life improved so much that I *almost* forgot about Ruby.

But at night, curled up on my big cushion by Kristin's bed, I imagined Ruby, her red hair and dark eyes glowing in the streetlight, hanging by our gate -- missing me and hoping I'd come out.

As I drifted off to sleep, some words would float around my brain like those fluffy dumplings in Dora's beef stew: *She walks in beauty, like the night ... like the night ... like the night ...*

10

When I was in Dog Detention, I missed Colette and the kittens. Especially Oliver, who had gotten to be my best buddy. (Actually, my only buddy.)

Now that I was at Dora's, he would streak across the street, then scramble over her fence to play with me in her escape-proof yard.

Oliver was kind of a pest. He liked to prank me. His favorite trick was dropping down from a tree onto my head when I least expected it. Super annoying.

Mostly, though, he was fun. Our favorite game was touch basketball. Dora gave me an old deflated ball that I could pick up in my teeth. I was always the L.A. Lakers while Oliver was the Boston Celtics.

(I got to be a Lakers fan by watching games on TV with Dora. On the sofa, we scarfed popcorn and cheer (I barked) when the Lakers scored. She promised me that someday she would get me a Lakers shirt.)

In my games with Oliver, I'd run with the ball, stop suddenly, spin around, and drop it on top of him. He would mew furiously, trash-talk me, and butt the ball back at me. Then I'd pick it up, do a slick evasive move and run for Dora's beat-up laundry basket, where I'd score a point. The Lakers almost always won, which is as it should be.

After our games, we'd hang out and talk. He told me that his mom hardly ever came out from under the house now, and the kittens had to bring dead mice for her to eat.

"Is it because she's sad that she can't have any more babies?" I asked.

"Maybe," Oliver said. "But really, I think she understands why Kristin did it."

"I still can't figure out why she's always been so afraid of people," I said.

"Me neither. She just tells us not to ever let ourselves become house pets."

"That's weird. There might be a few bad people in the world, but most, I'll bet, are kind. Like Kristin. And Jodi and Dora."

"Mama says you can't trust humans. She says that someday we'll find that out for ourselves."

Later, mulling over Colette's fears, a speck of doubt crept into my head. But I just did not want to think that people might actually hurt animals on purpose.

***

It goes without saying that daycare with Dora was great. But before long, I had a big problem: my weight.

I puffed up like a fur-covered black balloon, and Kristin was distressed. "Puppins, you need to go on a diet," she wailed. "Dora feeds you too much!"

During our evening walks, I no longer frisked ahead and pulled on the leash like I used to. But low energy or not, I still looked forward to those nightly events.

I liked to see the neighborhood kids jump rope and play street hockey. And sometimes the creaky old ice cream truck came crawling along, playing its tinkling tune over and over as the hot sun went down.

That green and yellow truck drew kids like our porch light drew moths. Kristin was not about to buy a treat for me, but I always hoped some little toddler would drop his Bombsicle on the sidewalk.

Almost every yard we passed had at least one dog, and most were friendly. But one house was patrolled by two seriously mean pit bulls. Kristin says pit bulls are only mean if their owners train them that way, so I guess that's what happened to those two.

As soon as they spotted us, they'd roar up to the fence and lunge against it with all their might. I'm pretty sure they wanted to kill us.

"Good grief!" Kristin would say. "Why does anyone want to have dogs like that!"

Their owner, a man with carrot-colored hair, sometimes scowled at us through an iron-barred window. I guess he was mad that we upset his monstrous dogs. We'd hurry past as fast as we could.

Thankfully, the other neighbors were nice. Miss Wisteria, for instance. Her last name is a kind of flower, and maybe that's why she grew up to be a lepi ... lepi ... butterfly scientist. Now she was too old to chase butterflies anymore, so she sat on her front porch and read her books.

Whenever we passed by, she'd call us over to talk. She was a small person with chocolaty skin; I liked her, but not her two cats, Harriet and Victoria, who sat inside the house and hissed at me through the window.

Next door to Miss W lived Mr. and Mrs. Quintero. They always worked in their small yard, and their cocker spaniels, Carmelita and Pico, romped around in the coarse grass and greeted me with friendly sniffs.

"Buenas noches, Kristeen," the Quinteros would call out. They talked mostly like Pepito but I understood more of their words. Mr. Quintero always told Kristin that she was lucky to have a big dog like me for protection.

"This neighborhood no good no more. Mi esposa and me, we move away soon," he'd say.

"It's a fine neighborhood, Mr. Quintero," Kristin would reply. "I hope you don't move."

We almost always took the same route. Most of the houses we passed were small, like The Cottage. But there were a few big old mansions sprinkled in. Some were turned into apartments; others had boards on the windows instead of curtains. Whenever we walked by an empty place, Kristin would say, "Puppins, look at that sad house. I wish I could buy it and make it happy."

Once, when we were in the car, we drove past an old dump with a red tile roof. Kristin slammed on the brakes and yelled, "Spanish Colonial!" Whatever that is. She dragged me across the overgrown yard and peered through the cracked windows. "What a great place this could be," she exclaimed. "If this were my house, I'd call it La Casa Royale. A house fit for a king!"

Give me a break. It was a pitiful wreck. But that shows you how weird she is about things that need to be rescued. She always sees possibilities in them, no matter how pathetic they are. (Wait. Does that apply to me?)

Anyway, I guess that's what happened with The Cottage. When her friends came over, she'd pull out her "before" photos and tell them how the house was more than a hundred years old and a rundown mess, inside and out, when she bought it.

It was Craftsman style, she told them. I don't know what that meant, but I liked the part about the roof, which swooped down and then curved up at the ends.

Apparently that's the way Japanese people built houses in the old days. The idea was that if a devil landed on your roof, it would slide down and fly right off, like those ski jumpers I've seen on TV.

Having a roof like that was comforting. I did not want any devils invading our house.

43

11

Kristin had been in The Cottage for a while when I came to live with her. By that time, it was cozy and nice, and the tiny front yard was filled with orange and pink flowers instead of weeds and rocks.

She painted the front door purple and made a sign that she hung above it. When I arrived, she read it to me so I'd feel welcome. It said:

Bare feet allowed, dogs and cats allowed
the sun and the stars and the evening
wind allowed.

I liked what the poem said, despite the cat reference. Kristin told Jodi that she saw it in a newspaper once and she didn't recall who wrote it, but she hoped they wouldn't mind if she painted it on her sign.

The front porch was my favorite part of The Cottage. On Sunday mornings, Kristin would sit queen-like on the swing, eating her granola and reading the Sunday paper, while I, the royal dog, lay at her feet, chewing my best rawhide bone.

By the way, that porch was a good place even after dark. There was a golden light on the ceiling that welcomed us home when we went somewhere at night. Whenever I saw it, some words would pop up in my brain: *Heaven is a house with porch lights.*

So true.

***

Those Sunday mornings on the porch were just about the only times Kristin sat still at home. She set aside 10 minutes per day to throw a tennis ball to me, and we had our walks, but otherwise she worked hour after hour on the house and in the yard.

One of her projects was what she called her archaeological dig: unburying old stepping stones that were hiding under weeds and dirt in the driveway.

She pried them up, cleaned them off and laid them out in a new pattern, while I sat in the shade and supervised. That was my job.

One morning, while we were doing this, a little girl with long dark hair suddenly skipped out from behind the shrubs next door.

"Hi! What's your name?" she asked Kristin in a sweet, bird-like voice.

"Kristin. What's yours?"

"Lin Lu. What's your dog's name?"

"Puppins."

"Is he friendly?"

"Very."

She came over, let me sniff her small hand, then patted me. "How old is he?"

"About 3, but I don't know for sure. How old are you, Lin Lu?"

"Six. I'll be 7 next week, but I'm not having my party until my grandmother and cousins come from Thailand. That's where I was born."

"You speak English very well."

"I practice a lot. My teacher says I talk *too* much."

"Do you have a dog?" Kristin asked.

"No. We move too much. But maybe I'll get one for my birthday."

"I hope so. Are you moving in next door?"

"No. My father is doing repairs there. Kristin, do you

believe in leprechauns?"

"Leprechauns? Why yes, I do. But I've never actually seen one. Have you?"

"I think so. I was with my father while he worked at a big house, and in the garden I saw a little man with a tall hat."

"Was the hat green?"

"No. Blue. That's why I'm not sure, because my teacher says leprechauns wear green hats. Anyway, I made a wish when I saw him. I wished for a puppy. Kristin, if you could make a wish on a leprechaun, what would you wish for?"

Kristin thought about it, then said, "I think I'd wish that I had more room in my house for people to visit me, and more space for Puppins since he's a big dog. What would you wish for, besides a puppy?"

Lin Lu smiled shyly. "Well, I would make a special wish -- that you would be my friend for my whole life."

What a great wish! Kristin's eyebrows shot up in surprise. But before she could reply, Lin Lu's father called her and she disappeared as magically as she had appeared.

We would not see her again for a very long time, but her memory stuck in my brain. If I had a wish on a leprechaun, I'd wish that Lin Lu lived next door.

***

Meanwhile, I grew fatter and fatter in Doggy Daycare. When Pepito's band of parakeets flew over Dora's yard, they screeched at me: "Gordito! Gordito!" That was rude. It hurt my feelings, but I didn't know how to answer.

Oliver teased me, too. When he dropped out of a tree onto my head, he'd say, "Thanks for the soft landing, Pudgy Puppins!" I'd call him Sir No Neck, the way Jodi did, because his fur stuck out around his face and made

46

him look like he had no neck.

Despite the name-calling, his pranking habit, and the fact that he was a cat, we were still best buddies. Sadly, I got too out of shape to be a Laker. But it was summer and too hot to play basketball anyway, so we just hung out under Dora's avocado tree.

One day, as we were vegging and Dora was still inside sleeping, a streak of red flashed by.

Oh my god! Ruby!

I jumped up and bounded over to the fence. "Ruby! Hey!" I yelled.

She turned and trotted back, and my heart took a crazy upside-down flip.

"What are you doing here?" she asked. "Don't you live across the street?"

"I stay here now while Kristin's at work. Did you look for me over there?"

"No," she said curtly.

Ouch. Obviously, she hadn't given me much thought. But what else was new?

"Where are you headed?" I asked.

"Anywhere. Want to come along?" She regarded me with a double-dare in her glittering eyes.

Whoa. Seriously? Of course I wanted to come along! But ... "I can't get out of here," I admitted.

"Really? Just jump over the fence."

"I'm not a jumper. Wouldn't make it."

"Too bad. See you around." Her eyes mocked me as she turned and sprinted down the street.

Aargh. What kind of wimp was I?

I eyed the fence doubtfully. If only I was in better shape!

Oliver pranced over. "Who was that?"

"Ruby."

"Ruby? The Ruby who ran away from Jodi?" I had

told him all about her.

"Yeah. Listen, I've got to get out of here!"

"Are you nuts? Why?"

"I've just got to, that's all." I began running back and forth along the fence.

"But you'll get in trouble!" Oliver warned.

"So what?" I replied, still checking out the fence. This might be my only chance, and I was going for it.

Getting as far back as I could, I drew a deep breath. Then, lumbering like a plus-size baby elephant, I catapulted myself straight for Dora's rose-covered fence.

Didn't make it. Crashing to the ground, I landed in a bunch of flowers. I hoped Dora wouldn't notice.

I tried again. Gathering all my strength, I ran ... I leaped ... I flew. Rose thorns raked across my belly, but I made it over!

"Wait for me!" Oliver cried.

I looked back. He was climbing over the gate.

"Stay there!" I yelled. "I'll be right back!"

He stopped and stared after me as I ran on.

Scratched, bleeding, heart pounding, I raced as fast as my awkward body could go. Ruby had a good head start on me, but I gave it everything I had. If I could just keep her in sight, maybe I could catch up with her.

She stopped at a corner up ahead. She was within reach. I pushed myself to the limit.

"Ruby! Wait!" I yelled.

She turned and stared at me. "You got out. Wow."

Yeah, she was mocking me. Still, as I pulled to a stop next to her, I thought I saw a spark of respect in her eyes. A spark just big enough to make all my pain fade away.

Suddenly, miraculously, I was a new dog.

12

We trotted side by side, the hot sun beating down on us. A wave of happiness lifted me up and carried me along.

"Where are ... are ... you headed?" I wheezed as we ran.

"Stop asking me that. What difference does it make?"

I had no answer. I just didn't get it. Why would she run like that, with no destination in mind? Or, maybe she had a goal but just didn't want to tell me. Whatever it was, she just ran on and on and on.

After a while, I gasped, "Can ... we stop and ... and rest ... for ... for a minute?"

"You can. I'm not tired," she replied, glancing at me, her eyes squinted scornfully.

Ouch. She did not slow down, and I fell a few steps behind. I wondered if she even cared if I was there. I forced myself to keep going, but there was no getting around the problem: Ruby was fit, I was fat.

And I was getting hungry. Wasn't it time for dinner? I saw garbage cans in alleys as we dashed by, and I imagined they held all sorts of good eats. Ruby kept going.

We got to an area I didn't recognize. Storefronts and little restaurants. A bunch of shabby houses crammed together, then larger ones that were more spread out.

By then, I was a robot. A starved robot, with legs

made of rubber. What if all four of them gave out on me at once?

Suddenly, Ruby stopped.

"Wait here," she said abruptly. "Don't come until I signal you."

I sank gratefully to the sidewalk as she crossed the street, heading to a yard where some kids were playing.

The smallest, a boy, spied her. "Look! A red dog!"

The kids ran up to Ruby, held out their hands so she could sniff, then petted her.

Ruby stood there, proud and beautiful, and my heart, tired as it was, skipped a beat.

The biggest girl said, "I'll bet it's hungry. Cara, go get something for it to eat."

"What should I get?" the small girl asked.

"Hot dogs. The ones left over from lunch. And a bowl of water, and ..."

"Potato chips?"

"Yeah. Chips."

The girl named Cara ran inside while the others continued to fuss over Ruby.

"I wonder where she lives," the boy said.

"She doesn't have a collar," the big girl answered. "Maybe she needs a home. Maybe Mom and Dad would let us keep her."

"We could ask. Maybe if we said she could be a watchdog ..."

Cara came back, carrying a plate loaded with food and a bowl of water. "The chips were gone but I got some cheese," she said.

Ruby sent me a look, and I wobbled across the street as fast as my exhausted legs and blistered paws would let me.

The kids spotted me coming. "Look! A black one!" Cara cried, and began to chant: "Red dog, black dog, puppies on the run!" The others laughed and joined in, as Ruby and I scarfed down the hot dogs and cheese.

Hot dogs are great, but I wish they had a more respectful name. Anyway, never had food tasted so good. Not just because I was famished, but because I was sharing it with Ruby.

Some words flashed through my tired brain: *All happiness depends on a leisurely breakfast.*

It wasn't breakfast. And for sure it wasn't leisurely. But that did not matter. Real happiness, I thought, is sharing stuff with someone you are nuts about.

No sooner had we finished than Ruby turned and sprinted down the sidewalk. Caught off guard, I stumbled, then picked myself up, following as fast as I could.

The kids shrieked at us. "Wait! We want to keep you!" They chased us as far as the corner before turning back.

***

We ran on. The food and water gave me new energy, but my legs and feet, and scratched belly, burned with pain. I managed to keep within a few paces of Ruby, but behind. Always behind.

Toward nighttime, we came to a small park with a few scraggly palms, a fountain, an empty playground, and a pond with some orange fish that looked like wiggly sliced peaches.

We crashed under some shrubs. "We probably can stay here all night," said Ruby, "but if the police or Animal Control show up, we've got to run in opposite directions."

"What ... would they ... do to us?" I asked as I tried to catch my breath.

"The police would just chase us away. But Animal Control would try to catch us."

"And if they did, then what?"

"Don't you know anything?" she asked impatiently. "They take you to the Humane Shelter. And after three days, if no one claims or adopts you, they put you to death."

"What!? No way!" I cried. "You mean ... they kill you, just because ... because you don't have a home? Why??"

"I guess not enough people come there to find a pet. And those that do – well, they mostly want cute little kittens," she sneered contemptuously, "or adorable puppies."

"But if no one adopts you, why can't you just stay at the shelter?" I asked. This scenario did not make sense.

"I don't know. Maybe they don't have enough food and kennels for a lot of animals."

I shuddered. I'd heard that shelters were not a good place to be, but I had no idea they were death chambers!

Then something clicked in my brain. "Were you in the shelter when Jodi and Kristin came looking for you?"

"Yes," she admitted with a smirk.

"I *thought* that was you. But you were so dirty! Jodi said she gave you a bath."

"I got in a sprinkler and rolled in the dirt after I ran away. Had to cover up this red fur. But some guy sneaked up and caught me. Jodi forgot to put my collar on, so of course he took me to the shelter. And when you came, they hadn't gotten around to cleaning me up."

"But why didn't you respond to Jodi and Kristin?"

"Because, stupid, Jodi wants to own me," she replied angrily. "I don't want to be owned."

She called me stupid. Sigh.

"Jodi was awfully good to you," I said, ignoring the insult. "All those toys, and canned food!"

Ruby stared at me, her dark eyes filled with scorn.

"Canned food? No thanks. The price for that is too

high. I have to be free."

"But why?" I still struggled to figure out where she was coming from.

"You're too dense to understand."

Ouch again.

"Try me," I said bravely.

"If you knew anything, you'd get it. Owners are for things, like cars or houses, not for dogs. Dogs were not meant to be owned. We were meant to be our own masters. That's our history."

Hmm. I'd heard Kristin talk about that with her friends. They said all dogs were descended from wolves.

Really? Poodles? Chihuahuas? No way. But even if it was true, things obviously were different now.

"That was a long time ago," I replied, "when dogs were wild, with no humans to take care of them."

Ruby wasn't buying it. "It's possible even now," she said coldly, "and even in the city. It's not easy, but it's the only way to really live."

"But what about Animal Control?" I persisted, thinking about her being caught and that 3-day rule. "What if you hadn't been able to escape from that shelter?"

"I can always get out of shelters," she stated flatly. "It's not hard, if you stay cool and know what you're doing. Anyway, I'd be adopted. Irish setters are popular and beautiful. It's the old mutts and over-the-hill cats that really have a hard time getting homes. And big black dogs," she added with a smirk.

That was harsh, but I figured it was probably true. A lot of people, like that mailperson I mentioned earlier, think big black dogs are fierce and don't make good family pets.

But I still had questions. "Well, if someone adopted you, would you run away from them?"

"Of course. Just like I did from Jodi. No one *owns* me. I told you that."

The idea of not being owned and taken care of was weird. I just could not relate.

"Haven't you ever been any place you wanted to stay?" I asked finally.

"No."

"But ..."

"Shut up. You give me a headache. Anyway, if you're going to keep up with me, you'd better get some sleep."

The way she said it was rude. But the words kept going around in my head, like one of those songs you hear on the radio. "If you're going to keep up with me... keep up with me ... with me ... with me ..."

To my ears, those words meant she wanted me to be with her. Leave behind my dull existence. Be part of her exciting life on the streets of L.A.

Wow.

The ground was hard, but somehow it seemed as soft as a pillow. Even better than my dog bed at home, the giant one that Kristin got for me at Costco.

Wait. Kristin! And Dora, and Oliver! They'd be really upset to find me gone. Dora would blame herself for thinking her yard was escape-proof. Kristin would cry. And Oliver would yell at me, jump on my back, sink in his claws and call me bad names.

I'd go back. But ... not quite yet. I'd spend one night with Ruby. Just thinking about that made my skin tingle.

I closed my eyes and moved as close to her as I dared. Heat from her body radiated through mine. Her feathery red fur felt soft and silky against my nose. Her scent was like ... like ... like her.

Despite the prickly grass, my swollen paws and raw scratches, I fell instantly asleep. A deep, wonderful sleep.

13

When I opened my eyes again, the sky was just lighting up. I stretched, yawned, gave myself the usual shake, and looked around.

Ruby?

Gone! I ran frantically around in circles. Did I lose her already? Aargh!

As I've mentioned, my nose isn't the greatest because of when that car hit me, but I was able to catch a faint scent of her on the grass. Tracing it down a narrow path, I turned a corner, and there she was. Drinking from the little pond, looking as fresh and unconcerned as the golden fish swimming in lazy circles.

"You passed the first test," she announced.

"Test?"

"Finding me when I disappeared."

"But ... why did you disappear?"

"Survival training. You're a wimp. You wouldn't last two days out here on your own, you know."

Harsh. "That's not true," I said lamely. "I think I was on my own in Seattle."

"Ha. You don't know that. Anyway, next test: You need to get rid of that collar. Collars are the mark of a kept dog."

"But I have to wear it all the time, in case I get ..."

I stopped, as the ridiculousness of it sank in.

Ruby laughed.

"Okay, okay," I told her. "I'll get rid of it. But how?"

She trotted over. Close. Very close. My heart did a triple flip.

"Lie down," she ordered. "I'm going to chew it off."

I obeyed. Gladly. She lay down next to me, her head on my shoulder, and began to chew.

Whew! Why did I suddenly feel so hot?

She chewed the collar clear through. Too soon, it fell off. I wanted that chewing thing to go on and on.

"Th ... thanks, Ruby," I stuttered. "Could you ..."

She wasn't listening. Grabbing the collar in her teeth, she ran to the pond and dropped it in. Then she took off, her mocking words trailing back to me. "Catch me if you can, wimp!"

I caught her. Well, maybe she let me. We danced on the grass, spinning, chasing, tagging. After a while, the sprinklers came on, making our fur gleam with sparkling stars of water.

The morning sun was gentle. The sweet smell of jasmine, which I recognized from Kristin's garden, mixed with the rich scent of Ruby and made my head spin.

It was just me and her. No fences, no closed doors. No one to scold me and say I was bad.

Something flashed through my feverish brain: *let's touch the sky...*

Yes. I was with Ruby, and we could touch the sky!

When we finally keeled over, she licked my face with her pink tongue and nuzzled me with her soft nose -- just long enough, in my opinion, to count as a kiss. My first.

Wow.

She jumped up. "Come on," she called, her eyes flashing. "Let's get breakfast." She ran off down the path, her leg plumes flaming in the bright sunlight.

I followed her, sore paws and belly scratches

forgotten.

As we ran, I thought about everything that had happened since I met Ruby, and some new words flew into my brain: *How sad and bad and mad it was, but then how sweet!*

***

After that morning, I lost track of the days. We ran. We found food when we could -- things Ruby begged for, but mostly garbage. I soon got used to the hit/eat/run routine: knock the can over, gulp down the edibles, run off before anyone comes to investigate.

Some days we found nothing. But on garbage collection days, when a lot of overflowing cans sat on the curb, we ate pretty well. It's surprising how much good stuff people throw out sometimes.

After a while, all the running made me stronger. It got easier for me to keep up with Ruby, and I felt like I was losing some of my fat. Good riddance.

Survival lessons continued. I followed her lead when she sensed danger. She was really good at dodging Animal Control. Actually, I think she enjoyed it, like a game. But I was terrified when it happened. If I got caught, would Kristin and Jodi come to the shelter to look for me before three days were up? Or had they forgotten me by now?

At those times, I promised myself I would say goodbye to Ruby and go back home. But when the danger passed, I'd put that vow off for another day.

***

One early morning, Ruby led me to a little mall lined with scraggly palm trees. The shops seemed to be closed, except for one that had a flickering sign in the window.

"That's Yin's donut store," Ruby told me. "Behind the shop is Donut Alley. Come on."

We trotted past a line of dumpsters to the back,

where a stack of boxes sat on steps by the shop's backdoor. "Leftover donuts," Ruby explained. "The Yins put them out for people who live on the streets, but they don't care if dogs take some too."

Donuts? My kind of food!

"Do you come here a lot?" I asked.

"No. Donuts weigh me down. But they're okay once in a while. Anyway, there's good entertainment here, as you'll see, and the Yins like me."

Just as she said that, the backdoor opened and a tiny old man emerged. He spied Ruby. Clapping his hands and bowing, he cried, "You back! Wait here! No go away!" He disappearing inside.

A moment later he was back, an equally tiny woman by his side. She smiled and bowed and smiled and bowed at Ruby. Then she smiled and bowed at me, chattering in words that clacked together like the chopsticks Kristin uses to eat sushi.

Mrs. Yin held a plate of steaming donuts that she set on the ground, and she and Mr. Yin watched, smiling, as we stuffed ourselves. Then they made one last bow and went back inside.

I licked the sugar off my paws. That was one great breakfast. But it made me think of Dora, and I felt a stab of guilt. She loved donuts. Sometimes she took me with her to Johnny Donuts, the best there is.

Just then, a wild-eyed man appeared, dressed in black trash bags that were wrapped around his skinny body and tied on his feet with strings. His hair and beard were as shaggy as an ungroomed English sheepdog.

In one hand he carried a long stick. Waving it at Ruby and me, he shouted, "Blessings on you, creatures of the Earth! Come and share the Bread of Life!"

"What's he talking about?" I asked Ruby.

"He's crazy. But harmless. Calls himself Joshua, and

spends his days telling people to repent before it's too late. He claims his other mission is to bless the donuts for the multitudes."

"Multitudes?" I asked, glancing around at the near-empty alley.

"The homeless. They'll be here, don't worry."

Sure enough, they began to drift in. An odd assortment of folks carrying bags and pushing overloaded shopping carts. Ruby knew them all.

The last to arrive was an old woman, hobbling down the alley with a beat-up baby stroller.

"That's Odette," said Ruby, "and Loofah."

As they got closer, I could see a little white dog in the stroller, peeking out of a grimy blanket, almost buried under piles of plastic bags. She had a sweet face, sparkling black eyes, small round paws, and soft curly fur the color of marshmallows.

"Hello, Loofah," said Ruby.

"Hi, Ruby. How have you been?" Loofah asked in a squeaky little voice.

"Alright," Ruby answered. "How about you?"

"I'm fine. But I'm worried about Odette."

"What's going on?"

"The homeless center has a new rule. They won't let her sleep there if I'm with her. They want her to take me to the Humane Shelter, and of course she won't do that."

Loofah stopped, took a breath and continued, her words tumbling out. "We sleep outdoors, which is alright for me, but what if she gets sick? Who will take care of her? Who will take care of me?"

Before Ruby could respond, Joshua got up on the back steps of the donut shop and told everyone to be quiet.

"Let us begin the service," he proclaimed loudly. "Blessings on each of you, my friends. Let us be thankful for this glorious day. And for how blessed we are to be in Southern California. For two years, I lived in Florida. A God-forsaken place! Hotter than the fires of Hell! Mosquitoes like the Seventh Plague! The poor suffered, of course. The rich had air-conditioning, and their neighborhoods got sprayed."

His listeners shook their heads at the unfairness of it all. Then he went on. "And let us be thankful there's no snow in L.A. For two years, I lived in Cleveland ..."

"Just say the blessing and get on with it!" a thin man yelled. Joshua quickly waved his stick over the stacked-up boxes, crying, "Bless these donuts, oh Lord, and bring us more tomorrow!"

Everyone shouted "Amen!" Then, as each person filed by and took some donuts, he tapped them lightly on the shoulder with his stick.

Odette picked out a couple of cream puffs, stuffing one in a bag and breaking the other into bits for Loofah.

"Why do they wait for the old guy to bless the donuts?" I asked Ruby. "Why don't they just grab them and run?"

"I don't know. I guess they like what he does. Maybe they want to feel like they're part of something. You know, like they belong. People seem to need that."

The whole thing was strange. For starters, I didn't know there were people who had no homes. How did that happen? Were they like Ruby and just wanted to be free? Somehow, I didn't think that was it.

It was time for us to go, so we said goodbye to Loofah. But just as we turned to leave, a terrible voice rang out, shattering the calm like a rock hurled through a window.

"Get outta here, you f****** stupid bums! Dis is our territory!"

14

Ruby sprang up and flew toward the far end of the alley. "Come on!" she yelled, as two ugly men appeared around the corner.

One of them had a big knife that he waved menacingly at the homeless people. The other held a bag of fried onions in one hand and a heavy chain, attached to a huge Rottweiler, in the other.

That dog was a demon. It snarled and foamed and strained on its lead, ready to kill whoever got in its way.

Needless to say, I sprinted after Ruby. We made it to the end of the alley and hid behind a trash bin.

Looking back, we saw Mr. Yin open his door a crack and then, seeing those men and that dog, quickly shut it.

The homeless cleared out fast. Even old Joshua booked it. But Odette, gasping and clutching her chest, was left behind, bent over the stroller to protect Loofah.

The hoodlum with the knife screamed at her. "Are ya deaf, ya ol' scumbag? Get outta here, or we'll kill that stupid little mutt, an' you too!"

Odette toppled over. The guy, cussing and waving his knife in her face, yelled, "When will you worthless bums learn ta stay outta here?"

I turned to Ruby. "Sh...shouldn't we go back and ... and try to help them?"

"Are you insane? No way! They'd like nothing better

than to trap us. Especially you."

"Trap me? Why?"

"Don't you know who they are? It's Stites and Onions. And that Rottweiler is Tolliver Yar."

"Stites? Onions? Tolliver ... who?"

"Tolliver Yar. The dogfight champ. How could you not know about him?"

"Dogfight? What are you talking about?"

"The dogfight ring, dummy! Stites and Onions get paid to bring in dogs, and Tolliver helps them. They could use you, even though you are a wimp."

Ouch. She called me dummy. And ... was I still a wimp? I thought I'd toughened up.

"I don't even know what a fight ring is," I protested.

"So what? They just want dogs to throw in the ring. To be bait, if nothing else. Come on, we've got to get out of here." She turned and ran.

I glanced back. Odette was still on the ground, her tiny dog trembling in her arms. Those goons tore the bags off the stroller and dumped her shabby belongings on the ground, then kicked them aside.

Tolliver Yar, saliva dripping from his massive jaws, stood over Loofah and snarled at her.

I had to do something. Screwing up my courage, I called out, "Loofah!"

She didn't answer. But the men stopped in their tracks and peered down the alley.

"Hear dat?" the onion guy said. "Sounds like a big dog! Want me ta send Tolliver after it?"

Fear gripped my heart. I couldn't take on those two guys and their frightful dog by myself. And I did not want Ruby to leave me behind. I turned and shot after her.

When I caught up, she stopped running and stared at me angrily. "That was stupid! You might have been caught. Show some smarts, will you?"

"But Loofah is so helpless! And that poor woman!"

"There's nothing you could do," Ruby snapped. "When you're on the street, you take care of yourself. Forget about anyone else."

"But ..."

"No 'buts.' You're an idiot. You have no idea what can happen to a dog out here."

Ouch again. She had a talent for deflating me like that old basketball at Dora's.

I tried to regroup. "How do you know about the dogfight ring?" I asked meekly as I caved down to the sidewalk.

"Any dog on the streets knows about it," she said shortly, "and knows to stay clear of those two criminals."

"Did they ever try to catch you?"

"I'm not easy to catch," she stated flatly. She lay down next to me and then went on.

"Someone I know was captured not long ago. I saw it happen. They sneaked up and shot him with a kind of gun that knocked him out."

"That's horrible!"

"They picked him up and threw him in a van. I haven't seen him since." She got up abruptly and quickly trotted off.

Something in her voice sent a stab of jealousy through me. I pushed myself to catch up to her.

"What was his name?" I asked.

"Bill. Bill the Boxer," she answered, increasing her pace.

Subject closed.

We ran on. After a while, we came to an area with big houses surrounded by gardens. Tall palms lined the streets, their green fronds fanning the hot blue sky.

I recognized that place: Pasadena, where Kristin

sometimes drove with me just to look at the houses.

"Aren't these mansions beautiful, Puppins?" she would exclaim. "And the roses! No wonder they call this the City of Roses."

Pasadena was nice, but the sun was burning down on me and frying my brain. I started fantasizing about watermelon. A cold, juicy slab, like the one Dora shared with me once on a summer afternoon.

Ruby slowed to a walk, and I ventured another question. "Why did those men -- Stites and Onions -- scare the street people away? And why were they so cruel to Odette and her little dog?"

"Bullies. Like all bullies, they smell weakness and go after it. Maybe it makes them feel powerful. Their job is to find dogs, but they don't mind having a little fun with the homeless along the way."

I just could not relate. When we finally stopped to rest, I picked up the subject again.

"Is a dogfight like boxing? Once on TV, I saw two guys with big gloves try to cream each other. Dora turned it off -- too violent. But I never saw a dogfight on TV."

"That's because dogfights are against the law, stupid," she snapped.

Why does she keep calling me stupid? I ignored it and pushed on. "What exactly happens at a dogfight ring?" I asked.

"They train dogs to fight each other."

"But if it's against the law, how can they ...?"

"They keep it hidden. They do it to make a lot of money. People pay to come and watch, and they bet on the dogs."

I shuddered. "But why would a dog go along with it? If they captured you, why wouldn't you just refuse to fight?"

"You don't have a choice. They throw you in the ring

with a dog that's been trained to attack. You fight back and win, or you are dead meat."

Wow. I had seen dogs fight each other, but for a reason: to protect themselves, or their food or their territory. This seemed monstrously different.

"I still don't understand. Why would people want to see dogs kill each other?"

"Who can explain people? Some like to do violent things. Some like to watch it. And others find ways to make money off of it."

I didn't know what to say. I never knew any bad people, at least not that I could remember. But Colette talked about it, and now Ruby.

And that very morning I had seen Stites and Onions in action. They were evil, for sure.

Everyone is a moon and has a dark side...

Those words crept into my brain, but I pushed them down. I did not want to think they might be true.

"Where is this dogfight place?" I asked Ruby.

"Not that far from where you live. Maybe you went by it on those walks you told me about."

"No way. Not in my neighborhood. I never saw any dogs fighting, except a skirmish or two over a bone."

"Ever go by a house that looks like a fortress, with two pit bulls guarding it?"

Gulp. Oh, yeah. I knew which house she meant. But how could such a bad thing be right in my neighborhood?

"Wouldn't the neighbors know about it and call the police?" I asked, shaking my head.

"Maybe. But maybe if they know, they don't want to get involved. Or they are too afraid."

Would Kristin get involved, if she knew about it? I think so. She is brave. Much braver than me.

15

I had more questions, but Ruby shut me down. I could tell she was losing patience with me and my cluelessness.

She got up and took off again, me following. We ran with the sun beating down on us, she with her usual unknown purpose, me just trying to keep up.

We had not eaten since the donuts, and that energy was long since burned off. What I wouldn't give for a cold bowl of ice cream!

Wait. Stuff like ice cream is what got me so out of shape. Why did I eat everything Dora put in front of me? Was it just because it was there and tasted good?

I thought about the time Kristin went away for a few days and I stayed at Dora's. To feed Oliver and his family while she was gone, Kristin got a thing that had a big upside-down jar for the kibble, and it trickled down a little at a time when the cats ate from the base.

When Kristin got home, the jar was tipped over and all the chow was gone.

"Those greedy little creatures!" she told Jodi. "Oliver was as swollen as a tick!"

I gave Oliver a hard time about that. "Couldn't you see there was enough in that jar to feed you for a lot of days?" I asked.

He got defensive. "When you live in the wild, you eat whatever you can get, when you can get it. That's what Mama says."

"But you don't live in the wild. You have a home."

"Mama says it's not our home. We're just staying here until she's stronger, then we have to move on."

Bad news. I was not surprised that Colette felt that way, and maybe the girls too. But I hoped that Oliver, at least, would stay. He was my buddy.

Anyway, to get back to the greed issue. Maybe the cats had a reason to stuff themselves, but what was my excuse? I could blame Kristin for depriving me of things I liked, which made me want them more. I could blame Dora for tempting me too much.

I could also blame my out-of-control impulses on having a teenage brain. But maybe I should just own up. I had made some bad choices about food, not to mention other things. Sigh.

Ruby and I ran on. And even as I put myself down for overeating, I thought about food.

I was hungry, for sure. And exhausted. And missing home. Still, I forged on. The fear of losing Ruby was stronger than anything else, even my hunger.

Why did I want so much to be with her? It made no sense. Some words crept into my tired brain: *The heart has its reasons, which reason does not know.* So true.

***

Finally, we stopped. Another little park, with a few benches, some ragged palms and a big cactus that seemed a little threatening.

"I suppose you're tired," Ruby commented, her voice dripping with disgust.

"Yeah," I mumbled, collapsing. "And hungry." At the moment, I was not too proud to admit my inferiority.

"Stay here. I'll find some food and bring it back," she said tersely.

Wow. She was offering to get me food, despite being

annoyed with me. But wait: Was I really such a wimp?

"Thanks, Ruby ... but I'll ... I'll come with you. ... I can make it," I panted.

I struggled to my feet, took a step, then fell back down in a black heap. Ruby gave a little laugh, just this side of nasty.

I forced myself to get up again. "I'm getting my second wind," I gasped.

"Your 'second wind' will be gone in a second," she said with a snort. Tossing her head, she turned and was gone.

Staggering to a shady spot under a bench, I licked my bruised ego. Waiting for her return, I fought to keep my eyes open, but it wasn't long before I lost the battle.

***

I woke up. It was dark. The heat of the day had drained out of the sandy ground, and I shivered as I stared into the shadows.

"Ruby? Are you there?"

No answer. My heart did a nosedive. Was this another of her survival tests?

I limped around the tiny park, trying to pick up her scent with my less-than-perfect nose. A thousand smells competed for my attention, but none of them was hers.

Famished and chilled to the bone, I had to face reality. If Ruby meant to return, she'd be back by now.

I stumbled off in the direction she had run. Could I find her? On the other hand, did I really want to?

16

The streets were dark, deserted. I saw a stray cat and tried to ask for directions, but it streaked off, terrified at the sight of me. I trotted on blindly, down one ghostly street after another, no idea where I was.

Suddenly, rounding yet another corner, I tripped over a lumpish thing huddled up against a vacant storefront. The lump let out a pitiful yelp.

"I'm sorry!" I cried. "I didn't mean to step on you."

Trembling, it looked up at me, eyes full of fear, and I saw that it was the little white dog we'd left back in Donut Alley.

"Loofah! What are you doing here? Are you alright?"

"Who ... who are you?" she stammered.

"Puppins. Ruby's friend. I met you this morning in Donut Alley, remember?" Was it really only this morning? Unbelievable.

"Oh Puppins, I didn't recognize you. It's so dark."

"Did those terrible guys hurt you?"

"I'm not hurt, but Odette ..." Her voice trailed off.

"What did they do to her?"

"They pushed her down on the ground," Loofah cried. "They wanted our money. We only had a little, and that made them mad. They thought she was hiding more."

"What happened then?"

"They were going to turn that Rottweiler loose on us. Then we heard a police siren -- I think the donut man called them -- and the bad guys ran off."

"Was Odette hurt?"

"Yes. I licked her cheeks and forehead and finally she opened her eyes. She whispered that her chest hurt something awful."

"Poor Odette!"

"She told me that they'd probably take her to hospital, and then they would take me to the Humane Shelter, so I should go to Mariah's as fast as I could, and she'd come and get me when she got out of hospital."

"Mariah's?"

"Yes. I didn't want to leave her, but I ran and hid behind a trash can. The police came and talked to the donut man. They looked at Odette, then the emergency truck came and put her in and drove away. I ... I heard one of them say, 'The poor old thing -- she's not going to make it.'"

"Oh, Loofah, I'm so sorry!"

"Puppins, I know he was wrong. She's going to be alright. She has to be."

"I'm sure she will be," I lied.

"She's taken care of me most of my life," Loofah cried. "She found that stroller for me so I wouldn't have to walk. And she saves up her coins to buy a can of dog food and we share it."

She paused, then whimpered, "What am I going to do, Puppins? I'm afraid out here all alone. What if Animal Control picks me up?"

"I think you'd get adopted really fast, Loofah. People will like the way you look."

"But I don't want to get adopted!" she wailed. "I want to be with Odette!"

"She'll come for you if she can, but ... but she might not be able to for a long time."

Loofah wasn't listening. "Maybe she's already better

and they let her go. Maybe she's trying to find me. I should go back to Donut Alley and wait for her there."

"You can't do that, Loofah. What if those goons and their Rottweiler show up?"

She shuddered. "Then I'd better go to Mariah's, like Odette said."

I didn't have a clue what she was talking about. When I didn't answer, she peered at me. "Where's Ruby?"

"She left me sleeping in a park. When I woke up, she was gone," I admitted, hanging my head. "I think she ... she might have dumped me."

"I'm sorry, Puppins. But I'm not surprised. Lots of dogs and homeless people have tried to be her friend, but she never stays with anyone very long. Odette says she's a serial loner."

I knew in my heart that was true. But I wanted Ruby to be what I wanted her to be -- someone who would appreciate my wonderfulness and be my (gulp) girlfriend. Was that asking too much? Apparently.

"Were you with her very long?" Loofah asked, breaking the silence.

"No. Well, actually, I'm not sure. I've lost track of time. Anyway, I think I'm ready to go back home."

"Home? You have a home? I thought you lived on the streets. Except most street dogs aren't ..." she paused.

"Plus size?"

She nodded.

"Well, at home I ate too much people food and junk food, then I didn't have much energy for exercising. Out here, well, you know how it is. I think I've actually dropped some weight."

"How did you get lost from your home?"

"I didn't. I ran away. Following Ruby," I said, ducking my head in embarrassment.

"Oh, dear," Loofah sighed sympathetically.

I hurried on. "Anyway, I want to go home, but I don't know how to get there."

She thought for a moment, then said, "Maybe you should come with me to Mariah's. She's helped lots of lost dogs and cats find their homes."

"Really? Who is this Mariah, anyway?"

"A greyhound. She's ... well, it's hard to explain. You'll see. Will you come? I don't like walking alone."

What did I have to lose?

We started out. She led the way, but her legs were short and soon she fell behind. I was glad to be in the lead for a change, but Loofah decided which streets to walk on, and she seemed sure of the way.

"Do you know this area?" I asked.

"Oh, yes. Odette and I spend most of our time around here."

We kept trotting along. Then, I started noticing that although it was still dark, I could tell that the streets were suspiciously familiar.

"Loofah, where are we headed?" I asked.

She got a sheepish look on her face. "Donut Alley. Then I promise we'll go to Mariah's."

"Donut Alley? Oh, Loofah!"

"Just to make sure that Odette hasn't come back for me. If we're careful, we'll be alright. And I feel safe with you, Puppins." She gazed at me with those pleading eyes.

"Well ... okay," I agreed reluctantly. Maybe *she* felt safe, but I didn't. Life on the streets seemed to be one trauma after another. How did Ruby deal with it?

A thought went through my brain: *Safety is all well and good, but I prefer freedom.* I guess that's how Ruby felt.

Freedom seemed great to me for a while, then -- not so much. Sigh.

17

The rising sun peered at us over the foothills. It was going to be another scorcher, but Loofah trotted briskly along, picking up speed as we came close to the dreaded alley.

For me, the closer we got, the harder my heart beat. It echoed in my chest like those big Japanese drums Kristin and I heard once at a festival in Little Tokyo.

I slowed down and called out, "Loofah! Stop!" But she kept going.

Holding her white plumed tail high as she purposefully ran ahead, she disappeared out of sight down the alley.

I thought about turning around and heading the other direction, but I just couldn't abandon the little thing, no matter how foolish she was.

I reached the alley just as she was slowly coming back out, her head and tail down. "Odette's not there," she mumbled. "No one's there."

Whew. I stopped holding my breath. I walked with her back down the alley and, sure enough, it was deserted.

The donut boxes were gone, and Odette's belongings and Loofah's stroller were piled in the dumpster.

I was hungry. Nosing around, I found a couple of

dried-up cream puffs underneath the dumpster and ate one, leaving the other for Loofah.

She shook her head. "I'm not hungry. You can have it," she said.

"Loofah, you'd better eat. You need something before we start out again."

"I can't. My tummy hurts. Puppins, look at my stroller! It's all bent up. Maybe if we pull it out and push it along with us, Odette can fix it."

"Odette's in hospital," I said lamely, swallowing the other cream puff. I couldn't bring myself to say what I really thought about Odette.

"She'll be out soon," said Loofah confidently. "She's got a strong will. How else would she have lasted on the streets so long?"

"I know. But she might be in hospital for days and days. It's better for her to be there. She'll have people to take care of her, and good food and a warm bed."

"She hates hospitals," Loofah replied. "Once, before she got me, she was in a hospital. She told me they made her leave before she was well, just because she couldn't pay her bill."

"That's harsh!" I cried. "But maybe all hospitals aren't like that. Anyway, let's rest for a while."

I gently pushed her to the ground and flopped down beside her.

"When did you and Odette first get together?" I asked, wanting to change the subject.

"A long time ago, at Mariah's hideout. I was born there. My mama was in bad shape after I was born, and Mariah took care of both of us."

She paused, remembering, then went on. "Odette stopped there sometimes to pet the dogs and cats, and she happened to come the day Mama died."

"Oh, Loofah, I'm sorry!" I cried.

"Mama was in so much pain that I think she was ready to go to heaven," she continued. "Odette buried her in the yard and said some words for her, then took me away. She says I'm the best thing that happened to her since she got homeless. And she says I'm the best dog she's ever known. She says I'm a bichon frise, and if she had papers to show that I'm purebred, I could be a show dog. I don't know who my father is, but Mama ..."

"Wait!" I interrupted. "You're going too fast. This place of Mariah's. What is it?"

"It's a big old empty house. Mariah has been there a long time. It's a secret place for strays. She calls it our Tribal Base."

"Tribal Base?"

"Yes. For the Tribe of Street Animals. You know, ones that are lost and homeless. It's a place where we can be safe. The Tribe is kind of like a family, except that animals come and go."

"Hmmm. I don't get it."

"I think you have to be there to understand. Mariah helps the animals and teaches us to help each other. And she keeps our historical memories."

"Historical ...what?"

"Memories. I'm not sure what it means. But she knows about different breeds and what is special about them."

"I'm a Labrador retriever, but I don't know anything that's special about me."

"Mariah could help you with that. She also tells us things we need to know to survive on the streets. How to find food, what places are safe, which people are bad."

"Like those guys in Donut Alley?"

"Yes. Those two. They're part of a dogfight ring, you know."

"Yeah. Ruby told me. But ... are there other bad

people around here?"

"There's Animal Control, but I don't think they are bad, they're just doing their job. The dogfight guys are the ones Mariah warns us about the most. Them, and the people at Puppy Haven."

"Puppy Haven? That sounds nice."

"It's not. Mariah told me not to ever let myself get picked up and taken there. I asked why, and she said she'd explain it when I'm older."

Just then, the back door of the Donut Shop opened and Mr. Yin peeked out. He saw us and smiled. Then he called to his wife, who came to the door and smiled also.

He said something to her in their language and she went back inside. When she came out again, she had a big bowl of noodles swimming around in golden broth.

Even with her tummy ache, Loofah couldn't resist.

As we slurped up the noodles, a young man came out the back door.

"I finished the last batch of donuts, Ma," he said. "What's up out here?"

"We feed dogs. They hungry," Mrs. Yin said.

The young man laughed and gave Mrs. Yin a hug. "You old softies. Feeding stray dogs is not a good idea. These look like nice ones, though. Look at that little white one. Cute."

Mr. Yin turned to his wife. "This little dog I think belong to dead lady. We keep?"

Loofah turned and bolted down the alley, and I raced after her.

"Bye-bye! Have nice day!" Mr. Yin called as we rounded the corner.

Loofah didn't stop until we were blocks away.

"Why ... did you ... run away, Loofah?" I panted. "I'll bet the Yins ... would take good ... care of you. You'd have all ... all the donuts and noodles you want!"

"They're nice, but … but I don't want to live with them. I … I want to stay with you and … and go to Mariah's. I have to be there … when … when Odette comes for me."

Didn't she hear what Mr. Yin said about Odette?

***

Full stomachs and the hot sun on our backs turned us into snails. Loofah had to stop and rest more than me; after all, she was used to riding in a stroller. Anyway, I was okay with taking it easier. The thorn scratches on my belly had healed a long time ago and I was a lot stronger, but I still got tired, and sometimes my legs and paws still hurt.

We found a shady place to wait out the hottest part of the day. Lying there with Loofah made me think of time spent the same way with Oliver, and that made me homesick again.

Yeah, I knew that running away was a crappy thing to do. But on the other hand, if Ruby came trotting by right now, wouldn't I leap up and run after her? Even if it meant leaving little Loofah behind? That would be harsh, but it was hard enough for *me* to keep up with Ruby.

I studied Loofah as she slept. In the daylight, I could see that her curly white fur was grimy and matted. Ruby and I rolled around in sprinklers to get clean, but Odette probably had no way to give Loofah a bath.

Thinking about abandoning Loofah made me feel guilty. But what was the point of wishing I could be with Ruby? She obviously didn't want me around.

Suddenly, a new thought struck me. What if Ruby was in trouble? Maybe she got caught by Stites and Onions, like that boxer she told me about. Maybe right now she needed help, and I was just lying here vegetating.

"Loofah," I blurted out, waking her up, "I'm worried

that Ruby's been hurt. Or kidnapped by those dogfight guys. Maybe I should look for her, just in case ..."

Loofah shook her head and cocked a bright eye at me. "Puppins, Ruby gets into scrapes, but she is smart and always gets herself out. And I think she really likes to be alone. Odette says she's never stuck with anyone for very long."

I didn't want to think about that, so I changed the subject. "It always seems like she is looking for something. What do you think it is?"

"I don't know. But I don't think she's looking for a companion. Odette says that if people and dogs are alone, it's usually because they want to be."

"But maybe it's because they haven't found the right friend, or the right partner."

"Not everyone needs someone else. You might, and so do I. So does Odette. But not everyone does."

It was really hard for me to accept that Ruby had no need for long-term friends. But I suppose I was in denial about her, just like Loofah was about Odette.

Some words snuck into my brain: *The house of denial has thick walls and very small windows, and whoever lives there will turn to stone.*

Yikes. The words made me shudder. Were Loofah and I doomed to turn into statues and have birds poop on us?

Loofah nudged me out of my dark thoughts.

"Puppins, please don't go off looking for Ruby. You will stay with me until we get to Mariah's, won't you?"

Looking into those mournful eyes, how could I say no?

18

We slept. When I woke up, Loofah was still deep in sleep. She was a cute little thing, for sure, but so needy. That was a bummer.

Despite the nap, I was still tired. And hungry. Wouldn't it be dinnertime at home?

Home. There it was again, the twisting knife of homesickness.

Still, there were times when I felt that it was kind of nice not being responsible for Kristin -- having to protect her and The Cottage, cheer her up when she was blue, take the blame for any messes.

I also didn't miss her anti-dog rules. Or, having to obey those "7 basic commands" for canines: Come! Sit! Down! Heel! Stay! Off! and, especially, No!

As for the danger, the uncertain eats, the lack of a person to love you back -- well, maybe if you lived on the streets long enough, you got used to all that. Maybe.

Suddenly, Loofah cried out in her sleep: "Odette! Are you hurt?"

She woke herself up. "Oh, I guess I was having a bad dream!"

"About Odette?"

"Yes. We were in Donut Alley and I licked her face but she didn't talk to me. Oh Puppins, I miss her so much. When will I find her?"

"It might not be for a long time," I said, trying to be as gentle as I could. "For now, don't think about it."

"Alright. But do you think I'll ever see her again?"

"I hope so," I replied. Not much of an answer, but I didn't want to hurt her.

But my brain shot out a warning: *Numbing the pain for a while will make it worse when you finally feel it.*

Yeah, I should tell her what I really thought happened to Odette. But I just couldn't do that.

We stretched and shook ourselves.

"Where is this Tribal Base?" I asked.

Without looking me in the eye, she mumbled, "I haven't been there for a while, Puppins, and Odette always knew the way. I'm not sure exactly where it is."

"Then how do we know which way to head?"

She thought hard, wrinkling up her forehead and squinting her eyes. Then she said, "I think it would be toward where the sun goes down. Yes, I'm sure of it."

She trotted off down the street. I followed, not so confident. The neighborhood around us was filled with shabby houses, metal bars on the windows, weeds, trash and broken glass in the yards.

Big kids with ragged pants sat on doorsteps, looking bored. One of them threw rocks at us, but missed when we ran hard. Some chained-up dogs barked meanly as we passed, reminding me of those two brutal pit bulls.

We tipped over a couple of garbage cans to look for food. Only some stale french fries and bits of salad.

We shared the fries, but I let Loofah have the salad; I'm not big on greens. Anyway, they reminded me too much of Kristin.

We walked on. I began to worry. We were on a steady course toward the setting sun, but Loofah gave no hint that we were getting close.

As we left that sketchy neighborhood behind, I

started to see a lot of cute little houses like The Cottage, puncturing my heart with another stab of homesickness.

Loofah, suddenly nervous, stepped up her pace. "I think we'd better get out of here," she whispered.

"Why? It's pretty here. And it smells good. Look at the colors on that house and those yellow flowers."

"Odette says nice neighborhoods mean trouble. They don't want stray dogs or homeless people. They call Animal Control or the police if they think you don't belong."

Her little legs, churning faster and faster, became a blur. As she sped along, she glanced anxiously from side to side, trying to stay in the shadows.

Darkness was coming, and I thought we should be making a serious search for food. In that kind of neighborhood, I figured there would be really good garbage. But Loofah just wanted to get out of there as fast as possible.

Finally, we reached a street that backed up to some woods. Plunging quickly into the trees, Loofah sank gratefully to the ground.

"We made it!" she panted. "This will be safe."

I stretched out beside her. "Are we close to Mariah's now?" I asked.

"I ... I'm not sure," she stammered.

Aargh. That's what I was afraid of. I didn't say anything, but I was not happy.

"I'm sorry, Puppins," she said mournfully. "We missed the street I was looking for. Now I think we're near the Old Bridge."

I had no idea what she was talking about.

"Old Bridge?"

"Yes. It's a way to get from here to L.A. over the river. It doesn't have much traffic, and there's a walkway. But Odette says it was shut down to be repaired a while ago, and I don't know if it's open."

"River? I never heard of a river in L.A.," I said.

"The Los Angeles River. It's called that, but there's no water in it. Unless there's been a big rain in the foothills, and how often does that happen? Odette says it was lined with cement a long time ago, and it looks like a big ugly ditch."

"If there's no water in it, why couldn't we just run across?"

"Because it's fenced off. You can't get to it."

"Crazy. Who ever heard of a cement river with a fence around it?" I asked.

"Only in L.A. That's what Odette says."

"Well, isn't there some other way to get back to Los Angeles?"

"There's the freeway ..." she paused.

The freeway. Even in the car with Kristin or Dora, I was scared of freeways. Hundreds of cars and trucks whizzing by at top speed, and no sidewalks to walk on. A dog alone on a freeway would be a goner. I'd been hit by a car in Seattle, and once was enough.

"I don't want to go on the freeway," I said.

"Me neither. Odette says you have to have a death wish to do that."

"Can't we go back and look for the street we missed?"

"I don't think I could find it from here. And I don't want to go through that nice neighborhood again. That was scary." She shivered, then went on. "Puppins, do you think I'll be able to see Odette soon?"

"Go to sleep, Loofah. We'll figure out what to do later."

19

Loofah slept like a rock, but I couldn't get settled. Finally, I got up and stretched.

A full moon was just rising over the foothills, lighting up Loofah's snowy fur and giving the trees a soft glow. Everything was peaceful.

Deciding to look around, I made my way through the woods. Suddenly, right in front of me, a bridge loomed up like a ghost in the moonlight.

It was kind of pretty, with fancy metal arches underneath and unlit globe lamps lined down each side.

I trotted over to where the land dropped off by the bridge, and scanned below.

Way, way down, at the very bottom, was a ditch covered in concrete, blocked off on the sides by a chain-link fence.

Just as Loofah had said. Creepy.

As I stood there, taking in the eerie scene, my eye caught a slight movement in the nearby brush.

Another movement.

Then, in the pale moonlight, I made out four dogs. Three were asleep on the ground, while the fourth circled restlessly around them.

A moonbeam touched the pacing dog's fur and set it on fire.

"Ruby?" I cried out.

At the sound of her name, she turned abruptly and stared through the shadows. "Who's there?"

"Me! Puppins!"

"Puppins? What are you doing here?"

"Trying to get back home. What are *you* doing here?"

"Nothing. Just passing by," she said curtly.

An awkward silence. I moved closer. Then the big question just fell out of my mouth before I could stop it.

"Why didn't you come back to the park? Were you hurt? I've been worried about you."

Lame. As soon as I blurted it out, I wished I hadn't. Even in the dark, I could see the contempt in her eyes.

"I just didn't make it back," she replied coldly. "I figured you'd be able to take care of yourself by then."

"I can take care of myself," I said defensively. "That's not the point."

"What *is* the point?" Her voice dripped with sarcasm.

"The point is," I mumbled dumbly, "that I thought we were going to travel together for a while."

"We did."

"Not very long," I countered. OMG. Why was I making such a fool of myself?

She turned away and didn't answer.

I was humiliated, but that didn't stop me from trying to regain her attention, so I plunged on. "Anyway, I've got Loofah with me, and we're going to cross the bridge."

She turned around. "Loofah? What's she doing with you? Where's Odette?"

"I'm pretty sure she's dead, but Loofah doesn't want to believe it."

"Oh," she said shortly. "So where are you and Loofah headed?"

"She's trying to find a dog named Mariah. And she says this Mariah might help me get back home."

"Mariah? She's probably at the Tribal Base. What are

you doing here?"

"We were trying to get there but got off track. Is it true that the bridge is closed?"

"Yes. They're still working on it. But it is possible to get across."

I brightened up. "That would be better than going on the freeway, wouldn't it?"

"Depends on whether you'd rather die by falling or by car."

Gulp. A shudder traveled down my back from my neck to the tip of my tail. "Neither, actually," I replied, trying for a light tone. "Which way would you choose?"

"The Old Bridge. I've done it before. I'm going again soon with these other dogs." She paused, then added, "You can come along if you want."

My stupid heart quivered in my chest. Another chance to be with Ruby.

"Alright," I replied, faking casual. "I'll get Loofah."

As I ran off, Ruby called to the snoozing dogs: "Max! Bobo! Felicity! Time to go!"

***

I roused Loofah, explaining quickly what was going on. She shook her head when I said Ruby's name, but followed me back to the bridge.

I thought about making a quick search for food, but maybe a death-defying bridge crossing goes better on an empty stomach.

Ruby stood by the big yellow barriers blocking the bridge, and next to her was one of the other dogs.

"This is Felicity," Ruby told us. "Felicity, Puppins and Loofah."

Felicity was small, brown and tan short hair, long body, and a ruff of shaggy fur around her neck. She was, I guess you'd say, plain.

When she stepped forward to greet us with a friendly

sniff, I saw that one of her legs was twisted, and she walked with a limp.

"Where are the others?" I asked Ruby.

"Max and Bobo decided not to go. Last-minute attack of nerves," she said with contempt.

Okay. I could not back out now, no matter what.

"Alright," she said, "let's get started. We need the moonlight, and it will be gone pretty soon."

"Couldn't we wait for daytime?" asked Loofah nervously.

"The workers come early. They'd never let us get on the bridge. It's now or never." She turned and surveyed the structure.

"I'll go first, since I've done it before," she said. "Don't walk too close together. If someone panics, we don't want them taking anyone else down with them."

Uh oh. This could be even worse than I feared.

Ruby continued, "Don't look over the edge. Keep your eyes straight ahead, so you can see what's coming up. There are big gaps where parts of the floor are gone, and you have to balance on the narrow beams."

She paused, then went on: "It will get slippery when the morning dew comes. Don't walk fast. And don't make any sudden moves. You might startle someone into falling."

Loofah and I stared at each other, then at Felicity. How could a dog with a crippled leg make it across? Still, she did not seem the least bit nervous.

Ruby continued. "Puppins, let the two smaller dogs go in the middle, then you bring up the rear. It shouldn't take us long to get across. Let's go."

20

We started out, Ruby in the lead. She squeezed through the barricade, then called back to us: "Looks like more sections of the road are done. Should be easy."

Following her, we fell into a single file -- Ruby, Felicity, Loofah, me. The bridge seemed sort of magical, with those ornate arches underneath and the moon throwing silvery shadows on its surface.

I felt my anxiety drain away. It was going to be alright. Best of all, Ruby was back in my life! Finally, I'd be able to show her that I wasn't a wimp after all.

The first stretch on the bridge was paved. Then came gravel and bumps -- hard on my paws, but no danger. We trotted on.

Suddenly, Ruby stopped. Then Felicity, then Loofah, then me. The roadway had ended. Now, only a narrow beam. Ruby had warned us about this, but actually seeing it was something else.

The beam was just wide enough for our paws. To make matters worse, a slippery film of dew, like silver icing on a dark chocolate cake, had spread over the beam.

My heart thumped. Gulping in a big dose of night air, trying to calm myself, some words flashed through my brain: *To die will be an awfully big adventure!*

True. But not the kind of adventure I was looking

for.

Ruby started up again, much slower. The rest of us followed. I tried to concentrate on each step. Watching my feet without letting my eyes stray over the edge was really hard, and I moved as slow as a sleepwalking slug.

I glanced up at the others. Felicity was moving along steadily behind Ruby, despite her bad leg. But Loofah – right in front of me -- was in trouble. Each trembling step she took was slower than the one before.

Ruby warned us not to walk too close together, but Loofah slowed down so much that I couldn't help it.

"I'm right behind you, Loofah," I said quietly, trying not to startle her. "Don't worry. You'll be alright. You're doing fine."

"Oh Puppins, I ... I'm not! I'll never make it!" She stopped, her soft pompom tail brushing against my face. I wobbled, then recovered.

"Don't look down," I told her. "Close your eyes for a second, and take a deep breath."

"A-a-all r-r-right," she stammered.

I took a deep breath myself, then said, "Okay, let's start out together. Take it slow. Look ahead as you go. Remember, don't look down. Ready?"

"Y-y-yes," she answered. She took a step, then another, then another. Gradually she was going at a steady though snail-ish pace.

"Am...am I doing alright?" she called back.

"Fine," I told her. "Just keep going."

"It's better, knowing that you ... that you are right behind me."

But I was not right behind her. The stop had thrown off my rhythm and I couldn't get it back. To complicate things, the moon was starting to go down, painting the bridge in deeper shadows and making the beam hard to see.

Then the wind came up. The Old Bridge seemed to sway like a broken tree branch. I stumbled. Scrambling to get my footing, I accidentally glanced over the edge.

There was the great yawning ravine, ready to gobble me up in its jaws like the giant crocodile I saw once on Animal Planet. My head swirled. In the fading moonlight, the concrete river far below turned into a waiting deathbed.

***

The next thing I knew, I was lying on the beam, my legs folded under me, a soft tongue licking my face. A quiet voice said my name. Was it an angel? Was I in dog heaven?

"Puppins? Can you hear me?"

I opened my eyes. Felicity's plain little face was next to mine, her dark eyes filled with concern.

"What ... what happened?" I managed.

"Everything's fine. Ruby and Loofah are across. I came back to see how you are doing."

Aargh. Ruby had made it, and little Loofah. Felicity, with her crippled leg, not only got to the other side but came back for me. How could that happen?

Felicity spoke again. "Now that you've had a rest, we can go on. I'll be right in front of you, so don't go too fast and bowl me over."

Ha. Some joke. Anger shot through me. If those three girls could do it, so could I.

I stood up, slowly, my legs like cooked spaghetti. Then an awful realization hit me: Felicity was facing me - - the wrong direction!

Not to worry. With a sudden twist, she turned herself around. Just like those gymnastic girls Kristin watches sometimes on TV. Amazing.

"Coming?" she called back.

"Yeah," I answered fiercely. I'd show her. And Ruby

and Loofah. They'd regret thinking I was a yellow-bellied coward, which I knew they did.

One step. Then another. And another.

Then I stopped, my determination crumbling like a stale cookie.

Felicity glanced back and saw me, paralyzed and shaking. "Puppins," she said, "I'm going to sing a bridge-crossing song. Listen to the words and step to the beat."

Howling softly, a little off key, she sang:

"Over the Old Bridge
Under the moon
A leisurely crossing
With land coming soon.
Over the Old Bridge
Breakfast is near
Pancakes and syrup
Will bring us good cheer."

The song went on and on, sillier and sillier. I knew she was making it up, and listening to see what she'd come up with next kept my mind off the ravine below. My steps to the beat of the song got steadier. Before I knew it, I was across.

Collapsing on solid ground, I looked back at the Old Bridge, slinking like a criminal into the shadows. I hoped I'd never see that -- or any bridge -- ever again.

Loofah ran up and rubbed noses with me. "Puppins! It's a good thing I didn't know you weren't right behind me, or I never could have ..."

I interrupted her. "Where's Ruby?"

"She went on. She said she was in a hurry."

Aargh. I tried not to show my bitter disappointment. Dumped again! Why was I such a loser?

Much later, I realized that I was so bummed about Ruby that I forgot to thank Felicity for saving my life.

Loser, for sure.

21

Worn out by the ordeal, the three of us lay there for a while. I didn't feel like talking, but Loofah couldn't stop.

She told Felicity, in great detail, about how Stites and Onions and Tolliver Yar terrorized her and Odette. How Odette got taken away to hospital. And how I got ditched by Ruby. Ouch.

She went on to relate how I joined up with her, how lucky that was for her, what a good friend I was. And now I had helped her across the Old Bridge.

Loofah had become the upbeat one, while I was down in the dumps. Some words crept into my sorry brain: *A cheerful heart is good medicine, but a crushed spirit dries up the bones.*

My spirit was crushed, for sure. Loofah's heart was cheerful at the moment, but was she going to be good medicine for my dried-up bones? Not likely.

"Where are you headed?" asked Felicity, when Loofah finally wound down.

"To the Tribal Base," Loofah told her. "I'm going to wait there for Odette, and Puppins will ask Mariah to help him find his home."

"The Tribal Base? That's where I'm going!" Felicity said.

"Really? Why?" I asked.

"I go there once in a while to see Mariah. I've known her a long time."

"Then you know how to get there? Loofah's not too sure."

"Yes. We can all go together," she replied.

Whew. That was a huge relief.

Then Felicity looked me in the eye. "Puppins, I'm sorry about Ruby. She doesn't seem to really need friends."

I wished Felicity hadn't brought it up. I put my head down on my paws and didn't answer.

Ruby did not want my friendship. There would be no more chances.

Some new words worked their way into my brain: *It's over, and it can't be helped, and that's one consolation...*

Yeah, it was over, and it could not be helped. But how was that a consolation?

***

After we rested awhile longer, Felicity suggested looking for something to eat.

"Yes! I'm hungry!" Loofah cried. "Puppins, you lead the way."

My ego took another hit. I wanted to redeem myself for the bridge fiasco and be firmly in command. But I had no clue where we were, or where to find food.

Felicity spoke up. "Puppins is in strange territory. I'm very familiar with this area, and I think I know where we might find some food."

Once again, I licked my wounded ego. Someday, but obviously not that one, I'd be the alpha dog.

***

We set out. The sky got lighter, and a band of orange, like one of Kristin's scarves, spread over the hazy foothills. It was going to be another hot day.

So far, though, the air was as fresh as a gulp of cold milk. (I had cold milk once. Dora put out a bowl for

Oliver, and he actually shared it with me.)

As the day went on, tiredness, and the growing heat, got to us. No food where Felicity thought there might be. No generous café owners, no promising garbage cans.

Just as I started hallucinating about Dora's grilled cheese sandwiches, a boy appeared and ran toward us.

"Hey, dogs! Where'd you come from?" he yelled in a friendly way. Loofah and Felicity trotted up to him. I hung back, afraid I'd scare him. He held out his hand for them to sniff, then patted them while eyeing me cautiously.

We followed as he ran to a nearby house. "Do you want to live with me?" he asked. "I need a dog. Maybe two. Wait here."

He disappeared inside, returning quickly with his mother. Sitting on the steps, they petted Loofah and Felicity, then the mom called me over. I trotted up to her, wagging my tail.

It felt so good to be petted!

"I'll bet you're all hungry," she said. "I'll get you some food, but then you have to go. We can't afford to keep two or three dogs, or even one!" She laughed.

She went inside and soon returned, carrying a bowl of water and a tray loaded with enchiladas, beans, rice and tortillas. We ate like pigs, no time for manners.

When the tray was licked clean, the mom and boy patted us again. "Now go!" the mom said cheerfully.

We trotted away, hearing her tinkling laugh as her kid begged, "Can't we keep one of them, Mommy? The little white one?"

***

We ran along with new energy. Suddenly a wind came up, hot and dry. I knew about such winds. Kristin and Jodi call them the Santa Ana's because they blow in from the Santa Ana Desert. And when those winds come, they heat up the city like an oven turned on high.

They burn your eyes and dry out your nose. They fill you with a kind of uneasy dread, and they make you a little crazy.

Some words crept into my brain as we slowed to a walk: *The sun hung like a stone; time dripped away like a steaming river.*

If we didn't find a shady place to rest and get some water soon, we'd be in trouble.

Just as it seemed like we'd die on the sidewalk like desert rats, we stumbled upon a grassy park with a little pond. We drank our fill, trying not to slurp up any of the tiny fish, then slumped under a shrub.

I closed my eyes. Right away, scary scenes flashed across my brain's big screen: grotesque beasts with knives swam in a river made of broken glass. Then a monstrous red dog appeared, mocking me, while hot winds destroyed my newly groomed hairstyle.

I woke up, shaking. Worst movie night since Kristin and her friends binge-watched horror films last Halloween.

Rearranging myself on the hard ground, I went back to sleep. Then a new dream came. As I tried to get a drink from a lake, its water blue and tempting, a giant dog-eating fish swam just under the surface. Getting brave, I leaped in the lake. Cool water washed over my feverish skin and the menacing fish disappeared.

I opened my eyes. I was drenched. The sprinklers had come on.

I couldn't help remembering that time Ruby and I played in a sprinkler. *Love, genuine, passionate love, was mine for the first time ...*

Wait. Seriously? Was that what it was? I think not. Time to stop dreaming about her. Enjoy my new friends. Have some fun.

"Hey, Loofah and Felicity!" I called out. "Wake up! Wanna play sprinkler tag?"

***

We romped through the sparkling waterdrops for a long time. Then, all refreshed, we trekked on.

Felicity was a good guide. She was upbeat and kept her cool, even in the face of Loofah's constant worries.

As we trotted along my stomach made rumbling noises, sounding like that old truck in our neighborhood that Kristin says needs a new muffler.

Just then, we came to a church with a big stone angel on the lawn. She had a nice smile on her face, so we figured we'd be welcome there.

A picnic was going on. Grownups sat at tables while kids -- all different skin colors like in my neighborhood – chased each other and played games.

Great-smelling food overflowed the tables. I remembered the church supper Dora took me to once.

"There's nothing like a church potluck for good eating," Dora told me, and she was an expert.

Keeping a polite distance, Felicity, Loofah and I surveyed the amazing spread. There was a lot of food like I had at Dora's, along with the kind of stuff Kristin's friends brought over for parties: egg rolls, lumpia, adobo, tamales, fruit salad, curry and kale.

My mouth watered and my empty stomach growled louder.

Suddenly, a tall woman came rushing toward us. She did not look friendly.

"Shoo! Go away!" she cried, waving her arms.

We turned to run. But just then, a young man appeared. He had skin the color of caramel syrup, and he wore a black suit with a white collar. He reminded me of a Boston terrier -- in a good way.

"Welcome! Would you travelers like something to

eat?" he called out.

"Oh Father," scolded the tall woman. "They're strays. They might be dangerous." I wondered why she called him Father. He appeared to be a lot younger than her.

"Harmless strays, I believe," the young man replied. "Jesus said to feed the hungry, and I think that includes our animal friends."

He turned to us again. "Come along, compadres." As the woman shook her head and stalked off, we followed him.

A horde of kids swarmed around us. They called him Father, too. He must have a really big family, I thought.

Leading us to where some girls scraped leftovers into a garbage can, he asked them, "Have you any delicacies for these wayfaring strangers?"

They giggled and began piling stuff on paper plates for us. Some of everything except corn on the cob, fried chicken and brownies, which, sadly, are not good for dogs.

We wolfed it down. Then the Father brought over a bucket of water. While we drank, the kids petted us – Loofah got the most attention, because she's small and fluffy and white.

We wagged our tails to say thanks, then it was time to go.

"Come back and visit us again sometime," called the Father as we trotted off.

Technically, it was garbage. But that was the best meal I'd had since I left Dora's.

22

The moon appeared above us, lighting our way. Then it sank on the other side of the sky a long time later, leaving a lonely darkness behind.

Felicity set the pace, despite her limp. Occasionally she asked if we wanted to rest, but we voted to keep going. It was hard, especially for Loofah, but all three of us were anxious to reach our destination.

The sun was just coming up over the hills when I began to get hungry again. Thoughts of Dora's waffles with syrup and bacon rose up to torture me.

But before I could suggest looking for breakfast, Felicity turned and headed down an alley and Loofah, lagging behind, suddenly came to life. She sped past me, past Felicity, down the alley and up to the back gate of a rickety old house. A big, spooky-looking dump.

"This is it!" Loofah cried. "The Tribal Base!"

"It is indeed," Felicity affirmed.

Loofah flew through the unlatched gate into a dusty courtyard, with Felicity and me close behind. The little white dog bounced up the steps like a tennis ball, then pushed the peeling door open with her nose.

"Mariah! It's me, Loofah! I'm back!"

We heard stirrings from the next room. Then in trotted a brindle greyhound, the ex-racer that Loofah had described as graying, but still as fast as the wind.

Mariah and Loofah pranced and danced, delighted to

see each other. Then Mariah spotted Felicity and leaped over to rub noses with her. "It's been so long since you were here, Felicity. I've missed you! How are you?"

"Fine. It's good to be back, Mariah. I've missed you, too."

Felicity introduced me to Mariah, saying, "Puppins has been helping Loofah since Odette's been gone."

"Welcome to our Tribal Base, Puppins," Mariah said. "But Loofah, where is Odette?"

The little dog lowered her head. "Those bad men from the dogfight ring robbed her and knocked her down. She went to hospital, and I think she's still there."

"That's terrible!" cried Mariah. "You haven't heard how she is?"

"N-n-no. But before they took her away, she told me to come here and wait for her. I know she'll come for me as soon as she can."

Mariah was silent for a moment, then said, "You can tell me more about it later, dear. Now come with me. You three must be thirsty."

She led us out to the courtyard, where a chipped stone fountain held a shallow pool of water in its wide bowl.

"The hot winds have dried up most of our water," she said, "and it hasn't rained for quite a while. Anyway, help yourselves. We'll find another source when this is gone."

We thanked her and took a few sips. I was surprised that she would share her precious water with me, a total stranger. Like that Father who invited us strays to share his food -- unexpected, but really nice.

Then I thought about what Felicity did on the Old Bridge. I was a stranger in need; she put herself at risk to save me, and I still hadn't thanked her.

***

Following Mariah back inside, we passed through some junk-filled rooms, then into a room that was cleared of trash. It had a peaceful vibe, and big windows that let in the early morning sun.

"This is the Tribe's Gathering Room," said Mariah. "We're a small family right now, but that can change from day to day."

She introduced two dogs lying on the floor: Sparkles, a blonde cocker spaniel, and Zeke, a German shepherd. Sparkles wandered out of her yard and got lost, and Zeke was going to help get her back home.

I guess Loofah was right. The Tribe really does help pathetic lost dogs like me.

A few cats were in the room, and Mariah introduced them. Kara and Matzov, two orange alley cats; Romeow and Julicat, a pair of Siamese who were dumped when their owner died; and Kudos, an old black-and-white gentleman who had seen better days.

Seeing those cats made me think of Oliver. I missed him. He was a pain in the butt, but a BFF is a BFF.

Suddenly, a round gray mouse popped out of a hole in the wall and scampered wildly around the room.

"That's Pasadena Fats," Mariah said, "our resident rodent." To my surprise, the cats didn't pounce on him. Instead, Matzov let Fats ride on his back, yelling "Giddyap!" as he clutched the big cat's fur.

Fats tumbled off and we all settled down. Then Mariah asked Loofah to tell her story, and she tearfully described what happened in Donut Alley.

"Man, that's flaccid!" Fats cried, as the others nodded in sympathy.

Then Loofah told how I joined up with her, and helped her get across the Old Bridge. "Puppins saved my life!" she exclaimed, and everyone cheered.

"Turgid, my man! Totally turgid!" yelled Fats.

Loofah scowled. "I'm not your man!" she cried.

"That's just the way Fats talks," Mariah assured her. "Don't take it personally."

I was embarrassed, but glad she left out the bad parts: Ruby ditching me twice, and my wimpy meltdown on the bridge.

The talk turned to Zeke and his plan for helping Sparkles. The chatter went on, but I was out of it. Time for a nap.

***

The next thing I knew, Felicity was standing over me with questions dancing in her dark brown eyes.

"Good evening, Puppins. I was wondering if you would sleep forever!"

"Is it nighttime already?" I mumbled. It was.

Felicity said Zeke and Sparkles had set out a while ago, promising to return if they couldn't find the cocker spaniel's home in a day or two.

I stumbled groggily to the window. It was dark outside, but I could see Mariah and Loofah in the courtyard. Had Mariah figured out the truth about Odette? If so, I hoped she could help the little dog face up to reality.

I went back and flopped down near Felicity, who was watching me with friendly eyes. Maybe now was the time to say what I needed to say.

"Felicity," I began, "what you did on the Old Bridge ... I just ... I just want to ..."

She smiled, shaking her head. "No need to say anything, Puppins. Just doing my job."

"Your job? What job?"

"I'll tell you sometime. Right now, it's time for all of us to go forage for dinner. Come on!"

23

The following days fell into a nice routine: sleeping while it was hot, going out to search for food after dark, then coming back to talk and tell stories. (In my case, mostly listen.)

Mariah made us laugh with funny tales about greyhounds she called dogsfunctional.

She also told us that when she was a racer, she learned about greyhounds and a lot of other breeds by listening to the trainers.

"They talked about dogs all day long," she said. "They said that greyhounds came from the country of Egypt, and if you go there now you can still see drawings of greyhounds in burial places that are thousands of years old."

She paused, then continued. "Greyhounds were not only hunting partners and companions for people, we were practically worshipped like gods."

Wow. That was impressive. I wondered if anyone every worshipped Labs like gods. Probably not.

To the Egyptians, Mariah went on, the birth of a greyhound was almost as big a deal as the birth of a child.

"And when a pet greyhound died," she told us, "the entire family shaved their heads and wailed, and didn't eat for two days."

"That's weird," Loofah giggled, and everyone nodded

in agreement.

"How fast can you greyhounds run?" I asked Mariah.

"Almost as fast as a horse. Of course, I'm a little too old now to take on a horse," she joked.

Mariah then told us about our own breeds. Loofah's, the bichon frise, used to be the favorite pets of kings and queens, she said. They also performed in circuses because they can walk on their hind legs and twirl and do other tricks.

"I'd rather be in a circus any day than sit on a king's lap!" Loofah exclaimed, demonstrating how she could twirl.

Mariah went on to talk about my breed. She said Labrador retrievers are known for how smart they are. (That would surprise Jodi, who says I have no brain.)

"Labs are strong, and good workers," she continued. "In the country of Labrador, they helped fishermen haul in heavy nets loaded with fish.

"Now, they are used as hunting dogs and guide dogs for blind people. Or trained to sniff out drugs and explosives, since Lab noses work so much better than human noses."

Whew. I guess that means I'd never have to do bomb duty, I thought. My nose was damaged when that car hit me, remember?

Felicity, it turns out, is a border terrier. "They are one of the smallest terriers, but they are fast enough to keep up with horseback riders in a fox hunt," Mariah said.

"Their bodies are so thin and flexible that they can squeeze into fox holes. And they are brave -- they aren't afraid to take on a fox, or even a much tougher badger."

I glanced over at Felicity and thought about what she did on the bridge. She lived up to her breed, for sure, even with her limp.

According to Mariah, even mutts should feel good about themselves.

"Those trainers at the racetrack said that mixed breeds usually are healthier and stronger than purebred dogs and can make the best pets," she told us.

I loved hearing Mariah's histories. And it was nice that the Tribe was sort of like a family -- whoever showed up at the backdoor was welcome.

I felt welcome, too, although I really wanted to get home.

***

In the meantime, I sometimes caught myself wishing I had one more chance with Ruby. Sigh.

One evening, trying to sound casual, I asked Mariah if she knew Ruby.

"Yes. Why do you ask?" she replied.

"No reason," I muttered. "I ... I just wondered."

"I don't know her very well," Mariah said. "She's only been here a few times, and she never stays long."

"Do you know where she comes from, or why she lives on the streets?"

"No. Unlike most dogs and cats who come here, she hasn't shared her story. I can just tell you that according to those trainers at the racetrack, Irish setters are headstrong and not usually good at obedience. As for Ruby herself, she's made it clear that she doesn't want to get involved with the Tribe."

"Do you know why?" I asked.

"Maybe it's because it would mean getting close to others, and that's something she doesn't seem to want."

That was Ruby, alright. She didn't want to be close to Jodi, and for sure she didn't want stay close to me.

***

Later, going out to find something to eat, we took back alleys and walked solo or in twos, like Mariah said we should.

"If people see a lot of strays together, they think it's a dangerous pack," she explained, "and they call Animal Control. Especially if there's a big black dog in the group."

She smiled at me when she said it, but it was no joke. So unfair.

That night, Mariah and I walked together. "Loofah tells me you ran away from home, and now you want to go back. Is that right?" she asked.

"Well, yes," I admitted vaguely.

"You don't sound too sure."

"I am sure, Mariah. I miss Kristin. And Dora, and Jodi and Oliver, and Colette, and ..."

"It sounds like you have quite a circle of friends," she broke in. "Tell me about them. Tell me your story, from the beginning."

I told her the only beginning I could remember – how I was saved by Kristin's mom, the Seattle vet, after that car thing happened. And I told her about the two big mysteries in my life: who my first owners were, and why weird brainy things sometimes pop into my head.

"Can you give me an example?" she asked.

"Oh, no. When I *try* to think of something intelligent, I can't."

"Alright," she said with a smile. "Go on with your story."

I explained how Kristin adopted me. And about Oliver and his family under house. About Jodi and how she tried to tame Ruby. About Dog Detention, and Doggy Daycare with Dora, and how I got to be a fat furry balloon.

"Why did you leave home?" she inquired.

Good question. I didn't answer.

"Was it because of Ruby?"

"Yeah," I admitted. Then the words just tumbled out like a river of M&Ms spilling out of a torn bag (which happened once at Jodi's -- a memorable day).

"I ran away to be with Ruby but she ditched me and then Loofah turned up and needed help and then I ran into Ruby again at the bridge but made a fool of myself and she dumped me again and now I don't know where my home is but I want to go there."

A full confession. Whew.

Mariah took all this in. Then she asked, "What if Ruby turns up again?"

"I ... I don't know," I stammered. "It sounds really dumb, but I might want to be with her again. Maybe my brain's gotten curdled."

She didn't say anything for a while. Then she asked, "What happened at the Old Bridge?"

I told her about my blackout shame.

"Loofah got across. And Felicity did it twice, with her bad leg. And I had to be rescued by a girl."

"I'm not surprised about Felicity. She is one of the strongest and bravest dogs I know," Mariah said.

"I didn't mean to put her down," I said quickly. "She was great. It was amazing how she turned around on that beam. But if I wasn't such a wimp, I could've made it on my own."

"God gave Felicity the feet of a deer, despite her lame leg. And, as I've mentioned, border terriers are very flexible."

She regarded me closely. "What do you think your strengths are, Puppins?"

"Eating," I answered ruefully. "I'm good at eating, pooping and sleeping. That's about all."

She laughed. "That's not all. You showed so much caring when you stayed with Loofah, after Odette got taken away. And by the way you encouraged her on the bridge. You weren't as brave then as you wanted to be, but that doesn't mean you won't have courage next time. Don't lose faith in yourself."

Easier said than done. And there'd probably be no next time, where Ruby was concerned.

***

A breakfast place that stayed open all night was our dinner destination. Felicity said it was called the 3G's because they served grits, gruel and granola.

I didn't know what grits and gruel were, but they sounded lethal. And a breakfast place with no bacon? Give me a break.

Then I thought about Kristin. She was a nut about granola, so this would be her kind of place.

Maybe, if I ever got back home, I should stop complaining about Kristin's ideas on food. It's possible she was right, much as I hated to admit it.

***

At the backdoor of the restaurant, Mariah barked politely. A young guy came out, patted us and gave us a huge pan of cold gruel -- which turned out to be oatmeal. Who knew?

In fact, it was like the oatmeal Dora made: thick and creamy, dotted with raisins and covered with a blanket of brown sugar. Super.

***

On the way back, we broke the dog-pack rule and walked all together. Even though it was very dark and the streets and alleys were deserted, it did not seem scary.

Funny how a full stomach and being with a pack of pals can calm your nerves.

As we walked, Loofah piped up. "I think I'd better go look for Odette tomorrow. She would've come for me by now if she could. She's probably not strong yet and needs my help."

Silence. I guess everyone knew that was not a good idea.

Loofah turned to me. "Puppins, will you come with me? As soon as we find Odette, she and I will help you get back home."

I stalled, turning to the Tribe's greyhound alpha.

"Mariah, what do you think?"

"I've told Loofah that I'd like her to wait. I believe Mr. Pegasus is coming soon, and he always has the latest street news. Maybe he'll know what's happening with Odette."

Waiting for Mr. Pegasus, whoever he was, sounded like a good plan for Loofah. But for me, not so much.

I was ready to leave for home, with no more delays.

Mariah guessed what I was thinking.

"Puppins, I know you are anxious to go home," she said. "Someone else can go with Loofah."

I looked at the little white dog. She'd been through so much. Leaving home was my own bad choice, but Loofah didn't choose what happened to her. Besides, she was my friend now.

"Okay, Loofah," I said slowly, "I'll go with you."

She rushed up and gave my face a few hundred licks. Messy, but sweet.

Then Felicity spoke up. "If you like, Puppins, I'll tag along with you and Loofah."

Are you kidding? That was the best news I'd had in ages.

With Felicity's help, things were bound to go faster -- and, I hoped, turn out better.

24

As we trotted into the Tribal Base, Pasadena Fats popped out of his hole like a cork out of a bottle and scampered up to Mariah. He was in a frenzy.

"Something's happened! Something totally flaccid!" he cried.

"What is it, Fats?" asked Mariah.

"People! People inside the Tribal Base! They snooped all around!"

"Could you tell what they wanted?"

The overstuffed mouse ran in circles. "I don't know. They said stuff about what bad shape the house is in. After they left, I ran out front and there's a big sign stuck in the ground."

"That's bad news," Mariah said, her face creased with worry.

Yeah. I knew from things Kristin and Jodi said that a sign in the front yard meant the house was for sale. What if someone bought the Tribal Base and moved in?

"Oh Mariah," Loofah wailed, "are people going to take away our secret place?"

"This has happened before," Mariah told her calmly. "A sign goes up and people come to look. After a while the sign goes down. This house needs too much work."

For now, she continued, "we'll do what we've done in the past. Fats, you're the early warning system. Keep watch. When you sound the alarm, we'll hide out back in the Carriage House. Most people don't get that far. If we need to, we'll find another hideout."

"You can always stay at my camp by the Old Bridge," Felicity offered.

Camp? By the Old Bridge? Hmmm. Maybe it was that place where Loofah and I first met her. There was a lot about Felicity that I didn't know. But just hearing those words "Old Bridge" made me shudder. I had no desire to go back there.

The Tribe was in an uproar, milling around and barking, mewing, yipping and wailing. I figured I'd be long gone before anything happened, but I felt bad for the rest of them. The Base was the only place most of them had ever felt safe.

To distract everyone from the bad news, Mariah gathered us around and told us stories about some of her nutso relatives that made us laugh.

I asked about her life at the track. "What was it like, Mariah? Why did you leave?"

"Well, as a new racer I had to prove myself," she said. "They give you six chances to finish first, second, third or fourth. I didn't make it. I could have, but it just seemed silly to me. I loved to run just for the fun of it, not to win."

"What happened then?" I asked.

"I knew they'd get rid of me. If I was lucky I'd get adopted, but there aren't enough adoptive homes for all the ex-racers. Chances are, I'd be put to death."

"Whaaat? That's way harsh!" I cried, echoed by all the others.

"That's just the way it is," she said. "So, I slipped away one night when they brought us back from a race. I ran across the freeway, dodging cars, to get as far away as possible.

"Living on the street was hard, because I was used

to being taken care of. But in most ways, my life was better. As a racer, when you aren't racing or in the exercise runs, you're caged in a small crate. You have no chance to be free or to make friends."

She paused, then went on. "After being on the street for a while, I got the idea of finding a safe place where stray dogs and cats could come and help each other.

"I stumbled across a vacant house -- not this one -- and it became the first Tribal Base. When it was sold, we had to move on. We found this place, and we've been here ever since."

I examined the Gathering Room. It was dirty and full of spider webs. The floor was stained, the walls faded and peeling, and the big window was cracked. But that window let in sunlight during the day and moonbeams at night. It seemed perfect. I hoped the Tribe would not have to find another hideout.

***

Mr. Pegasus didn't show up that night, or the next day. That evening, as the rest of us sat in our circle, Loofah trotted around anxiously, worrying out loud about Odette.

"What if she forgot how to get here? Her brain might not be working too well. She got knocked down by those criminals, you know."

"I don't think she would forget," said Mariah. "Anyway, I'm sure Puppins and Felicity will do all they can to help find her. Now lie down and rest, little one."

Loofah crumpled down next to her. "Mariah, will you tell Puppins why you are the Tribe's Keeper of Memories? I tried but I couldn't explain it very well."

Mariah smiled. "Well, I have a good memory, and I know the streets -- what goes on, where food might be, where danger is. I try to pass that information along, so homeless animals will have a better chance to survive."

"But wouldn't it be better for them to find real homes?" I asked.

"Yes, but that's not always possible. And some, like you, already have homes, but are lost."

"Can any dog or cat come here? Even bad ones?" Loofah asked.

"They can," answered Mariah, "but they have to be willing to follow the rules."

Rules. I never liked Kristin's rules. But if troublesome animals did come to the Tribal Base, it would be good, for sure, to make them behave.

"There are some really awful cats out there," put in Tamminy, an orange tabby. "You wouldn't help them, would you, Mariah?"

"Yes, Tamminy. Everyone deserves a chance. If they see what it's like to be treated with kindness, they might stop being mean. Sometimes bullies just need to be loved."

Loofah coughed, then put her head down on her paws. I guess she was thinking about Tolliver Yar, and had doubts about what Mariah said.

I had my doubts too. "You mean we shouldn't be afraid of vicious animals?" I asked.

"You have to use common sense, of course, and protect yourself if you need to," Mariah replied. "But you don't want to be ruled by fear. Fear and hatred cause hardening of the heart."

Loofah raised her head, her little face wrinkled up tight. "I think I've got that. Hardening of the heart."

"You?" asked Mariah. "Why do you say that?"

"Well, I used to like everyone, but now I don't. And I don't trust anyone. Except you. And Puppins, and ..."

"You've had a terrible experience, Loofah, so that's understandable. And it's hard to trust strangers. Sometimes, if we don't know someone, we take

111

shortcuts."

"Like what?" Loofah asked suspiciously.

"Well, like bunching them together by breed, and thinking they are all alike. Pit bulls, for instance. They aren't all bad. They should be judged on who they are as individuals."

Seriously? I thought about those two pit bulls on my walks with Kristin. They were bad for sure. I guess it's possible that other pit bulls could be nice, but I was still afraid of them.

Some words went through my brain: *To fear is one thing. To let fear grab you by the tail and swing you around is another.* Maybe I'd gotten swung around by the tail a little too often.

Mariah turned to me. "Puppins, how many strangers are afraid of you, just because you are big and black? They don't know that your heart is as soft as a marshmallow."

The others laughed, but I cringed. Why couldn't I be a good guy and still have a heart of steel? Still, I don't like it when someone thinks I'm going to bite them, just because of the way I look.

Everyone fell silent. For me, the whole thing was too much to digest. Kind of like that big chocolate rabbit I stole off Jodi's table once. I wolfed it down in two bites and Kristin had to take me to the vet to have my stomach pumped.

With my brain on overload, I trotted over to the window and gazed out at the night sky. As usual, only a couple of faint stars were up there.

Kristin says you're supposed to make a wish on the Wishing Star. I didn't know which of those stars was THE ONE, so to be safe I made a wish on both.

Then I curled up on the floor next to Loofah and closed my eyes. Maybe soon my wish would come true.

25

The next day, still no Mr. Pegasus. Dinner that evening was hard to come by: nothing at the usual cafes, so we ended up raiding garbage cans. Not my top choice, but better than nothing. And, not that unusual.

As we made our way back home, Loofah's anxieties tumbled out again. "Puppins, Odette might not survive much longer without me. I can't wait for Mr. Pegasus. If he doesn't come tonight, can we leave in the morning?"

It was so hard to say no to her. I hedged. "It's been so hot the last few days, Loofah, and it'll probably be blistering again tomorrow. Why don't we wait until tomorrow night? Mr. Pegasus may show up in the meantime. Anyway, we'll do better if we travel on full stomachs and when it's cooler."

Reluctantly, she agreed.

***

He came late next afternoon. A fine-looking, black greyhound, Mr. Pegasus, like Mariah, was an ex-racer, aging but still buff.

Mariah bounded out to greet him and they rubbed noses like old friends. After introductions, she gave him a sly look. "Why don't you rest for a while, Mr. Pegasus? Then if you're not too tired, perhaps we can go for a run."

He pranced around with a lot of tail-wagging, his booming voice filled with laughter. "A run? A run? Why not a race? And who needs to rest? Who needs to rest?"

"*I* need to rest," she said. "And so do you. Anyway, it's too hot to run right now. Let's wait."

While we all chilled out under the ceiling fan, Mr. Pegasus told his story. He raced for a long time at the track, retired, and then got adopted. His new owner, an old man, treated him well. But one day, while in the park, his owner let him off leash. Big mistake.

"A greyhound, even a pet, will run away if turned loose. Run away!" Mr. Pegasus said. "We can't stop ourselves. Our instincts take over. Just take over."

That's what happened. Mr. Pegasus bolted. He just kept going, running with all his might. When he finally stopped, he was hopelessly lost.

Since then, he'd lived on the streets. Now and then he stayed at the Tribal Base, and he and Mariah were special friends, and they loved to race each other.

As the sun went down, the two greyhounds headed out to the alley with the rest of us trooping along to watch. They toed the mark.

"Ready, set, go!" yowled Romeow the Siamese, and off they went. Mariah flew down the street, her light-colored tail curved neatly underneath her. Mr. Pegasus, whose long, spindly legs seemed to trip over themselves when he walked, suddenly became a black bullet. Turning the far corner, nose-to-nose, they disappeared.

"Who wants to bet? I'll take Mr. Pegasus!" cried Romeow. Several Tribe members sided with him.

"I wouldn't bet against Mariah if I were you," advised Felicity. "She has incredible endurance."

Julicat, who never agreed with Romeow about anything, took Mariah also. "I think she's too smart to be beat," she said. I agreed, and so did several others.

We waited. Excitement grew. Finally, the greyhounds reappeared, barking madly as they rounded the corner and thundered down the alley toward us, neck and neck.

"Go, Pegasus, go!" screamed Romeow and his followers, as the rest of us tried to out-cheer them:

"Come on, Mariah! Faster! Faster!"

Dead heat. The two sank to the ground, out of breath. "That was a ... a good run," Mariah gasped. "You're always an ... an able ... challenger, Mr. Pegasus."

"So are ... you. So are you," he replied. "I've beaten ... you easily in the past, Mariah. ... Easily. Now I ... I'm just glad to keep up. Just ... keep up."

Romeow was sore because Mr. Pegasus didn't win. "Why do you greyhounds like to run so much, anyway?" he grumbled. "Cats only run if they have to."

"Why?" repeated Mariah with surprise. "We run just for the joy of it, of course!"

After they rested, we set out to find dinner. Mariah and Mr. Pegasus trotted ahead, followed by Zeke, just back from delivering Sparkles safely home, and Felicity.

I walked with Loofah. She had paid no attention to the race. She was a nervous wreck, waiting for Mariah to ask Mr. Pegasus about Odette.

"Puppins, do you think I should talk to him myself?" she asked me. "Maybe Mariah forgot."

"I don't think she could forget, with you reminding her all the time. She's just giving him a chance to relax. I'm sure we'll find out tonight if he knows anything."

"But I want us to be on our way tonight!"

"If that's what's called for, we will," I said curtly. "Otherwise we'll wait."

She was silent, and right away I felt bad for being short with her. She scrutinized my face, then said, "Puppins, do you really want to go with me to look for Odette?"

I hesitated. "Well, I want your mind to be put at ease about her. If I can help with that ..."

I was saved from saying anything more. We had arrived at a place where the smell of greasy burgers, onions and fries got everyone's attention -- even

Loofah's. We did the usual polite barking, then dug in.

***

Back at the Tribal Base with full bellies, we settled down around Mr. Pegasus. As Mariah had told us, the streets were his beat. He knew what was happening out there, and he was ready to give us his report.

Mariah turned to him. "What news do you bring, Mr. Pegasus?"

"Well, well," he said. "Not much to report. Not much. But let's see. Animal Control. Animal Control picked up a couple of dogs you might know, Buster and Carla."

"Oh, poor Carla! I wonder if someone will adopt her," cried Mariah.

"Maybe. Maybe not. Not a good watch dog. Too friendly. Way too friendly. People in the city want a protective dog. Protective."

Mariah shook her head. "Oh dear. And Buster? I don't think I know him. What breed is he?"

"Poodle-terrier mix. Strange-looking guy. Strange. Not likely to find a home either. Not likely. Not cute, and too old. Too old. People like puppies."

Ruby had told me about that. Harsh. Why are humans so picky?

Mr. Pegasus continued, "And, let's see. I heard that the city's cracking down on street people. Cracking down. Not good for tourism, the mayor says. Sweep them up. Sweep them up."

"Oh no!" Loofah cried. "What happens to them?"

"They get rounded up if they stay in one place too long. Too long. Or sleep on the sidewalk. Sleep anyplace in public. They have to go to the new homeless center."

"That sounds okay," Zeke commented.

"For some it's alright. For some. But, others can't adapt. Or won't. Won't. They walk away. Then they're picked up again. In and out. In and out. Revolving door."

He paused, then went on. "In Donut Alley, they got old Joshua and his followers, right in the middle of a sermon. Right in the middle. I was there. Sad. So sad."

"Donut Alley? When was that?" Loofah cried.

"A couple of days ago. Couple of days. I don't go there much anymore. Dangerous. Too dangerous. But sometimes I get a craving for cream puffs. Nothing like a good, day-old cream puff to soothe the soul."

"Did you hear anything about Odette? An old woman who got attacked there a while ago?" Loofah asked anxiously.

"Odette? Hmm. Yes ... Yes. Odette."

"What did you hear?" Loofah cried.

"Joshua said prayers for her. Prayers. He said he went to the hospital and asked about her. They told him she died. Died! Heaven would welcome her, Joshua said. She loved animals. Especially her little white dog."

Loofah moaned and crumpled to the floor. Mr. Pegasus, not noticing, went on.

"Joshua gave thanks that the old woman was free. No more pain. No more sleeping in bushes, no more eating out of garbage cans. No more garbage. He said he hoped those dogfight criminals who frightened her to death would be rot in Hell. Rot in Hell!"

Loofah wailed. Mariah, Felicity and I rushed to her side and tried to comfort her.

"Oh, dear!" exclaimed Mr. Pegasus. "Are you her dog? The little white dog? I didn't know. Didn't know! I'm sorry. So sorry!"

The whole Tribe made a tight circle around Loofah, nuzzling her with our noses. That's all we could do. How do you fix a broken heart?

26

Next day, under the camellias in the courtyard, Loofah gazed at me with teary eyes.

"Oh, Puppins, I feel so alone. I'm so afraid. Who will take care of me now?"

"Why don't you stay here?" I suggested, licking her ears to comfort her. "Mariah loves you. She'll take care of you."

"That's not how it works. Mariah isn't able to keep all the dogs and cats that come here. You come to get better when you're sick or hurt, or to get some rest. Or help with finding your home, like you. You don't stay very long. It's one of the rules."

"But wouldn't she make an exception for you? She's practically like your mom. And you could help her."

"No. Odette said Mariah is here for you when things are bad, but she wants you to learn how to help yourself."

"That sounds like a good thing. Don't you want that?"

She hesitated. "I guess so. But I've always had Odette to take care of me. I don't know anything else."

We were silent for a while. Then she asked, "Puppins, how did you get along when you had to be on your own?"

"I can't remember how it was before I got hit by that car," I told her. "After that, Dr. Holly took care of me until I was well, and then Kristin. Then when Ruby ran off and left me on the street, that's the first time I remember being by myself. It was scary, but I wasn't alone very long before I joined up with you. That was a really good thing for both of us, wasn't it."

"Still, you'd be able to take care of yourself. You are big and strong, and brave."

"I don't *feel* big and strong, or brave. Remember what happened to me on the Old Bridge? Anyway, I am not a loner. I think I need a home. I'm not like Ruby."

Loofah didn't reply. Then, with her sad eyes on mine, she said, "Puppins, you were going to help me find Odette. Now I'm going to help you find your home, like I promised. We'll leave tomorrow."

***

In the Gathering Room that night, it was pretty quiet. Loofah slept, worn out from all the emotions of the day, and I napped.

Mr. Pegasus, after resting awhile, loped down the alley to get back on his beat. Zeke took off to hang with friends in the foothills, and Kudos, left behind when the other cats went out on the town, snored on his shelf; he was too old for feline nightlife.

Then Felicity came in and settled down next to me.

"We haven't had a chance to talk for a while, Puppins," she said. "I've missed that."

"Me too," I replied, a little embarrassed. "What are your plans, now that we won't be going to look for Odette?"

"I'd like to go with you and Loofah to find your home, if that's alright."

It was more than alright. I thanked her with all my heart.

Then I had a sudden thought. What would become of Loofah when I got to The Cottage? Jodi probably wouldn't adopt her; she prefers big, strong-willed dogs like Ruby. And I doubted it either Kristin or Dora wanted to take on another dog.

Wait. What if Kristin took Loofah to that kill shelter? She'd probably be adopted right away because she's adorable. But if she wasn't, she'd be put to death! I couldn't bear to think about that.

I went out to the courtyard. The cool night air calmed me down, and I settled under a little palm tree.

In the early evening sky, I saw a thin slice of moon, like a piece of lemon pie on a deep blue plate.

Pie! How long had it been since I shared a whole pie with Dora? Sigh.

After a time, Felicity came out and joined me under the palm.

"Puppins, I've been wondering. Do you think Loofah might find a home with you and Kristin?"

"That's been on my mind too," I told her. "I don't know. Maybe Kristin or Dora would fall in love with her and let her stay, but if not, then what?"

"I could stick around the neighborhood until they decide," Felicity said. "If necessary, I'd bring her back here. I'm pretty sure Mariah would let her stay until we figured out something else."

"But what if Kristin takes her to the kill shelter?" It was my worst fear.

"You'll have to keep your ears and eyes open. If she decides to do that, you'll need to help Loofah get out of the house as fast as possible, then I'll take over."

I could see lots of potential problems with the plan, but I had nothing better to offer.

"Okay," I said. "Let's ask her if she wants to live with me or at Dora's, *if* it's okay with them."

We went inside, woke up the little dog and asked her the question.

"Oh, Puppins! I was secretly hoping for that!" she

cried, jumping up and twirling around and around.

"But if neither of them can keep you," Felicity warned, "you have to leave fast so I can bring you back here."

Loofah kept on spinning. Bichons are good at that. "It will work out, I know!" she exclaimed. "I'm going to think positive thoughts to help make it happen." She stopped twirling, closed her eyes, and scrunched up her face in concentration.

Felicity and I laughed. Positive thoughts have rough going with Loofah.

***

We three went outside. As we watched the night sky give way to early morning, a sudden blast of squawks broke the peace.

Down came a swirl of green, swooping to a landing on a nearby fig tree.

"Puppeens!" screeched Pepito. "Que pasa?"

"Pepito!" I cried. "Hola!"

I was really glad to see him and his flock. But before I could try to say another word, they took off.

"Hasta luego, Puppeens!" Pepito's voice trailed off as the wild parakeets disappeared down the block. "Adios, amigos!"

I had never seen them at the Tribal Base. What were they doing here? If they had only stayed a little longer – and if I knew better how to talk to Pepito -- I might have found out how to get back to The Cottage.

***

Just then, Mariah came bounding out.

"Come inside," she called to us. "There's something I want to show you!"

She turned and loped back into the Base. We followed as she trotted through the Gathering Room, up the broad, curving stairs, down a dark and dusty hall, and into a large room.

I'd never been upstairs; it always seemed kind of out of bounds. Mariah trotted over to the window, trailed by Felicity, me and Loofah, and we looked outside.

The wind had blown away the morning smog and haze, uncovering a rare sight. Mountains. The ones Kristin calls the San Gabriels. She always got excited when they came out.

Some words flowed into my brain:
over my sleeping self float flaming symbols of hope & i awake to a perfect patience of mountains

A perfect patience of mountains, right outside our window! I stared at them. Were they flaming symbols of hope?

Maybe. That's what I wanted them to be.

Hope that I would soon be home, and that Loofah would get to be my little sister.

27

That afternoon, resting in the courtyard with Mariah and the pack, I tried to figure out a plan for finding The Cottage.

Loofah would not be much help. She was an emotional mess. Besides, she didn't know anything about the area where I lived.

Felicity was calm, steady, and organized. But she didn't have much to go on either. I knew the streets on my walking routes with Kristin, but the rest of the city was pretty much a blank slate.

Just then, a commotion at the back gate got my attention. Two dogs appeared: a borzoi, tall, thin, kind of elegant-looking, with silky hair the color of vanilla ice cream. And a black and tan bloodhound, low to the ground, with long, floppy ears and an enormous nose. His eyes looked really sad, but as he got closer I could see sparks of fun in them.

Mariah leaped to her feet. "Sue! Columbo! Welcome back!" she cried. And the whole Tribe rushed over to greet them. Obviously they were a very popular pair.

Later, when we all headed out for dinner, Felicity filled me in about the two. The borzoi, Oglala Sue, once lived on the Oglala Sioux Indian Reservation with her owner, a member of the tribe. As a sight hound, she loved to hunt on the wide-open lands of the "rez." She and her owner moved to L.A. for work and when he was killed in a construction accident, Sue got dumped on the streets.

Columbo had the friendliness of most bloodhounds (who, according to Felicity, get a bad rap because of their looks). Like a lot of other scent hounds, he tracked criminals as a police dog. After retiring, he was adopted by a man who drank too much alcohol and was mean to him, so he ran away.

Columbo and Sue met at Mariah's. They were an odd couple, for sure, but a great team. Felicity said borzois are brave, faithful, and protective of the ones they love, and the one Sue loved most was Columbo.

When Felicity described their tracking skills, I had a brilliant thought: Maybe they could come with us to help find The Cottage! The more the merrier, right?

Back at the Tribal Base, Columbo, in high spirits, played tag with the cats. Sue watched, shaking her head.

"Wouldn't you think a dog his age would act more dignified? It drives me crazy."

Mariah laughed. "That's just Columbo. How can you not love him?"

"I do love him. But I'd *like* him better if he took things more seriously. He's almost blown a couple of searches with his clowning around."

Uh oh. That sounded kind of ominous. Still, from what Felicity had told me, their success rate was high. Anyway, what did I have to lose?

"Sue," I ventured, "I need help getting back home. Loofah's coming with me, and Felicity. But some expert tracking would probably make things go faster."

Felicity gave me a look. Maybe she thought I doubted her abilities. But she quickly recovered. "That's a great idea. Sue and Columbo are the best."

"Should we?" Sue asked Columbo, who had heard the conversation. He turned to me. "When are you leaving?"

"Tonight," I said.

Sue shook her head. "No. We just finished a job, and we need to rest. But if you wait a day or so, we'll do it." Columbo nodded his agreement.

Loofah looked relieved at the delay, so I decided to go with the flow. "Cool," I told them. "We'll start day after tomorrow."

Columbo broke into a song and shuffling kind of dance. "Work, work, work, all day long, I'd rather sing my bloodhound song!" Sue sighed.

Over the next couple of days, I told Columbo and Sue as much as I could remember about my neighborhood. It sounded like a hundred other neighborhoods in L.A., they said. Still, they were confident they could find it.

The night we were to leave, I went out with the others to forage for dinner. Felicity fell in beside me.

"Puppins, I'm going to miss you," she said in her straightforward way.

"Aren't you coming?" I asked in surprise.

"I don't think it's a good idea. So many dogs would attract attention. And there's no need for me to go, really."

That did not seem right. I wanted her to be part of the search. She had become a good friend, and it was going to be hard to say goodbye to her.

"I wish you'd come," I said. "Let's ask Sue and Columbo if they think it's okay."

Sue was with Loofah, listening to her tale of woe. I jumped in at the first pause and explained the situation.

"It does make things a little more difficult to have that many dogs," she said, "but I think Felicity should come. We can't wait around to see if Loofah needs to come back here."

Great! We were set. We'd leave as soon as we got back from dinner.

28

Goodbyes to the Tribe were really painful. Loofah choked out a tearful farewell to Mariah, and I thanked our greyhound friend for all she had done for me. I only hoped that someday I would see her again.

She wished us good luck. "If you run into any trouble, try to get word back to us and we'll come to your aid," she said.

And so we were off. Columbo led the way with a croaking road song, then he and Sue broke into "Razzle Dazzle," a song and dance routine that he'd made up. It was kind of like a Dog Channel version of that TV dance show Dora liked to watch.

The rest of us wagged our tails to the rhythm, enjoying their little show. Then it was time to get serious.

Sue and Columbo had a general plan, based on what I'd told them. But right away they started arguing over which streets to turn down, which alleys to use.

"This is the quickest way," Columbo would say.

"But it's also the riskiest," Sue would reply. "We'd have to cross the street at some point, and there are way too many cars, even at this time of night."

She was the more cautious one, he the one who got carried away by the thrill of the hunt.

They also had what they called the "War of the Senses."

Columbo kept his nose to the ground, while Sue's tracking skills were based on what she could see. She thought his way was too slow. He said hers was not so accurate.

Somehow, they always managed to work things out after a few heated exchanges, some give and take, and some touching of noses.

As I said, they were a good team.

Sometimes Felicity helped them decide which way to go. I was cool with whatever was decided, as long as they didn't take us on the freeway or across the Old Bridge.

***

We walked all night. Probably wasn't the most direct route, but we did the best we could.

Toward morning, Loofah needed a rest so we stopped at a small park with a pond.

It seemed familiar. Then I remembered. "Hey, I know this place," I told them. "I came here once with Kristin. We played Frisbee on the other side of that picnic area."

"Then it must be close to your home!" exclaimed Columbo, dancing a few surprisingly agile hip hop steps.

I thought about it, then I remembered that we had come by car.

"Was it a long ride?" asked Sue.

"I don't know. I was probably asleep. I don't pay much attention in the car."

We got a drink from the pond and found a shady place to stretch out. A couple of other dogs were lying in some nearby shrubs, and one of them turned his head toward us.

"Mr. Pegasus!" Loofah cried.

He jumped up and loped over. He knew Columbo and Sue, and we all greeted each other in the usual nose-to-butt way.

"What are you doing here?" I asked.

"Taking a breather," he said. "A breather. Where are you headed?"

"We're trying to find my home." I told him.

"Quite a crew, quite a crew," he commented. "If numbers count, success is certain!"

"What news have you heard since you left Mariah's?" asked Felicity.

"Well, let's see. Let's see. The biggest thing is the dogfight ring."

"What about it?" Loofah asked anxiously.

"A sorry tale. Sorry. Those two villains. Those unspeakable characters who gave your mistress a heart attack," he said.

She began to wail.

Felicity spoke up. "Stites and Onions? What about them?"

"They went on a rampage. A rampage. Rounding up dogs right and left. Some, like Ruby -- you know, that Irish setter -- not even fighters. Not even fighters! But the dogs they don't want, they'll sell to Puppy Haven. They'll sell."

Wait. Ruby? Caught? I couldn't believe it.

"Are ... are you sure they got Ruby?" I asked.

"Yes. Yes. Her and a few others. Those hoodlums put knockout powder on some food. Knockout powder. I happened by and found them passed out. Passed out! Nothing I could do. Nothing."

Wow. How much more bad stuff could those evil guys do?

Mr. Pegasus went on. "I tried to rouse them, but no use. No use. When those criminals came back, I hid and watched. They threw the dogs into a van and drove off. Easy as pie. Easy. As. Pie."

"Who else did they get?" asked Felicity, concern stamped all over her furry brown face.

"Some they'll probably keep for the fights: Sam, a Doberman; Jocko, a shepherd; and Bertie, some kind of mix. He's got a mean streak they'll like. Mean.

"And Ruby, like I said, and Custard. Can you believe it? Custard!"

"Not that sweet little cream-colored pup!" Sue exclaimed.

"Yes. Puppy Haven will get her, and Ruby. For sure."

"What's Puppy Haven?" I asked, my brain reeling.

"I told you about it, Puppins," Loofah cried. "I told you that Mariah warned me about it. Don't you remember?"

"But what is it? Why is it bad?"

Felicity stood up, shaking with anger.

"It's a puppy mill. A place with bad breeding and terrible conditions. Puppy Haven is barbaric. You don't ever want to go there."

I had never seen Felicity so upset. We all fell quiet.

Suddenly I realized there were more bad things in the world than I ever dreamed of.

29

After a while, Columbo got up and stretched. The others followed, but I didn't move.

Sue scrutinized me. "Puppins, the sooner we get started, the sooner we'll find your home," she said.

I still didn't get up.

"What's wrong, Puppins?" asked Felicity. "Don't you feel well?"

"I ... I'm worried. About those dogs that were captured. About ... about Ruby."

Sue looked disgusted. "Ruby can take care of herself. She's famous for escaping from tight situations. By now, she's probably long gone from that place."

"But what if they keep her drugged? What if they locked her up somewhere, and she *can't* escape? Or what if some vicious dogs at the ring tear her up? And ... and what about that little dog Custard -- what will happen to her?"

"They'll take Custard to Puppy Haven, like Mr. Pegasus said," Sue replied. "And Ruby too, if she doesn't escape. Stites and Onions can make money by selling them to the mill."

"But Felicity says the mill is not a good place either."

"True. True. But what can be done? Nothing. Nothing," Mr. Pegasus sighed.

Columbo began to dance, a twinkle in his eye. "Let's rescue them!" he boomed.

Sue glared at him. "Are you insane? How could we

possibly do that?"

"We can do it!" he exclaimed. "We'll go to the dogfight place, sneak in, and let Ruby and Custard out. And the other dogs they've captured, too. Liberation! Freedom for all captive dogs!"

"Columbo, you've had some outrageous ideas, but ..."

I interrupted Sue. "I think Columbo is right," I said. "We could do it. We *should* do it." Columbo and I did a paw bump.

The others just stared at us.

"What if they already took Custard and Ruby to Puppy Haven?" asked Loofah.

Felicity turned to Mr. Pegasus. "When were they captured?"

"Day before yesterday. I came straight over here afterwards. Wanted to get away from that neighborhood. It's not safe. Not safe."

Felicity spoke slowly. "They may still be at the dogfight place. They'd want to get them cleaned up and in good shape, so they could get more money for them."

I looked at her. "Felicity, do you think we could rescue them?"

She hesitated, then said, "I don't know. But I think we should try."

Columbo danced a four-legged breakdance like the two-legged ones I've seen on TV, only clumsier.

"Hooray! A real adventure!" he cried.

When he said that, some words spiraled into my brain:

Life is either a daring adventure or nothing at all ...

Crazy as the idea was, I was up for a daring adventure. As long as it didn't involve the Old Bridge, didn't take too much time, and gave me one more chance to redeem myself with Ruby.

Columbo taunted Sue: "Are you brave enough, dear?"

"It's not a question of bravery," she scoffed. "It's a question of common sense. We know where the dogfight place is, so that's no challenge. But remember how it's like a fortress, with those two pit bulls patrolling it? No thanks."

What did she say? I stared at her. "You know where that fortress house is? And those pit bulls? That means you know my neighborhood! I used to walk by there with Kristin, but I didn't know it was a dogfight ring until Ruby told me."

"You never mentioned that you lived close to that house," scolded Sue.

"I never liked to think about that house," I told her. "It's not high on my list of treasured memories."

Felicity turned to me. "Puppins, you must have some idea of how difficult it would be to get inside that house."

A nightmare vision of those pit bulls appeared before my eyes. "It would be hard. Very hard. Those dogs are barbarians. But ... maybe there's a way," I replied.

"Oglala Sue, any ideas?" Felicity asked.

Sue was indignant. "No. We're trackers, not rescuers."

Loofah piped up. "If we could think of a way to distract those pit bulls, one of us could sneak inside and let the dogs out."

We looked at each other. "Maybe bichons are smarter than I thought!" teased Columbo.

"It's a good idea, Loofah," Felicity said. "We'll create a ruckus in front of the house, and then someone ..."

A seed of the rescue idea had put down roots in my mind and was growing fast. "I'll volunteer to try and get inside," I said.

Wait. Was that me?

"Me too!" cried Columbo. Not the most sensible

partner. Felicity would be better, or Sue. But if Columbo wanted to come along, I guess it was okay.

"Alright. We've got a mission," said Felicity. "Mr. Pegasus, are you joining us?"

"Yes, yes! If you want to create a first-class uproar, I'm a good barker. A darn good barker. Want to hear me?"

"No, no," Felicity said hastily. "Not yet. Save your barks for those pit bulls."

***

As we set out on energy overload, one thought circled endlessly in my feverish brain: Rescue Ruby. Rescue Ruby. Rescue Ruby ... never mind the details.

Toward late afternoon, I began to recognize the neighborhood.

"We're close," Sue confirmed. "I think we're only a street or two away from the fortress house."

That meant we were close to The Cottage, too. But the dogfight thing had to come first.

It won't take long, I told myself.

"Let's review our plan," Felicity said. "We'll sneak up and see if any people are around. Then we'll start barking. Puppins and Columbo will move in. They'll have to work fast to find Ruby and Custard, set them free and get out before anyone comes."

Gulp. What had I gotten myself into?

"Maybe we should wait until dark," Sue suggested. "It would be much easier then."

Felicity agreed, but the rest of us had doubts. I thought people were more likely to be away from home during the day. Also, I just wanted to get it over with.

Sue and Felicity won out. We decided to look for something to eat while we waited for evening, but the only garbage cans we found were covered tight. We could have knocked them over, of course, but then someone might come to investigate.

Anyway, I didn't really want anything. My stomach churned. Was fear going to pick me up and swing me by the tail again?

Finding a hidden spot in an empty lot, we hunkered down to wait. I figure out how I could get inside that house. I didn't want to even think about the pit bulls. If they caught me in the yard, I'd be fresh hamburger.

Tossing and turning on the hard ground, I couldn't get comfortable. Finally Felicity noticed my restlessness and moved next to me.

"Are you alright, Puppins?" she asked.

"Not really," I admitted. "I'm worried."

"No wonder. You don't have to do this, you know. Like Sue said, Ruby is resourceful. She's probably already escaped."

"Maybe. But I can't help feeling that this time, she's really in trouble."

"Puppins, she's even escaped from humane shelters. That's almost unheard of."

"I know. Maybe you're right. But ... what about Custard?"

"We have to face reality. Maybe there's nothing we can do about her. Maybe ... maybe this is not a good idea, Puppins. It's a great risk to you and Columbo, and I don't know if it's worth it."

If I had thought about it with any smarts, I might have agreed. But where Ruby was concerned, smarts seemed to melt away like butter on Dora's hot popcorn.

Maybe the chance of saving Ruby was small, but I had to try. Then I'd go home.

30

Finally, but still too soon, it was dark. Agreeing to meet back at the vacant lot after the raid, we crept up to the fortress house like six goldfish headed for a pool of piranhas.

"What's your plan?" Sue asked me.

Plan? I still had no plan, beyond getting past the pit bulls, getting inside, finding Ruby and Custard, setting them free, and getting out. I had no idea how to make any of that happen.

"Any suggestions?" I asked weakly.

"See if there's a low spot in the fence to jump over. The owners probably wanted it to be super strong to keep the dogs in, but making it high wouldn't be as important. Pit bulls aren't jumpers."

I'm not much of a jumper either, I thought, recalling my badly scraped belly when I barely made it over Dora's fence. Who knew if I could do it again?

My gang took their posts. Then, like a canine war cry, they let loose a great storm of howling.

The pit bulls rose to the challenge. Lunging violently against the chain link, they doubled the noise level in an instant.

My fur stood on end. I could almost feel those steel jaws clamp down on my skull, cracking it open like a nut.

Suddenly, I knew I had to go it alone. Columbo was too excitable, too unpredictable. And two of us were twice as likely to get caught.

"I think I'd better go inside by myself," I told Columbo over the din.

"No way! That's the bold part! Staying out here is lame. Lame and tame!"

Some words flew into my brain and I said them out loud: *He also serves who only stands and barks.*

Felicity overheard. While the others kept up their unbearable uproar, she turned to Columbo and said firmly, "Puppins is right. It will be easier for him to get in alone. And we really need your commanding voice out here."

He shook his head disapprovingly. "Oh, all right," he grumbled. "But if you're not back soon, Puppins, I'm coming after you, even if I have to dig my way in."

If I'm not back soon, I thought, it's because I'm dead meat.

Columbo joined Felicity and the others as they marched back and forth in front of the house, barking their heads off. The pit bulls were not used to such open provocation, and they roared in response. The neighborhood exploded with sound and fury.

Racing as fast as I could along the fence, I found a low spot, just as Sue predicted. I backed up, tensed every muscle in my body, and ...

SPLAT! Something furry dropped on my head from above. A soft body draped itself around my neck, and a round whiskered face appeared before my eyes.

"Dude! It's me!" cried a familiar voice.

"Oliver! You almost gave me a heart attack! What the heck are you doing here?"

"I like to come and tease the pit bulls when I'm bored," he answered smugly. "What are *you* doing here? And *where* have you been!"

"Can't explain right now. Got to get inside. It's a

dogfight place, and they've captured Ruby."

He snorted. "Ruby? That redhead? Are you still chasing her? Man, your brains are poached!"

"I know, I know. Later. Wait here."

"No way!" he cried. "I know where those fighting dogs are. Let me at 'em!" And before I could stop him, he scrambled up the fence and tumbled down into the yard.

Okay. My turn. Gathering all my strength, I hurled myself toward the fence. Leaving the ground at exactly the right moment, I sailed over the chain link like those Olympic hurdlers I saw once on TV, and landed smoothly on the other side.

"Wow," Oliver cried. "That was great, Puppins! You've really slimmed down and beefed up!"

Slimmed down? Beefed up? Really? No time to wonder. "Quick. Where are the dogs?" I yelled.

"That building in back. Follow me!"

I raced after him. There was more to the place than you could tell from the street. Behind the house was a parking area, dog runs, and a building with no windows, all screened from the neighbors by rows of tall shrubs.

"What's that disgusting ruckus up front?" Oliver called back to me.

"My friends ... a diversionary tactic!"

"You have friends? Seriously?"

I ignored that. We reached the building. The door was shut, but I pushed hard on it and it opened wide enough to let us in.

In the dark, I could make out dog pens along the walls and, in the center, an open space surrounded by seats. I shuddered. That must be the fight ring.

Then the dogs saw us. Barking furiously, they threw themselves against their kennel gates.

All four of my knees shook as I called out over the bedlam: "Ruby? Custard? It's ... it's me, Puppins!"

"Ruby ain't here!" a deep voice boomed. "Custard neither. Who're you?" It was a boxer – a huge, angry-looking boxer.

"It's ... it's me," I replied. "Puppins. A friend of Ruby's. Are you ... Bill?"

"How d'ya know my name?" He growled, bared his teeth.

"Ruby. She told me about you. I ... I came to get her and Custard out of here. Where are they?"

His voice toned down a little. "Puppy Haven. They got taken there before Ruby had a chance ta get away. Quite an escape artist, she is, but she'd been drugged. Say, how about gettin' *me* outta here?"

Oliver, hiding under my legs, was trembling, and so was I. But Bill was a friend of Ruby's. He'd been kidnapped too. I couldn't just run off and leave him.

"We'll ... we'll try," I said. "Any ideas?"

"The latch on my kennel. Reach up 'n push it."

I tried, but even on my hind legs I couldn't reach it.

"Oliver, get up on my head. See if you can get that latch open," I yelled. He did, stretching his paw up toward the latch.

"I ... I can't," he squeaked. His bravado had disappeared.

"Come on, you can do it!" I urged. "You're the bravest cat I know!" That actually might have been true.

"Okay, but ... but don't let that boxer get me!" He reached up again, digging his back claws into my head to keep his grip.

"Ouch!" I cried. "Take it easy!"

"Sorry!" Wriggling up as far as he could toward the tip of my nose, he managed to push up the latch.

The gate swung open and Bill rushed out, heading for the door.

"What about these other guys?" Oliver yelled at him.

(I guess, in the face of success, he got his courage back.)

Bill stopped short and shook his huge square head. "Some of those dogs would tear ya to shreds. But the rest … well, they hate this place as much as I do. I'll show ya who to let out, but we gotta move quick."

We ran from pen to pen. Bill and I took turns being Oliver's stepladder, yelping as those sharp little daggers sank into our heads.

And one by one, we freed the chosen dogs: a couple of Dobermans, another boxer, a mastiff, three German shepherds, and an unidentified large brown mutt.

Four others, roaring ferociously at us, got left behind. I recognized one: Tolliver Yar. The deadly Rottweiler in Donut Alley. Ugh.

"Bye-bye Tolliver!" I couldn't resist taunting as we ran for the door.

Oh my god. It was closed.

We were trapped. Maybe the wind did it. "We'll have to storm through," I yelled. "Come on, guys!"

I shoved all the dogs into a tight pack with Bill in front, me bringing up the rear.

"Oliver, get on my back!" I cried. Then, "Ouch! Let up!" He dug in deeper.

"Let's get outta here!" yelled Bill. We hit the door at full speed, a flying wedge of muscle, busting clear through and leaving a hole the size of a dog team.

Into the dark night we flew.

Silence was the first thing that hit me. Where were the pit bulls? Where were my friends?

***

Suddenly, red lights flashing through the shrubs caught my attention.

I saw a couple of police officers run into the backyard. I sped to the low spot on the fence and leaped over, the other dogs following hard on my tail.

Oliver, still clinging to my back, dug in his spurs.

"Whooeee! Giddyup, Puppins!" he cried.

"Oww! Stop that, you little punk!" He didn't.

Once out of the yard, the liberated dogs scattered to the winds. All except Bill, who raced after me to hide behind some shrubs.

Oliver hissed at me. "Dumbo! What are you doing? Keep going!"

"I want to see what's happening," I said, shaking him roughly off my back.

As the three of us peered through the fence, the backdoor of the house opened and three men I recognized came running out: Stites, Onions, and the red-haired man Kristin and I had seen once in the window.

"Look!" exclaimed Bill. "Those jerks are runnin' right into the cops' arms!"

Indeed they were.

The officers, pulling their guns, jumped out of the shadows. "Stop! Put up your hands!" they yelled.

One held the hoodlums at gunpoint while the other went to check out the back building.

"Hey," he called to his partner, "somebody's broke clean through this door!" Crawling inside through the big hole, he set the caged dogs inside off on a new barking frenzy.

A moment later, the cop reappeared. "Joe, looks like we stumbled onto something!" he yelled.

Oliver pummeled my nose. "Come on, Puppins, we've seen enough. Let's get out of here!"

"But what about the pit bulls?" I asked.

"Don' have time to worry about them," said Bill. "Let's go before Animal Control shows up!"

31

As we dashed down the street, Loofah suddenly popped out in front of us.

"Puppins! You're safe!" she squealed.

Close behind her were Felicity, Mr. Pegasus, Sue and Columbo. My crew. All okay. Whew.

"How did it go inside?" Felicity asked anxiously.

"It was a ... a fail," I blurted as I tried to catch my breath. "Ruby and ... and Custard weren't there. Already taken to ... to Puppy Haven."

"Ain't no fail for me," Bill declared. "Puppins 'n Oliver saved me, and a lot of other dogs too!"

Introducing the boxer and Oliver to the gang, I told them how Oliver appeared out of nowhere and helped with the raid.

He strutted around with his chest puffed out. It was hard to admit, but he deserved the praise he got. In fact, I felt kind of like a superhero myself.

But wait. If I was such a hero, how come I'd been so scared? Anyway, didn't the rest of the gang deserve credit too?

"Great job," I told them. "We couldn't have got past those pit bulls without you guys."

"I guess the neighbors called the police when they heard us barking," Loofah said, "and when we saw their car come around the corner, we ran across the street to watch."

"Some of the neighbors came out and talked to the police," Sue added. "They must have told them that something was going on in the backyard."

"But how did the police get past the pit bulls?" I asked.

"Spray," Mr. Pegasus said. "Anti-dog spray!"

He told us it was time for him to get back to his news-gathering rounds. We said goodbye with big thanks for helping us, and the roving reporter loped off down the street.

Felicity turned to the boxer. "How long were you in that terrible place, Bill?"

"Dunno. Lost track of time," he replied.

"Did you have to fight other dogs?" Loofah asked, shuddering.

"Yeah. Ya gotta defend yourself, or you'll die. And defendin' yourself means killin' someone. Ya can't just walk away."

Ruby had told me about that. But now, hearing him tell about it, made the horror really sink in.

"Did you get hurt very much?" Columbo asked Bill.

"If it wasn't so dark, I'd show ya my scars," he replied.

"That's so awful!" cried Loofah.

"At least the ring is shut down now," Felicity said, shaking her head. "I hope those men will be in jail for a long, long time."

We fell silent. We were exhausted. But we had done it. We actually, really, truly, busted that dogfight ring.

Wow.

***

We slept until the sun came up like an over-easy egg on a milky white plate. Looking at it made me hungry.

"How about some food?" asked Columbo, echoing my thoughts.

"Yes!" I yelled. My appetite was back, big time.

Breakfast, then home. No more detours.

"Forward, ho! Food, ho!" Columbo sang as he danced down the street with the rest of us following.

As I trotted along beside Oliver, I asked, "How is your mom?"

"You wouldn't believe it," Oliver said. "Mama's gotten used to Kristin. She even lets Kristin pick her up and hold her."

"That's amazing! How did it happen?"

"Mama got sick. She didn't eat, and just kept getting thinner. Finally, Kirstin crawled under the house, threw a blanket over her and took her inside. Kristin got dirty."

Kristin dirty? Hard to believe.

"Then what happened?"

"We didn't see Mama for a long time. We thought maybe she died, and we were really sad. But one day, Kristin opened the backdoor and out came Mama. We almost didn't recognize her. She was plump, and washed, combed, and wearing a collar with a little tag on it."

"Was she over her sickness?"

"Yes. She said Kristin got her some medicine, then made a nest for her in the kitchen. All she had to do was sleep, eat and get better. At first, she was too sick to complain when Kristin picked her up. Then she started trusting her."

"Wow. I never thought that would happen, did you?"

"No. Her fears just melted down like a dead mouse on a hot sidewalk. She's back outside, but sometimes she still lets Kristin hold her and fuss over her."

I got quiet, thinking about how good Kristin is. I never appreciated it. Then Oliver gave me a hard look.

"Puppins, are you ever coming home?"

"Of course! That's where we're headed, you know. How is Kristin? And Dora and Jodi? I've missed them so much!"

"Well ..." he hesitated. Then, squinting his eyes at me, he said, "There's some bad news. Dora doesn't live across the street anymore."

"What?! She's gone? Where?"

"She sold her house and moved up north. Some new people live there now."

"Why? Why did she do that?"

"She told Kristin she got laid off from work, and she never liked living in the city, and L.A. was too hot for her, and with you gone there was nothing to keep her there."

"But ... but didn't she know I'd come back?"

Oliver bristled. "How could she know that, you big jerk! She and Kristin and Jodi really took it hard when you left. They called the Humane Shelter every day and Kristin put an ad in the newspaper. And they made some signs and put them up all over the neighborhood, with big red letters and a picture of your ugly mug. Kristin told Jodi she was going to give a reward if someone brought you back."

"Reward? She was going to pay a reward for me?"

"Yes, you creep. They never dreamed you could jump over the fence. They thought someone nabbed you out of Dora's yard. Jodi went ballistic, yelling about low-down dog thieves. As if someone would steal you!"

"That's terrible!" I cried. "I feel awful!"

"You should. Running after that stupid redhead, without a thought in your lame brain for anyone but yourself. Anyway, it's good they thought you were stolen. If they knew you ran away on purpose, it would *really* break their hearts."

It was true. How could I have been so selfish?

"Kristin blamed herself for you being in Dora's yard," Oliver continued. "She told Jodi that if she wasn't such a workaholic, none of this would've happened. She said she was going to change, even though it was too late to bring you back."

She blamed herself. I guess my heart knew all along that I had let her down, but my brain would not own up to it.

Some words crept into my brain: *It's such a secret place, the land of tears...*

I dropped back behind Oliver and the others. Big dogs aren't supposed to cry. If I was going to the land of tears, I wanted to be there by myself.

***

Later, in back of a small restaurant, we found some leftover enchiladas in a garbage can. They smelled good and ripe, but I had no appetite.

All I could think of was how much Kristin would hate me if she knew I ran away. She'd be so mad she'd never speak to me again. There's nothing worse than not being spoken to.

In the middle of those dark thoughts, Felicity and Loofah circled back and joined me. I told them about Dora moving away and they tried to cheer me up.

Then Felicity said, "Puppins, we'll be at your house before long. As soon as you and Loofah go inside, I'll leave. Then I'll check back, as planned, to see what's happening with Loofah."

"What if Kristin throws me out on the street before you come back?" Loofah cried.

"Kristin won't throw you out," I said to Loofah. "She's kind. If she can't keep you, I'm sure she'll find a good home for you."

Loofah whimpered. I didn't have a clue about what else to say to her. I didn't want to raise her hopes.

145

***

It got really hot, so we found a shady spot and settled down to rest. While the others talked about the raid and everything that had happened, Oliver was unusually quiet.

Then, talking low so no one else could hear, he said, "There's something else I haven't told you, Puppins. It's about Kristin."

Uh, oh. Ominous.

He went on. "Kristin is ... she is moving too."

"No way!" I choked. "How do you know that?"

"She was petting me one day and said she found another house and she wanted me and Mama and my sisters to live there with her. She said someone was buying The Cottage and they had a nasty dog, and they might not want to feed us."

"But Kristin loves The Cottage! She put so much work into it. Why would she ...?"

"Well, she told Jodi that someone wanted to buy it and they made a really good offer. And that the house had too many memories of you."

Aargh. That *really* hurt. "Where? Where is she going?" I stammered.

"I don't know. I guess she'll take me there when she goes."

What unbelievably awful news. It felt like that time an earthquake shook our house and left a big hole in the middle of the street. This time, though, the sinkhole was in my heart.

I let the others know about Kristin. Loofah began to sob. "Oh, Puppins, what should we do?"

As if I knew.

Felicity turned to Oliver. "When do you think Kristin will move?" she asked.

"I'm not sure. She was putting stuff in boxes the last

time I was in The Cottage, but that was a while ago."

"We'll go ahead. Maybe she'll still be there. If she's gone, we'll try to figure out where her new house is."

"But what if we can't find her?" Loofah wailed. "I want her to adopt me. I want a home, and I want Puppins to be my big brother."

That was sweet. I didn't know she felt that way.

She turned to me, her eyes shiny with tears. "Oh Puppins, what is it like to have a home? Odette and I had a place to sleep under the freeway and a blanket to put over us, but we never had a real home."

The question hit me right between the eyes. I'd had two homes that I could remember: with Kristin, and with Dora (sort of), and I ran away from both. Now Dora was history, and maybe Kristin was history too.

Shoving down that awful thought, I tried to answer Loofah. "Well, having a home is ... it's having your own doggy bed to sleep on. Or a special spot on your person's bed -- some people let you sleep with them. You get plenty of water and food, at regular times and in your own bowl. No eating out of garbage cans.

"If you're lucky," I went on, "there are treats and toys. And when it's cold or rainy outside, you can be indoors where it's warm and dry, with a closet to crawl into when the neighbors shoot off fireworks on special days and it hurts your ears and makes you scared."

I stopped to think, then continued. "It's having someone to take care of you when you are sick, like that time I ate the humongous chocolate rabbit. And it's having someone call your name, and laugh at your silly tricks, and give you lots of pats.

"It's being safe from the dog catcher. And it's feeling like you belong, that somebody loves you and needs you. That's what it is."

Loofah sighed. "That sounds so nice," she said,

shaking her head wistfully. "But what about a home just with animals? Like the Tribal Base. When I'm there, I feel safe and dry. And like I belong. We love each other and take care of each other. We don't need humans."

I thought about that. "It is good at Mariah's, in lots of ways. But you can't stay there, remember? A real home is someplace where you can stay until you die."

"But what if your people move to a different house, like Dora and Kristin?" she persisted. "That's not forever."

"I know. I don't understand that part of it either."

"And why do people move, anyway?" she asked. "Why don't they stay in the same house so their animals won't get upset?"

"Maybe some people is like Ruby," Bill put in. "They get bored bein' in one place with one person."

"Maybe," I said shortly. I did not want to discuss Ruby, especially with Bill.

But Loofah did. "Doesn't Ruby want to ever have a home?" she asked Bill.

"She never had none, that I know of. Maybe she jus' don't know what it's like."

"But ..." Loofah began.

"Shhh," I said. "Try to get some rest, Loofah. Everything's going to work out."

If only I believed that.

I closed my eyes. Talking about having a home made me think about Odette and Joshua and those other people I saw on the streets. Did any of them ever have a real home? And if they did, what happened to it?

Then, of course, I thought about The Cottage, and about Kristin selling it. That thought made my insides feel empty.

It had nothing to do with wanting something to eat. I was hungry for home.

32

We napped, then got up and stretched, ready to go on. But Oliver was missing.

Everyone helped search for him; I even checked the tree, in case he was planning to prank me.

Nowhere to be found. I knew he was really upset with me for making Kristin so sad, and Jodi and Dora too.

But he never held onto bad stuff very long, so I was counting on him forgiving me. Isn't that what BBF's are supposed to do?

"Maybe he went ahead to see if Kristin is still at The Cottage," Felicity suggested. "Let's go on and hope for the best. When we get there, I'll wait to see if Loofah will be staying. That was the plan, remember?"

Of course I remembered, despite all that had happened. But hearing Felicity say it once more raised another sad thought: she would soon be going away, no matter what happened at Kristin's.

"Let's get some eats!" Columbo boomed, interrupting my funk. Like me, he was a chow hound (excuse the pun). His nose led the way to a deliciously stinky garbage can, and we all dug in.

After Loofah finished the last crusts from a ham-and-cheese sandwich, she trotted over to me.

"Puppins, are we almost to The Cottage?"

"Yeah," I told her, gulping down a final over-the-hill chicken strip. "We're pretty close now."

I should have been happy about that, but a feeling of dread settled over me like a blanket of fog. What would happen when we got there?

***

The day was hot, even for L.A. Loofah dragged behind us, and we had to stop and rest several times.

That was okay with me. The closer we got, the harder my heart beat. Finally, we rounded the last corner, and there it was. The Cottage.

The gate in the vine-covered fence was partly open so I pushed through. There the carob tree and Kristin's flowers, the old stepping stones, the swing on the front porch. My hopes took a leap.

But wait. Where were the white curtains at the windows? And where was the "dogs and cats welcome" sign that should be over the purple door?

The house had the look and smell of desertion, and I knew the terrible truth: Kristin was gone.

I turned and ran back through the gate. Racing past my friends, I streaked across the street and stuck my nose through Dora's fence.

A strange woman sat on the porch, fiddling with her cell phone, while two boys played kickball in the yard -- with my basketball. Aargh.

The kids ran over to pet me through the fence.

"Leave that big black dog alone!" the woman yelled. "It'll bite you!"

I dragged myself back to where my pack stood watching. Felicity's bright eyes were full of concern.

"Oh Puppins, I'm so sorry," she said softly. Loofah started to wail.

I put up a brave front.

"It'll be all right," I assured them, not really believing it myself.

"What about Oliver?" Sue asked. "Maybe he's under

the house."

"I'll see." I went back through the gate. It seemed like the new people hadn't moved in yet. I was glad. I couldn't bear to see someone else taking over The Cottage.

I trotted around the house to the place where the cat family ran underneath. Crouching down, I looked hard into the darkness.

"Hey fuzz-face! Are you there?" No answer. Nothing visible, except the usual mess of dirt and cobwebs.

I called again. "Oliver! Colette! Cleo! Patra!" Silence.

I dragged myself back to my friends.

"He's not here," I told them. "No one's here."

We slumped down under the carob tree. I closed my eyes, trying to think what I should do.

Suddenly, PLOP! -- a blob of grey fur dropped on my head.

"Ha!" shouted Oliver. "Surprised ya!" He laughed, and so did the others.

"Not funny!" I yelled as he rolled off. "What's the big idea, you little beast!"

Actually, I was glad to see him. But it turned out, unfortunately, that Oliver still had no clue where Kristin's new house was.

He thought his family probably was with her, and he assumed she would come back to get him. In the meantime, he planned to hang out at The Cottage and wait for her.

That was not an option for me. What if the new people showed up? What if their nasty dog attacked me? What if they called Animal Control?

There had to be another way.

Oliver suggested going on a hunting expedition around the city.

"It'd be a cool adventure," he said, "and maybe I could meet some new girls." Bill seconded the suggestion. He was a high-energy dog and liked the sound of a longer trek.

No one else thought that was a good idea, but no better suggestions came up.

Hope drained out of me like water from the dog bath when Kristin pulled the plug. We lay there, silently, for a long time.

Then, out of the blue, a ghastly blast of noise filled the air. Down from the sky came a familiar green funnel.

The wild parakeets!

They coasted in, making a smooth landing in the carob tree.

"Puppeens!" Pepito squawked. "Que pasa? Donde has estado?"

I guessed what he was asking, and since he always knows what's going on in the 'hood, I took a stab at answering with a question of my own.

"Donde Kristin? Que?"

Pathetic. But amazingly, he got it.

"Kristeen? Si. Vamonos!"

He and the flock shot out of the carob tree and headed down the street.

"Get up!" I yelled to my incredulous crew. "Follow those birds!"

"But we can't fly!" cried Loofah.

We didn't need to. The parakeets flew low and slow, right over our heads as we raced to keep up.

Pepito and his feathered followers led us down one street after another. We passed the fortress house, stopping for a brief moment to stare at the boarded-up windows and taped-over door.

No pit bulls. They, and the dogfights, were history.

We gave a cheer, then resumed our pursuit. When

Loofah got tired, the parakeets circled overhead while she rested. Then we all carried on.

Finally, screeching excitedly, the flock landed on an oak tree in an overgrown yard.

"Aqui esta, Puppeens!" Pepito squawked. And with hardly a pause, the green birds took off, disappearing over the rooftop.

I stared at the house. Kristin in that dump? Not a chance. Maybe he didn't understand me after all.

Then I looked closer. The house seemed strangely familiar.

Suddenly, I recognized it. The old "Spanish Colonial" where we once peeked in the windows. The one that Kristin dubbed La Casa Royale!

The yard was cleared of trash, the broken windows fixed. Otherwise, it looked pretty much the same.

Except -- there, hanging over the front door, was the sign from The Cottage.

I couldn't remember exactly what it said, but I knew what it meant: This was home, and I was welcome.

Just at that moment, Kristin came around the corner, wearing a summer dress, her light hair tousled like always, and her arms full of those flowers she calls bird-of-paradise.

She saw me.

"Puppins? Is that you??"

I ran and jumped on her. Against the rules, of course, but I couldn't help it.

"You're back!" she cried, dropping the flowers and enclosing me in her arms.

Breathing in her sweet familiar scent, I licked her face, wet with salty tears.

"No collar! And ... and you're so thin! But it's you!" she cried. She didn't scold me for jumping on her, or for ditching my collar, or for disappearing.

"Where have you been?" she exclaimed. "Who stole you? How did you find your way to my new house?"

I barked and barked, trying to explain it all. Probably just as well that she couldn't understand.

Oliver came strutting over, getting Kristin's attention.

"Did you bring Puppins back to me, Oliver? Thank you!"

He puffed out his chest as she petted him, taking all the credit as usual. Then he ran off around the house.

Good riddance.

Kristin turned and spotted Loofah cowering in the background.

"Who's this?" she asked, running over and picking up the little puffball. "Are you a friend of Puppins? You could use a bath, but you're so pretty!" Loofah glanced shyly at Kristin as she rubbed her soft ears.

Meanwhile, Felicity, Bill, Columbo and Sue were crouching out of sight in the bushes. I raced over to them.

"Come out," I urged. "Come and meet Kristin!"

"I don't think that's a good idea. Too many of us," Felicity said, a worried look on her face. "And Puppins, do you realize where we are?"

"At Kristin's new home!" I exclaimed. "And guess what? She and I saw this house a long time ago, when nobody lived in it. Isn't that amazing?"

"It's even more amazing than you think," Felicity said. "This is the Tribal Base."

"No way," I declared. "Not possible."

Felicity insisted that she was right. I thought about it. We always went inside from the alley. I'd never been around to the front. But if this really was the Tribal Base, where was the Tribe?

"Puppins! What are you doing? Don't you dare

disappear again!" Kristin hurried over with Loofah still in her arms. Then she saw Felicity and the others.

"Good grief! Where did all these dogs come from, Puppins? Do you have an entourage?"

I didn't know what that word meant; this was just my pack. I pranced around, licking each of their faces to show Kristin they were my friends.

She put Loofah down and beckoned them to come out, then let them sniff her hand.

"I'll bet you're all hungry," she said. "Come along. I'll get some food for you."

Maybe everything was going to be okay after all!

I followed her inside while the others waited on the steps. The first thing I noticed was the smell. Fresh paint, everything clean. Just like the smell of The Cottage.

The Tribe's Gathering Room was filled with Kristin's furniture. It looked really good, and it was not cramped like at The Cottage. I could actually turn around without bumping my butt on the coffee table.

I trailed Kristin to the kitchen. The Tribe hardly ever went in there -- too much trash, too many bugs.

Now, looking around, I had a new appreciation for Kristin's cleaning habits – the whole room sparkled.

Opening a cupboard, she brought out a bowl. My bowl. She still had it. I didn't even mind that she filled it with dry food.

As I sucked down the kibbles, Kristin ruffled my ears.

"Puppins, you really are too thin!" she said, tears welling up in her blue eyes. "Those dognappers didn't feed you enough. I wish I had some canned food for you."

Canned food? Wow. To a dog, nothing says love like canned food.

33

Kristin brought kibbles outside for the others, and I watched as they gulped down the meal.

"Puppins, what am I going to do about all these dogs?" Kristin said, hugged me again. Then she added, "Wait here. I'm going to call Jodi and tell her the great news about you!" She ran inside to get her cell phone.

What *was* she going to do about my pals? Maybe there was room in her heart for Loofah, possibly for Felicity. But there was no way she was going to adopt Bill, Sue and Columbo.

My friends quickly licked out their bowls. Then Felicity said, "We have to go, Puppins, and see if we can find the Tribe. I'll check back with you soon about Loofah."

Loofah and I said goodbye to them and they ran off.

Loofah cocked her head and looked up at me. "Do you think I'll be able to stay here, Puppins? Kristin seems to like me. She told me I was sweet."

"I don't know. We'll have to wait and see," I replied.

She went on. "Felicity said this is the Tribal Base. I don't believe it, do you?"

"It's true. When I went inside, I saw the Gathering Room and the kitchen. But Mariah and the others aren't in there."

"Oh Puppins, what if Kristin called Animal Control?" Loofah cried.

Would she? I knew she might think stray animals should be taken to the shelter, so I was plenty worried. But for Loofah's sake, I tried to stay positive.

"I think Pasadena Fats probably alerted them and they got away," I told her. "Felicity will find them." I only hoped that was true.

Just then, Oliver came bounding around the corner like a short-eared, long-tailed, loud-mouthed rabbit.

"Puppins! I've got news!" he yelled.

"Yeah, yeah. But first, fur face, there's something I have to say. I hate to admit it, but I goofed big time when I ran away. I apologize. I shouldn't have done it. Are you still mad at me?"

"Yeah, you jerk!" he said. "If I was taller, I'd kick your butt!"

Loofah laughed so hard she fell to the ground. Sigh.

"So what's your big news, bozo?" I asked him crossly.

"I'll show you -- come on!" He streaked off around the house and we followed.

Thankfully, everything in back was familiar: the alley, the gate, the courtyard with its old stone fountain, the sagging backdoor to the big house.

Oliver raced past the door and on to the Carriage House, which the Tribe had never used. He pushed through a new pet door, with Loofah and me close on his tail.

There was the missing Tribe! They welcomed us with a near riot of barking and spinning and tail-sniffing, a great and unexpected reunion.

"How do you like our new Tribal Base?" Mariah asked when things calmed down.

"It's awesome," I said. "But how ...?"

"We'll tell you the story later. First, Oliver just now

filled us in on your success at the dogfight ring. We're so proud of you, Puppins."

"I couldn't have done it without him," I said modestly, cuffing the little beast on the head.

"True," Oliver agreed, puffing out his chest like he always does.

"And," I added, "we never would have made it past those pit bulls if the others hadn't barked their heads off. It was a true team effort."

As I said that, some words bombed my brain: *When spiderwebs unite, they can tie up a lion.*

Or a ring of criminals.

***

I gazed around at what Kristin had done to the Carriage House, trying to take it all in.

On the floor were a lot of colorful rugs for the dogs, and under the windows and along the walls were shelves for the cats.

There on one shelf was Colette, contentedly grooming Cleo and Patra. She winked a friendly eye at me -- a first, for sure.

Stretched out on the shelf above them was a pure white cat with bright green eyes.

"That's Jade," Oliver confided. "She's hot, huh!"

I stared at him. "Wait. Is she your ... girlfriend?"

"Not yet. She and her family stowed away on a truck from Mexico, then she got lost from the rest. Someone on the street told her about the Tribe and brought her here. I'm going to be her ... uh ... mentor."

He leaped up beside Jade and boldly licked her on the face. Raising a paw, she swatted him soundly. He winked at me and curled up beside her.

OMG. Was the little pest going to have a girlfriend?

***

I settled down on one of the rugs. Loofah pulled

another next to mine, with Mariah on her other side. It was so great to be back with the Tribe again!

I couldn't help wondering, though, what was happening with Felicity, Sue, Columbo and Bill.

Then the door opened and Kristin came in.

"I saw you run back here with Oliver, Puppins. What do you think about all these fine animals?" She patted my head. "They can be your new friends."

Little did she know. But they were fine for sure, and so was the Carriage House. I nuzzled her hand with my nose to show my approval.

She counted the cats and dogs. "I'll bring your dinners soon," she told them, adding, "Puppins, come with me. Jodi is headed over to see you."

I trotted eagerly after her. I wanted to hear Mariah tell how the Carriage House got to be the Tribal Base, of course. But even more, I wanted to see Jodi.

***

Rushing out of her old yellow VW, Jodi hugged me so hard I could scarcely breathe. When she finally let go, I licked her face and wagged my tail as fast as I could.

I wished I could tell her and Kristin how much I loved them and how glad I was to be home, but I think they got the message.

"Puppins, I knew you'd get back!" Jodi exclaimed. "Those dognappers shipped you to Zambia on a freighter, didn't they! And then you got captured by pirates and threatened with death! But you escaped and hitched a ride back across the ocean on a tiny sailboat. You brave, intrepid dog!"

Kristin laughed.

Same crazy Jodi, I thought happily. And right in front of Kristin, Jodi gave me a red licorice rope.

Kristin just sighed.

"Is he alright?" Jodi asked. "Maybe he was tortured

by those pirates. Does he have any scars?"

"He seems alright, but I'll have the vet check him over," Kristin replied.

Wait. A visit to the vet? My favorite thing. Not. There should be a less embarrassing way to take a dog's temperature.

"Now if only Ruby would come back," Jodi said wistfully.

"Ruby? Haven't you given up on that dog?" Kristin shook her head. "Ruby's a gypsy. She's probably in Las Vegas right now, singing 'Don't Fence Me In.'"

Too true.

"No, no," Jodi replied. "She probably was captured too. Seriously, Kristin, there's a sophisticated dognapping ring operating in Los Angeles. I read about it in the Times."

"Jodi, we posted signs and ran ads offering a reward. Why wouldn't someone have contacted us for the ransom?"

"Hmm. Good question. If those pirates had sent a ransom note, I know you'd have paid zillions to get him back. But maybe he escaped before they could contact you, and he's been on the run ever since, trying to get home. Like in those old 'Lassie' movies. Ruby too. I know she'll turn up."

Kristin rolled her eyes. "You're nuts. Anyway, the important thing is, Puppins is home. And Jodi, he brought the sweetest little white dog with him. It's a bichon, I think. And some other dogs too, although they seem to have run off."

"Really? Maybe he freed all the dogs that those dognappers captured!"

I wished I could tell her what a liberator I actually was.

"Anyway, the bichon should have a home," Kristin

said. "How about it? Don't you still have all that gear you got for Ruby?"

"That stuff wouldn't work for a small dog. Anyway, little dogs are not for me. I like big, willful dogs. Dogs with spirit. Like Ruby."

Me too, I thought ruefully.

Kristin shook her head. "What good is a dog that's always running away from you?"

Ouch. That could apply to me, too.

Kristin went on. "I think Puppins' new little friend would be a much better pet than Ruby. She seems awfully sweet."

"Well, maybe *you* should adopt her," Jodi shot back.

"I don't want to have two dogs in the house," Kristin replied. "She can stay in the Carriage House with the others for now, but I think she should belong to someone."

"Maybe she already does, and is lost."

"She isn't wearing a collar. But tomorrow I'll do the usual 'found dog' routine. If I can't locate an owner, I'll try to find her a nice home."

That would be a good thing for Loofah, I knew. But it meant that sooner or later, she'd be leaving. She would not become my little sister.

Sigh. Another loss, another hole in my heart. Soon it would look like that cheese Dora liked to put on our grilled sandwiches.

***

Jodi drove off after giving me a few more hugs and another piece of licorice. Then Kristin and I went out to the Carriage House with dinner for everyone. She left me there, saying she had an article to finish up for work and would come back for me later.

***

Dinner done, Mariah asked about Felicity.

"She and the others left just after we got here," Loofah told her. "They had that boxer with them, too. We thought you and the Tribe ran away, and they went to look for you. Anyway, Felicity should be back soon. She's supposed to see if Kristin is going to adopt me."

I didn't want to deceive Loofah, so I told her the truth. "I heard Kristin talking to Jodi. She doesn't think she should have another house dog, but she is going to find a good home for you. A family."

"No!" Loofah sprang to her feet, her little face puckered up with anxiety. "I want to live here, with you and Mariah, and the Tribe. *This* is my family."

"Let's see what happens," Mariah said, nuzzling her gently. "It may take Kristin a while to find the right family, and you'll be here with us until then."

Loofah brightened. "Maybe it will take a long time. Maybe forever. In the meantime, I can get caught up on sleep. I've had *way* too much excitement lately."

Everyone laughed, but I could relate. I needed to get back to a more boring life myself. I looked forward to doing what I do best: nothing.

***

Soon, however, I discovered that lying around is not always a good thing; it can lead to too much thinking.

About Dora, for instance. When I thought about her, I felt awful. If I hadn't run off, she might still be living across the street. I don't know if I could still do daycare, but at least she could invite me over for snacks and to watch the Lakers. Now, that would never happen again.

And of course, I still spent too much time thinking about Ruby. Was she still at the puppy mill? Was she alright? Would I ever have another chance with her?

Yeah, sad to say, Ruby still had a choke-chain around my heart.

34

I finally learned how the Carriage House became the Tribal Base. When La Casa Royale was put up for sale, Kristin was the one who came to see it that day when we were out to dinner.

After that, Fats raised the alarm when anyone came. But on the day Kristin actually moved in, he was dozing in his hole. The Early Warning System failed, and Mariah and the others had no time to escape.

Miraculously, Kristin did not call Animal Control. Instead, she gave the Tribe food and water.

"I guess you must come with the house," she told them with a smile.

She and Jodi cleaned up the Carriage House, then herded the dogs and cats out there. She got a vet to come and check them out and give them shots. And every day since then, she continued to feed them.

"But ... dry food? Do you like that stuff?" I asked Mariah. "Don't you think it's kind of gross?"

She laughed. "Well, it's better than a lot of the garbage we used to eat, remember? Anyway, I had dry food at the racetrack, and I think it helped me have good energy."

"Can you keep the Tribal Base here forever?" Loofah asked Mariah.

"I hope so. Before, we always had to worry that we'd

get thrown out, or that Animal Control would come. Kristin is fine with us being here, and she doesn't seem to mind if we come and go, or if new dogs and cats show up.

"Jodi helps her with buying the food," Mariah continued. "And she told Jodi she's getting a license from the city to make this a private shelter."

"Really? Wow. That means you and the Tribe will always be right here in my own backyard!" I exclaimed.

"But what about me?" cried Loofah. "I don't want Kristin to find a family for me. I want to stay here. I've got a special rug now, and all my friends are here."

Mariah licked her ears. "When you get a real home, dear, maybe you can come back and visit us."

Before Loofah could respond, the pet door pushed open. In trotted Felicity, Bill, Sue and Columbo.

It turns out that while they were searching for the Tribe, they ran into Mr. Pegasus and he reported what was going on at the Carriage House.

They were thrilled with Kristin's new shelter. "Let's celebrate!" boomed Columbo, breaking into his song and dance routine.

The rest of us joined in. Soon it got kind of crazy. We barked and yipped and mewed and ran in circles, chasing each other's tails.

Some words flashed across my brain: *It is one of the blessings of old friends that you can be stupid with them.*

So true.

***

When the party finally wound down, Felicity asked me to go out to the courtyard with her for some fresh air.

The night was as dark and sweet as the hot chocolate Dora used to fix on chilly evenings. (I can't have much chocolate, of course -- it's the curse of being a dog -- but she always let me lick out her cup.)

Felicity and I settled down under a camellia bush that was bursting with red blooms. I liked it better than the pink one at The Cottage, because it reminded me of red licorice.

We were quiet for a while, then I broke the silence.

"Felicity, are you going to stick around, or do you have to go back to your camp by the Old Bridge?"

She regarded me with her steady gaze. "I wish I could stay, but I have my work. And there's something that I have to do as soon as possible."

"What is it? Can you tell me?"

She hesitated, then said, "Bill asked me to go with him to Puppy Haven to try to rescue Ruby. I agreed, because I want to get Custard out of there too. Sue and Columbo have offered to help us."

Wait. Bill was going to rescue Ruby? Aargh. The jealousy bug bit me right where it hurts.

I wanted to be the one to save Ruby, just like I had wanted to do at the dogfight ring. But Felicity and I both knew that I could not run off from Kristin again.

When I didn't say anything, Felicity squinted at me. "Puppins, do you still love Ruby?"

Yikes. Felicity is way too direct!

"I don't know," I said, probably blushing under my black fur. "I don't want to have any feelings for her. But sometimes they just won't go away, and I can't figure out how to get rid of them. It's stupid."

She smiled. "It's not stupid. Love can be a puzzle, I guess. Now that you are home, you'll have time to think it through."

Yeah, I thought darkly, I'll have time to do nothing but sit around and think, while she and Bill and the others go off to rescue Ruby.

Then the danger of the scheme dawned on me.

"Can you really get in and out of there without getting caught?" I asked.

"I don't know. But I have to try. It's not just about Ruby and Custard, you know. I hate that place. It's where I was born. The irresponsible way they breed dogs is what caused me to be crippled."

Wow. If I wasn't so dense, I might have figured that out.

"I'm sorry, Felicity. I wish there was something I could do," I said.

"There is," she replied quietly. "Just be here when I get back."

Ha. Like I had a choice. "I'm not going anywhere," I said with a sigh.

"That's what I want to hear," she replied, gazing straight into my eyes. "I really want you to be here."

Gulp. There was a softness in her brown eyes that I'd never seen before. Confusion washed over me like an unexpected spray from the garden hose.

Did she *like* me, or what?

Thankfully, Kristin showed up at that moment to take me inside. Whew.

***

That night, for the first time in ever so long, I would sleep curled up in my own cushy bed. Sweet.

I walked with Kristin around our new yard, she telling me the name of every flower and tree and shrub, just like she always did at The Cottage.

As we approached the house, I noticed a light by the front door. It gave off a comforting golden glow, reminding me of the porch light we used to have.

Some familiar words came into my brain: *Heaven is a house with porch lights.*

I was kind of sad that La Casa Royale had no porch. But it did have that outside light, and I guess that's just as good.

I followed Kristin inside and up the stairs to her new bedroom. She didn't have much furniture in there, but at the foot of her bed, right where it belonged, was the big plaid dog bed she got for me at Costco.

I sniffed to see if any trespassers had slept on it while I was living on the streets.

Hmm. A faint whiff of Oliver. I'd get even.

But wait -- maybe I owed him that much. Oh well.

I circled a few times before settling into the fleecy folds. Ahhh. Best bed in the whole world.

Kristin leaned over and gave my head a kiss. Then she scolded me: "Puppins, don't you ever disappear like that again!" I didn't mind. I knew it meant she loved me.

As I closed my eyes, that earlier brain bomb came back to me. The one about heaven and a house with porch lights.

I thought about it again. Did it mean that your house is heaven, or that heaven is your house?

And what if you had no light on your house? Or what if you were homeless, like Odette and Joshua? Would that mean there was no heaven for you?

Too deep for me. I snuggled down and breathed in the room's smells, new and old.

All good. I was home.

END of PART ONE

PART TWO

"This is the lesson: never give in, never give in, never, never, never, never..."

Winston Churchill

"Ask the animals and they will teach you, or the birds and they will tell you..."

Job 12: 7

35

Mariah wants me to continue telling my story. I'm not proud of a lot of it, but she says I don't need to be embarrassed or ashamed.

"Nobody is perfect, Puppins. Others can learn from your bad choices."

Ouch.

Mariah isn't shy about confessing her own past goof-ups at the greyhound track. She didn't care if she won or lost, she just wanted to have fun.

Anyway, lying on our rugs in the Carriage House, under the ceiling fan Kristin put up, we take turns telling chapters of our lives.

It's a good way to spend a hot L.A. afternoon, since we aren't allowed to fight each other.

I don't mean "fight" in a bad way, just the kind of friendly snarling and biting and wrestling that boy (and some girl) dogs like to do.

It's fine for us to do it in the courtyard, but not indoors. It riles up the cats, and it gives Mariah a headache. (She's getting old.)

When it's my turn to tell a chapter, I try to leave out the weird stuff if I can get away with it. But if I do admit my fails, Oliver twitches his whiskers and snickers rudely into his paws.

I guess that's the downside of having a cat for a BBF.

Anyway, I'm a teenager, remember? I figure I'm entitled to make a few mistakes. So, on with my story.

***

You'd think that after running away from home, living on the sketchy backstreets of L.A., almost falling to my death from the Old Bridge, helping bust a vile dogfight ring and getting ghosted twice by the same female, I'd be ready to enjoy a peaceful life with Kristin and the Tribe.

I was.

Then Felicity told me she was going to raid Puppy Haven, the breeding mill where she was born. Bill the boxer, and the trackers Oglalla Sue and Columbo, had volunteered to help.

Their goal was to rescue Ruby and the little dog Custard, who were captured by the dogfight slime, then sold to the mill.

Okay, I admit it. Trying to rescue Ruby was getting to be a habit. It was my original reason for raiding the dogfights, and now it was back on the table.

To make things worse, I was pretty sure she had "special feelings" for Bill, and I was jealous.

Shouldn't it be me who rescued her? Didn't I deserve one last chance to show her I was not a wimp?

Not happening. Hurting Kristin again was out of the question.

***

I stayed in the Carriage House with the Tribe while Kristin was at work. Like the other animals, I could go through the pet door into the courtyard to be rowdy or do my poop business.

Kristin always latched the alley gate, but any of the big dogs, including myself, could lift it with our noses. She was more worried about dognappers than about escapees, and felt I was safe because passing dog thieves could not see into the courtyard.

At night, while I slept in La Casa Royale, the other animals came and went from the Carriage House.

They were microchipped, just in case, but mostly they were happy to stay put in our backyard. They knew it was a safe place, and it served regular meals. Dry kibble, but still.

In general, life was pretty good for me. When Kristin came home from work, we had our customary walk -- a different neighborhood now, but still a nice mix of people and dogs. And thankfully, no killer pit bulls.

I usually ate dinner with the Tribe. Dry food, of course, although Kristin did allow treats on special occasions.

And when Jodi came over, she still sneaked me a red licorice rope, so the dietary scene was not entirely bleak.

Kristin was, as always, a clean freak. Her vacuuming addiction had not been cured, and I still hid under the bed when she brought out that fiend.

The vacuum caused a lot of grief for Pasadena Fats, too. "That flaccid thing is roaring all the time!" the Tribe's token mouse complained.

Fats liked to mock Kristin, racing around in circles, shouting "Vroom! Vroom! Vroom!" in his squeaky little voice.

Kristin hadn't spotted him or set any traps, but we all knew that life was uncertain for a mouse in the house.

The Tribe suggested that he move out to the Carriage House. But Fats was a gambler at heart, and being in La Casa Royale gave him more opportunity to steal eats.

Sadly, Kristin still clung onto her workaholic ways. Although she had vowed to reform, I didn't see much progress.

But at least she spent fewer hours at the newspaper now, because keeping up the shelter took a lot of time and effort.

She still had most of her other flaws, too, but I tried to overlook them. I guess that's what you have to do with someone you love.

***

When Oliver proclaimed one night that life in the new Tribal Base was "purrrrfect," a thought crept into my brain on little cat feet: *what in this world is perfect?*

Because for me, things were not.

Take my obsession with Ruby. I tried to convince myself that I was over her, but when Felicity or anyone else brought up her name, I broke out in an itchy rash.

No one could see it under my black coat, of course, but it was hard to hide those embarrassing fits of scratching.

Felicity herself was another problem. She had started to, you know, *like* me. Awkward.

Luckily, she spent most of her time at her camp by the Old Bridge, where she did some kind of work that I guess was important.

Mariah said that Felicity was the Tribe's warrior, "a beautiful spirit in a plain brown wrapper." To me, she was a good friend, nothing more. No way was I looking for another girlfriend.

***

Felicity had confided her Puppy Mill plan to me a while earlier. Then one evening, she showed up at the Carriage House with Columbo, Sue and Bill, and they announced their intentions to the whole Tribe.

"That's nuts!" exclaimed Oliver. "Why do you want to go there?"

"To get Ruby and Custard out. They should not have to be there," she answered.

"Ruby's an escape artist," Mariah pointed out. "She might be long gone."

"True, but I'm sure Custard will still be there. Anyway, there's another reason: Puppy Haven is where I was born, and I'm a good example of what they turn out."

"How did Puppy Haven cause your ..." I began. She had told me this before, but she'd never really explained how her leg got the way it was.

"It's what happens at all puppy mills," she said. "They didn't check my parents to see if they had problems that could be passed on to me.

"They don't care whether the dogs are strong and healthy. They only care about how many pups they can get and how much money they can make."

"But why would anyone buy a puppy from them?" I asked.

"They sell to pet stores. And pet stores count on people buying a cute puppy without finding out where it came from."

"No offense, Felicity, but would someone buy a puppy if it had a bad leg?" Columbo asked.

"A lot of problems don't show up until the puppy is older," Felicity said. "I was taken to a pet store as soon as I could leave my mother, and someone bought me.

"I didn't start to limp until a long time later, and that's when my owners found out that my hip was deformed."

"But didn't they love you anyway?" asked Loofah, our little bichon.

"Not enough. When my limp got worse, they decided they didn't want a dog with problems. They drove me to a new neighborhood, took off my collar and turned me loose."

"Oh Felicity! How could they do such a thing?"

Loofah cried, shaking her curly white topknot.

"They told me it was a nice area and I'd find a better home. Then they drove off."

"That's so harsh," I muttered, wondering once again if that's what happened to me in Seattle.

"Many dogs have told me they were dumped when their owners didn't want them anymore," Felicity went on. "Anyway, I met a stray who took me to Mariah. And she taught me that you don't have to be perfect to live a good life."

Trotting over to the greyhound, Felicity gave Mariah a grateful lick, then continued. "I'm lucky. I have my work, my camp, and a lot of good friends, including all of you."

"If I were you, I'd want to stay as far away from Puppy Haven as possible," Loofah said with a shudder. "And won't it be really hard to free Ruby and Custard?"

"Puppins and Oliver succeeded at the dogfight ring, and that inspires me," she answered.

Oliver jumped down from his shelf and strutted around the room. "I can help you, Felicity, just like I did then!"

"No, Oliver. You and Puppins have faced enough danger. Columbo, Sue, and Bill are coming with me for moral support. Once there, I'll get inside on my own. Then I'll play it by ear, like you and Puppins did."

Oliver deflated his chest and slunk off to a corner.

Then Bill spoke up. "I'm ready ta go, Felicity."

Bill was among the dogs we'd sprung out of the dogfight place. He and Ruby had something going, but I wasn't sure what. Maybe they had even ...

I didn't want to think about it.

Columbo, whose long, sad face and mournful eyes gave no clue to his clownish personality, broke into a clog dance.

"This time, I'm going to be in the frontlines!" he announced, stomping his big paws. "Give me action!"

Sue smirked. "Not much action at Puppy Haven, compared with the fight ring," she scoffed. She was a sight hound while Columbo followed scents, and they had been a team for a long time.

"Don't underestimate Puppy Haven," Felicity warned. "The owners have guns. They don't want anyone stealing their dogs. They make a lot of money off those puppies."

Columbo stopped dancing at the mention of guns. Then he quickly recovered.

"We can do it, Felicity! Piece of cake!" he crowed.

"Columbo, we're trackers," Sue reminded him, "and Felicity knows where Puppy Haven is, so there's nothing to track."

"You said that about the dogfight ring," he reminded her. "There's no excitement in tracking. No risk."

"Who needs more risk?" she asked, sniffing scornfully at him. "Just living on the streets of L.A. is enough risk for me." Despite the matts in her ungroomed hair, Sue still had the air of royalty.

Columbo bopped over and gave her elegant nose a lick. "Sue, you already said yes, remember?"

"I remember. But this is the last time we're doing a liberation," she replied shortly.

"Hooray! I'm a liberator!" he yelped. He executed a few steps of his Razzle Dazzle tap routine, croaking, "On with the hunt! On with the hunt!"

"This isn't a hunt," Sue insisted.

"We don't know what we'll find there, so it's a hunt!" he shot back, giving her a kiss.

She sighed and shook her head. "Hopeless. You are hopeless."

The rest of us couldn't help laughing.

36

Feeling glum about the puppy mill situation, I went outside, stretched out by the old fountain and closed my eyes. Maybe in the courtyard's peace and quiet, I could sort out the mess in my teenage brain.

Suddenly, a blast of screeches shattered the silence. The wild parakeets!

So much for peace and quiet. What were they doing here at night? Aren't birds supposed to be asleep after dark?

When we lived at The Cottage, Pepito and his flock came every afternoon to feast on the berries of our carob tree. But since we moved, they only dropped down once in a while, squawking hello and goodbye in parakeet words and taking off again.

Despite their frightful noise, I missed those longer visits. They were a cool shade of green, like that dropped lime popsicle I once slurped up from a sidewalk.

And they were my friends. If I knew more of their words, I could find out why they didn't live in cages like other pet birds.

This time, Pepito greeted me as always: "Buenos Dias, Pupeeens!" And I replied, as usual, "Hola, Pepito!"

Then I tried to ask what they were doing up so late.

He squawked something that sounded like "rap show."

"Que?" I asked, but they were already in departure mode. Pepito screeched "Adios, mi amigo!" and they were gone.

I shut my eyes again, deciding I might as well get some sleep before Kristin came for me. Then, just as I was drifting off, a warm body settled down next to mine.

"Are you awake, Puppins?" It was Felicity.

"Yeah."

"Alright to talk?"

"Yeah. What's on your mind?"

"I feel like you and the others don't approve of me going to Puppy Haven."

"Yeah. It's way too dangerous."

Her dark eyes shone with determination. "I wish everyone could understand that I have to go. I'll be careful. I don't think it will take long to do what I need to do."

I said nothing, just put my head down again. My stomach churned. What if she got hurt? If I was there, I might be able to help. I owed her that; after all, didn't she save my life on the Old Bridge?

And of course, much as I hated to admit it, I wanted to be the hero who saved Ruby. Not Bill.

***

Meanwhile, a new person had moved into La Casa Royale: Miss Wisteria, a former neighbor, who now lived upstairs in one of our spare bedrooms.

We met her when we lived in The Cottage and would stop and talk with her on our nightly walks.

Now she was too old to take care of her house, and she had no family to help. We have lots of space, so Kristin invited her to move in with us.

Her name is also the name of a flower, and when she grew up she became a butterfly scientist so I guess it's appropriate.

Miss W was nice, but her two cats, Harriet and Victoria, were another matter. They didn't like dogs, and they hissed at me if I came in the room with Kristin.

But other than the cat thing, having Miss Wisteria living with us was a good arrangement. Kristin watched over her, and sometimes Miss W, as best she could, helped out with our backyard shelter. And she also paid rent, which helped Kristin with expenses.

I didn't have anything against her being old, except that she couldn't throw the tennis ball to me. Kristin tried to do that a few minutes every day, but I could have used a lot more ball time.

***

The next morning after my talk with Felicity about her plans, Kristin, as usual, served up some healthy granola, kiwi fruit and coconut milk for herself and Miss Wisteria.

As they ate, Kristin informed Miss W that she was going to a writers' conference in San Diego with Jodi over the weekend. She asked her to check on the shelter until she got back, and Miss W agreed.

"The animals are well behaved," Kristin noted. "You'll just need to take their food to the Carriage House, and make sure their water dishes are filled. Puppins can stay out there with the others. I'll give you a phone number to call if you need any help."

I dragged myself over to my corner. Not only was Felicity leaving me behind, so was Kristin. Double bummer. I guess Jodi was right when she said I have abandonment issues.

Well, why shouldn't I? I've already mentioned how many times Ruby ditched me. And I probably got dumped by my first owners in Seattle, whoever they were. Why else would a mere pup be out alone on the street at night, hit by a car and never claimed?

I moped about all this, feeling sorry for myself. When Kristin goes away, she always gets a sitter if Jodi can't come over, and sitters are an uneven bunch.

One hag in recent memory did her social media thing on her cell the whole time she was there. She didn't even pat me or talk to me. Unforgivable.

And now I was going to be left with Miss W and her two snarly cats.

But wait.

Kristin would be gone. Couldn't I sneak out and go with Felicity, without getting in trouble?

I mulled it over. It'd be for a good cause, I told myself. We were going to raid an evil puppy mill. Kristin would approve of that, if she knew. But she didn't need to know. I could easily be back before she got home.

It was starting to make sense.

Miss W won't miss me, I continued assuring myself. She's ancient, and her eyes aren't too good. She reads with a magnifying glass. All dogs probably look alike to her.

Wow. A great plan. I could hardly wait to tell Felicity about it.

***

Ouch. Not the reaction I expected.

"Oh Puppins, no! That would be foolish. You don't want to take the chance of Kristin discovering you gone again. She'd be devastated."

"But that won't happen, Felicity. She said she'll be gone for three days. I'll have plenty of time to get back."

"But what about Miss Wisteria? She might be sharper than you believe."

"Nah. I told you, she's old. And too focused on those dumb cats of hers to know what goes on in the Carriage House. It'll be fine. Anyway, I'm going, and that's that."

She didn't say anything for a long time. Then, shaking her head, she said, "Puppins, if you insist on coming, you must promise that you'll stay outside the kennel house. I've made Sue, Columbo and Bill promise that too. I don't want anyone getting hurt."

"Cool. But if you do need me for anything, I'll be there."

She just sighed.

I couldn't believe it. I'd actually be going to rescue Ruby. I ran in circles, yipping like a chihuahua, until Mariah noticed and figured out what was up.

Same lecture as Felicity's, same result. I can be really stubborn when I make up my mind about something.

So it was settled. We'd leave the next morning, as soon as Kristin and Jodi were gone.

***

In the morning, I tried to wait patiently until Kristin finished breakfast, hugged me goodbye, got into Jodi's little car with her suitcase and drove off.

My team headed out immediately. Bill unlatched the alley gate with his nose, and the five of us set out at a fast trot.

Splitting up so we wouldn't call attention to ourselves, I pranced along with Columbo, both of us in high spirits.

It felt really good to be free again. No leash, no rules, no commands to obey. Awesome.

But as the day went on, the downside of running free came back to haunt me. The sun beat on our backs without mercy. The road got steep. My paws hurt. And my stomach rumbled, reminding me that I'd been too excited to eat breakfast.

The others were much more used to life on the streets. When I began to seriously lag behind, they agreed to stop so I could rest.

As we settled down in a shady spot, Felicity took in my exhaustion. Her eyes narrowed. "Puppins, do you think you can make it?"

Aargh. Was I really such a wimp? "Of course I can," I mumbled. "I'm just out of practice."

No way was I going back home.

"This road just has one direction -- up," Sue noted.

"Puppy Haven is in the foothills. It will be tough going from now on," Felicity replied. "Anyone sorry they came?"

As if.

We started out again at a slower pace. The uphill trek was torturous. We got hungry. Only one garbage can in sight, with nothing in it but a sticky pastry and half a stale burrito, both of which we shared.

Just after the sun went down, we reached our destination. It was a creepy-looking place. All by itself among some dark trees with no other homes around.

The colorless house stood next to a building with outside exercise runs, surrounded by barbed-wire fencing.

We found a spot in the brush to lie down on, and then Felicity revealed her plan.

"We don't need the barking diversion like at the dogfight ring," she said. "No vicious watchdogs here. But there are those fences to get past. And as I warned you, Master and Mistress have guns."

"Master and Mistress?" I snickered.

"That's what they call themselves," she replied. "They're strange people, and they are mean. They don't love their dogs; it's just a business to them. The place is filthy. The dogs are all crowded together. They don't get enough exercise, and they have barely enough to eat."

That's heinous, I thought. How could people treat their animals that way?

Felicity went on. "I'll have to get inside the kennel building where Ruby will be, if she hasn't escaped. Custard will probably be in the house. Mistress chooses one dog to be her 'pet,' and Custard fits the profile – small, white, and fluffy. The house dog gets better treatment, but as soon as it displeases her, it goes back to the kennels."

Felicity told us that she would dig a tunnel under the outer fence and another under the fencing around the exercise runs. Then she could get inside the building through the doggy door.

After freeing Ruby, she'd go on to the house. No lights were on in there, so that meant that if Master and Mistress were home, they'd probably be in bed.

"Under cover of darkness, it shouldn't be too difficult to get in and out of the bedroom," Felicity added.

Columbo jumped up and began clogging. "Let me dig the first tunnel! I'm a great digger! We bloodhounds are famous for that!"

"Maybe that would be a good idea," Felicity said after a moment's thought. "That would save me some tiring work. I'll dig the other one, and go inside alone. I know the layout, and I can get around more quickly by myself."

Columbo was really disappointed that he couldn't go inside with her, but Sue pointed out how helpful digging the outer tunnel would be. Soon he was dancing around again, wagging his ponderous tail, anxious to get started.

Felicity told the rest of us to stay in the shrubs. "If I'm not outside again within a reasonable time, all of you go straight back home. I'll get away as soon as I can."

We promised, and gave Felicity and Columbo "high-paws" for good luck, then settled down to watch.

37

At the first fence, Felicity stood guard while the big bloodhound began digging. Dirt flew out behind him, and soon he had a good start on a deep tunnel.

He raised his head to see where he was. Then ...

HSSSSS! A hideous sound ripped through the dark night. Blue sparks sprayed into the air, crackling like fireworks, and we watched in horror as Columbo flew out of the tunnel.

Felicity was at his side in an instant, with Sue, Bill, and me just behind.

"Columbo? Are you alright?" Sue wailed. No answer.

"Oh Columbo!" Felicity cried. "I had no idea the fence was electric!"

Columbo, with an awful burnt smell hanging over him, didn't move. Sue put her ear on his chest.

"Can you hear anything?' I asked her, my heart in my throat.

"I ... I'm not sure," she stammered.

"Let's get him hidden," Bill said. "Master an' Mistress might have heard something."

Putting our noses underneath his body, we pushed, trying not make his injuries worse. He was heavy. It was slow going. Finally, we got him to the shrubs.

His long nose was an angry mass of blisters. Sue tried again to get a response: "Columbo, can you hear me? Columbo?"

Nothing.

Maybe he was dying, I thought helplessly. How did this happen?

We huddled anxiously around him for a long time. Finally, he gave his tail a feeble wag.

"Lie still, Columbo," Felicity whispered. "We're all here with you."

He opened his eyes. "Sue? Wha ... what happened? Did I ... did I finish ... ?"

"Shhh. Don't move," Sue replied softly.

"But ... what ... ?"

"The fence. It's electric," Felicity choked out. "I had no idea. You bumped it with your nose. I'm so sorry!"

"You've got some nasty burns," Sue told him, "and you might be hurt inside, so don't move around."

He managed a slight grin. "Sue ... will you still ... still love me ... without my ... my razzle ...?"

"Don't worry. You'll get your razzle dazzle back," she said, tears in her grey eyes."

"But what about ... about Ruby? And ... and Custard?"

"Felicity hasn't gone inside yet," Sue replied grimly.

"After ... all that ... that digging?" His voice trailed off.

We closed in around him, trying to keep out the cool night air. It was all we could do.

Time dragged on. None of us felt like talking. Then, as the moon appeared between the scraggly trees, Felicity got up and shook herself.

"I've decided to go ahead," she announced. "You all stay here with Columbo."

"What??" Sue's voice was furious. "That's crazy! Isn't it enough that Columbo is hurt? Why risk getting yourself hurt and maybe killed, just to save Ruby? She's a selfish loner. Why should we care about her?"

"Sue, I can't tell you how sorry I am about Columbo," Felicity replied with a sob. "But I still have to go ahead with my plan."

As much as I wanted to see Ruby again, I knew Sue was right. "Why?" I asked. "Why do you have to do it?"

Felicity shook her head. "It's not just Ruby, or even Custard," she replied. "I remember too well what it's like here. Most of all, I know what bad breeding does to puppies, and how much pain it causes."

She stopped, sucked in her breath and then went on. "My plan was to free *all* the dogs, and that's what I'm going to do. I want to shut this place down."

Wow. I was shocked, and I know Sue and Bill were too. That was way beyond anything we had talked about.

"How can ya do that and get out, without bein' caught?" Bill growled.

"I'll finish the outside tunnel. I'm smaller than Columbo, so avoiding the wires won't be a problem. And digging under the inner fence will be a snap."

A snap? Seriously? My heart sank as she continued.

"Once inside the kennels, I'll free the mothers and puppies, and then the dogs waiting to be bred."

"But what if they touch the fence on the way out?" Bill asked.

"I'll find the switch and turn it off. And when I'm done in there, I'll go in the house for Custard."

"What's your plan for her?" I asked, filled with dread.

"I'll try to get her out of the bedroom before they wake up."

"Felicity, if they do wake up and see that you're just a small dog, they wouldn't shoot you, would they?" Sue asked anxiously.

"They'd shoot first and ask questions later," Felicity said. "Once when some kids tried to get into the runs to pet the dogs, Master came out with his gun. He shot up in the air, but it was scary. Anyway, I'll be out of there before they can grab their guns."

We begged her not to go, but she refused to listen.

Starting where Columbo left off, she quickly made it through. She ran to the inner fence and dug furiously, crawled into the runs and pushed through the doggy door, disappearing inside the building.

We huddled around Columbo, trying to stay calm. The night was filled with spooky sounds – the screech of an owl, the wind in the trees, the crackling of unseen critters creeping nearby.

Our ears were pricked up for just one sound, and finally we heard it: paws hitting the hard ground like beats on a distant drum.

In the moonlight, we could make out a rush of dogs tearing through the exercise pens and crawling under the inside fence.

Then they stopping short. One of the dogs grabbed a stick off the ground with its mouth, whirled around, and let it fly against the wires. Silence. No hiss, no sparks.

The dogs dropped to the ground and inched through the tunnel, one by one, then flew off in all directions. Except two grownups and a couple of pups who headed our way and sank down beside.

My heart took a leap. One of them was Ruby.

The others were a Bernese mountain dog and her puppies. The mom, breathing hard, said, "I'm ... Tasha ... and these ... these are my ... little ones, Hansel and ... Gretel."

The two balls of fur pushed up against their mom, trying to hide themselves under her thick coat. Then all three of them closed their eyes, exhausted.

"Where is Felicity?" Sue asked Ruby.

"She went to the house to get Custard," Ruby replied. Then she told us what had gone in in the kennels.

"Felicity said the outside fence was electric. She found where the switch was, shoved a chair to the wall, and pushed the switch down.

"Then she moved the chair next to our cages. The latches aren't very high and she could lift them with her paw."

"That's just what Puppins and Oliver done at the dogfight ring!" Bill put in. Ruby looked over, noticing him in the shadows for the first time.

"Bill! What are you doing here?" She sounded awfully pleased.

"I come with the others ta help Felicity," Bill told her. "Then Columbo got hurt by the fence."

Ruby gave Columbo a brief glance. "I know. Felicity said to test the fence before we went under, so I threw a stick at it."

I stared at her. She didn't seem at all concerned about Columbo, just continued telling what happened.

"Some dogs had to stay behind because their pups were too small to make it. Felicity told the others to run away as fast as they could, and look for places where they might find homes. They told her that even living on the street would be better than staying in that disgusting place."

"How many did she set free?" I asked Ruby, hoping to get some attention.

She answered without looking me in the eye. "I don't know. A lot of mothers with their puppies, and other dogs waiting to be bred."

Ruby abruptly got to her feet. She trotted over to Bill and whispered something in his ear. He jumped up and, without saying a word, the two of them took off.

38

"What the F***!" Sue yelped. I'm not big on swears, but that was my thought exactly.

"What's wrong with that dog?" Sue ranted. "She didn't even wait to see if Felicity and Custard are okay, or to thank Felicity for getting her out!"

Sue was right. I knew Ruby was self-absorbed, but this was unbelievable.

Columbo was still out of it. Sue and I sank down next to him again. We didn't talk. What was there to say?

I was angry too. Not just with Ruby and Bill, but with my own pathetic self. How did I get all dopey over Ruby again?

Sue and I kept watch while the Bernese, oblivious to the drama, slumbered on.

We listened as hard as we could for sounds coming from inside the house. Nothing.

Time dragged on.

Suddenly, shots rang out!

We sprang up and strained our eyes, trying to see in the faint moonlight. More shots! Doors banging, people yelling. Then the backdoor flew open and out raced two small dogs, running into the night. They quickly reached the shrubs where we were and fell to the ground beside us.

I could breathe again.

Turning my eyes back to the house, I saw a man in baggy underwear, firing his gun into the dark yard and screaming and cursing.

Finally, he went back inside, slamming the door behind him with a mighty bang.

"Felicity, you did it!" I exclaimed. "Are you okay? Is Custard okay?" The little white dog, breathing hard, had already closed her eyes.

"I'm ... alright," Felicity managed between ragged breaths. "Custard too. She ... she's a brave little girl. How is ... how is Columbo?"

"No change," Sue answered grimly. "He moans sometimes and I know he must be hurting. If only we could get him back to the Carriage House! Mariah knows about some healing plants in the courtyard. And Kristin could take him to the vet when she got home."

Felicity, gently licking Columbo's ears, didn't respond. Then she glanced around. "Where's Ruby? And Bill?"

Sue shook her head in disgust. "They ran off together. Ruby didn't even care that Columbo got hurt. And neither of them bothered to say goodbye."

Felicity's eyebrows shot up and her small face registered shock. She looked at me. She could guess, of course, how upset and humiliated I was.

Sue changed the subject, thankfully. "Tell us what happened in the house, Felicity. How were you able to escape with Custard?"

"It was easy to get inside," Felicity said. "The backdoor, luckily, was unlocked, and it opened when I pushed on it. I sneaked through the house until I saw a door that was open a crack. I figured that was to the bedroom, so I peeked in.

"Master and Mistress were asleep, with Custard curled up at their feet. Master was snoring -- an ugly racket, but it covered up the squeaks when I pushed the door open wider.

"I crept over to Custard and put my paw on her mouth so she wouldn't bark. Her eyes flew open. She was so surprised to see me! I nodded toward the door and she understood. She jumped off the bed without a sound and ran out of the room.

"Just then, Mistress woke up. Maybe she sensed something in the room. She yelled, 'Who's there?'

"That woke up Master. Right away he pulled his gun out from under his pillow and started shooting. Maybe he was still half asleep, but it was a miracle that he missed at such close range!"

Sue and I gasped.

Felicity went on. "He leaped out of bed and ran after me. I called to Custard to keep running as fast as she could and I'd be right behind her.

"Master was bumping into things in the dark, firing his gun, yelling and swearing, slamming doors behind him. I guess he thought there was a robber in the house. He yelled at Mistress to get the other gun and back him up, but she just kept on screaming. Custard and I flew outside and got away."

I shuddered. How close they came to being killed!

I asked Felicity if Master and Mistress would call the police when they discovered all those dogs missing.

"I'm pretty sure they won't," she answered. "They aren't supposed to have so many dogs, or keep them in such bad conditions. If the police came, I believe Puppy Haven would be shut down."

Her voice got sad as she continued. "They'll carry on, even though they lost a lot of valuable dogs tonight. I guess I'll have to come back here again for justice to happen." She put her head down on her paws and closed her eyes.

Oh my god. She already risked her life to free a lot of dogs. Would she really do it again? Unbelievable.

Words from another time and place came into my brain: *I want to cast aside the weight of facts and float above this difficult world.*

Yeah, that's what I wanted. To float above a world that seemed way too harsh.

***

Tasha, Hansel and Gretel didn't wake up even when those shots rang out. I stared at them. Tasha was gorgeous, and those two balls of brown, black and white fur were the cutest pups I'd ever seen.

But isn't it too hot in L.A. for mountain dogs? What were Master and Mistress thinking? They'd probably get a lot of money for them, though, so I guess that's what it was all about.

Felicity opened her eyes and saw me looking at the Bernese. "The puppies are just weaned," she said. "Master was going to deliver them to a pet store tomorrow. Tasha said she was willing to take her chances on the street rather than have that happen. She's hoping her family will be able to stay together."

Sue got up and stretched, then turned to the little border terrier. "Felicity, what is the plan for Tasha and her pups?"

"Puppins and I, and Custard, will try to help them find a home," she answered.

Custard, who was now awake, had other ideas.

"I'd rather stay and help Sue with Columbo," she piped up. "We can take turns going to find food. That way, she won't have to leave him alone."

Sue licked Custard's little black nose. "Oh honey, thank you. Help with Columbo, and having some company, would be wonderful."

***

We rested until morning. It would be hard to leave the others behind, but Sue assured us they'd try to get Columbo back to the Carriage House as soon as he could walk.

Suddenly, a blast of screeches filled the air. The wild parakeets!

Settling down like a bright green cloud in a nearby tree, they woke up Tasha and her pups, setting off a storm of barks and yips.

The racket got through to Columbo, who groaned, cracked open his eyes and tried to say something. When Sue finally got the mountain dogs and parakeets quieted, Pepito flew to the ground to see what was going on.

Spotting me, he squawked, "Puppeens! Dichosos los ojos!" New words; I didn't know what they meant or how to answer.

Then he saw Columbo. "Caramba! Que paso? Esta mal herido? Ees someteeng we can do?"

Felicity stared at him. "Could you ... could you fly to Mariah's? Bring back healing plants?"

He didn't understand. She tried again. Finally, he seemed to get it.

"Si! No problemo!" he screeched. "Vamonos! Adios, amigos!" The flock took off, disappearing down the foothills with a flash of sunlit feathers.

"Those squawkers will never come back," Sue grumbled.

Felicity shook her head. "We'll see. I hope they understood."

It was time for Felicity, me and the Bernese family to go. We said goodbye to Sue and Custard. Columbo was still out of it.

Each of us, including Hansel and Gretel, gave his long dark ears a hopeful lick before we left.

***

Tasha and the puppies led the way. She had her paws full with those two; they bounced and scrambled and ran in circles, playing tag and bumping into us. When Tasha scolded them they quieted down for a while, then went at it again.

But it wasn't long before they began to lag. "Mommy, where's our new home?" Hansel whined. "You promised."

"Are we there yet? Where's our dinner? We're hungry!" Gretel cried.

We stopped to rest, then trotted on. And as the day grew hot, we had to stop more and more often.

I noticed Hansel was limping and asked Tasha about it.

"I think he's just tired," she said slowly. "I hope he's not going to have hip problems. The breeding at Puppy Haven is not very responsible, you know."

Felicity nodded. She knew about that only too well.

Then the pups began fussing big time.

"Poor things, they're not used to this hot sun," Felicity observed.

"I'm not either," Tasha said. "I think mountain dogs are meant to live where it's cool. Once I heard Mistress and Master talk about going to a place they called Big Bear Mountain. They said it would be cold and they would see snow. It sounded so nice. I wonder what snow is like?"

Felicity and I had no clue; we were L.A. dogs.

***

We plodded on, finally coming to a park with a drinking fountain. Luckily it had a trough at the bottom that held enough water for us all to get a drink.

Hansel and Gretel crumpled down in a shady spot and Tasha groomed them as they slept, licking the dust of the road off their fur. Then she passed out too.

Felicity closed her eyes. So did I, but I couldn't sleep, worried about Columbo. And about the Bernese. How were we going to find a home for them? I wished the pups could stay with their mother, but I knew that doesn't happen much in the world of dogs.

Felicity must have had the same worries. Raising her head, she asked, "Puppins, do you remember those lovely neighborhoods we passed through on our way to Puppy Haven? Maybe in one of those, we'll be able to find someone to adopt Tasha and her puppies."

"Maybe," I replied, but it seemed doubtful. Then I had another idea. "What if they came back home with us? They could stay in the Carriage House until Kristin found a family for them."

Felicity shook her head. "The puppies would never make it in time. We need to be back before Kristin returns, remember?"

Sigh. How could I forget?

Felicity closed her eyes again, and I tried once more to get some sleep. But it seemed the universe conspired against me. Flies swarmed around my nose, and my stomach, long unsatisfied, growled in earnest. Even in the shade, the heat pressed down on me like that thing Kristin uses to smooth out her dresses. I guess if I had any wrinkles on me, they were gone.

To make matters worse, my brain would not stop its incessant chatter. Soon the most painful thought of all made its way to the top: Ruby and Bill, together.

Was I destined to always be the underdog (pardon the pun) in this triangle?

Some words bubbled up in that stew in my brain: *one plus one equals everything, and two minus one equals nothing.*

Math is not my thing, but my grasp of numbers was good enough to know that Ruby plus Bill equaled everything, while me minus Ruby equaled nothing.

Wait. Seriously? What's with that?? Ruby was history. Time to move on, right?

Yeah, right. Sigh.

Anyway, I figured I had a right to be angry with her for the way she ran off, showing no concern for Columbo and not thanking Felicity for the rescue.

Actually, I didn't recall ever seeing Ruby show gratitude to anyone, for anything.

Some new words flashed across my brain: *I have always depended on the kindness of strangers.*

The kindness of strangers got Ruby and me some pretty good meals, but she never even wagged her tail to say thanks.

What dog doesn't wag its tail in gratitude for food? I had to face the truth: Ruby was an ungrateful bitch. (Sorry. I guess that's a rude word in the world of people.)

And what about Bill? I couldn't let go of how he took off without even saying goodbye to us. After all, hadn't we liberated him from the dogfights, and welcomed him as a friend?

I suppose he was so anxious to be alone with Ruby that everything else just flew out of his head.

But wait. Let's get real. Look at the way I ran out on Kristin and Dora and Jodi and Oliver to chase after Ruby. Who was I to complain about Bill?

39

Time to get started again. Tasha had to rouse Hansel and Gretel, who right away began begging for something to eat.

To distract them, Tasha said she'd teach them a song. The pups perked up. "What kind of song, Mommy?" Gretel asked.

"A marching song," their mama said. "I'll make it up as we march along."

It was a good song, going something like this:

"Up, up, up, over the mouuuun-tain,
Marching along, singing our song,
Up, up, up over the mouuuun-tain,
We are Bernese mountain dogs!
Sing, sing, sing, join in the chorrrr-us,
As on we go, through ice and snow,
Sing, sing, sing, join in the chorrrr-us,
We are Bernese mountain dogs!"

I did join in the chorus, howling off key as usual, while Felicity yipped to the beat. Hansel and Gretel, puppyish again, bobbed along like those paper boats I saw once in a rain-filled gutter.

Suddenly, two big boys with mean faces raced up, throwing sticks and yelling swear words. Yikes!

Before I could react, Tasha, baring her teeth, growled ferociously at them.

They disappeared as fast as they'd come. I guess

even the most gentle mom gets fierce when her babies are threatened.

We slowed our pace when Hansel started to limp again. Tasha fretted over him. Finally, he lay down in the middle of the sidewalk and refused to budge.

"Mommy, I'm tired. And hungry," he whimpered.

"Me too!" echoed Gretel, falling down beside him.

Felicity called a halt. "Let's rest for a while," she said, "then concentrate on finding something to eat."

She led us to some nearby bushes where the pups, snuggling up to their mom, fell instantly asleep.

***

When Hansel and Gretel woke up, we trotted slowly on. We were all famished. We'd found some scraps in a tipped over garbage can, but far from enough for all of us.

Suddenly, I smelled something. Something really good. I lifted my nose in the air.

Meat on a grill!

The others followed as I traced the scent to a small yellow house with a fenced-in yard. A girl and boy played on a swing set; nearby, a smoking barbecue stood next to a table loaded with messy plates and leftover food.

I sent a look to Felicity. She nodded. Trailed by the Bernese, we trotted up to the gate and barked politely.

"Hey! Look at all those dogs! Where'd they come from?" cried the boy.

"I think they look friendly," the girl said. "Let's see." She ran to the gate, opened it and let us inside. The kids held out their hands for us to sniff, like people are supposed to do, then patted us.

"Are you hungry?" asked the boy. "Come on. You can have some leftovers." They led us to the table and filled plates with bits of burgers, buns, beans, and potato salad. We gobbled it all down, wagging our tails to show appreciation.

Just then, a woman came out of the yellow house. She saw us.

"Oh, my!" she cried. "Children, you should not let stray dogs come in the yard, or feed them!"

"But Mom, they were hungry. And they aren't fierce at all," said the boy.

His mother frowned and shook her head. Then she stared at Tasha and the pups.

"Are those Bernese mountain dogs? How strange!" she exclaimed.

She took a closer look. "Hmmm. No collars. What are such expensive dogs doing on the street?"

I didn't take it personally. Unlike me, the Bernese were much too nice-looking to be strays.

But suddenly I got afraid. What if the lady called Animal Control? Maybe we'd better get out of there.

Felicity must have thought the same thing. She gave me and Tasha a signal.

But before we could turn and run, the girl reached out and captured Gretel, and then her brother scooped up Hansel.

Tasha, racing back and forth between them, barked and barked, wild with anxiety.

"It's all right. We won't hurt your puppies," soothed the girl. Tasha kept on barking, and then Felicity and I joined in. We wanted those puppies back!

The mother, meanwhile, continued to stare at the mountain dogs.

"Wherever did you come from?" she asked, petting Hansel.

"Can we keep them?" begged the boy. "We could surprise Dad when he gets home from work."

"I don't think Dad would appreciate that kind of surprise," the mom said, smiling. "Anyway, they must belong to someone. Bernese are not that common."

She took Gretel in her arms and stroked her gently. "My, how soft you are!" she exclaimed.

"They're strays," said the girl confidently. "If they belonged to someone, they'd be wearing collars."

"Bernese mountain dogs would not be strays. Maybe they got lost."

"Mom, look at them. They need a place to stay," the boy pleaded. "The puppies are so cool. Can we at least keep them, and let the mother and the others go? Please?"

"If they really are mountain dogs," the girl put in, "we could take them with us when we go up to Big Bear next week."

Tasha stopped barking. She and Felicity and I stared at each other. Big Bear? That was the mountain Tasha had talked about!

The mother shook her head. "We could not keep the puppies without keeping the mother. But first, we'd have to make sure they don't belong to anyone.

"And," she continued, "I don't know what your father would say about three dogs in the house. These pups are going to get big, like their mama."

She examined Gretel. "This little one's paws are all cut up, as if she's been running a marathon. And the mother looks worn out. They should not be out walking in this heat."

She held out her hand for Tasha to sniff, then petted her. Felicity and I backed up toward the gate, waiting to see what was going to happen.

"Where did you come from?" the mother asked Tasha again. "Do you need a home?"

Tasha wagged her tail, then licked Hansel and Gretel protectively.

Time for Felicity and me to go. We yipped a quick

goodbye to the mountain dogs, then turned and sped out of the yard.

"Bye-bye!" the kids called.

We ran to the corner and stopped. We wanted to make sure Tasha and Hansel and Gretel really were going to stay behind.

They didn't come. They had found a home. Not in a fancy neighborhood like we planned, but it was a caring place and that's what matters.

It seemed like Tasha and her little ones would be able to stay together, too -- at least I hoped so. Maybe they'd even get to visit Big Bear Mountain.

***

We headed straight for the Carriage House, making much better time, of course, without the mountain dogs. But I missed them, especially those puppies!

When we staggered through the pet door, Mariah and the rest of the Tribe jumped up and welcomed us back, so relieved that we were safe.

Needless to say, I was exceedingly happy to get back before Kristin did.

"Do you think Miss Wisteria knew I was gone?" I asked Mariah.

"No. A black Lab named Joey happened to be here, and she thought it was you. You were lucky this time, Puppins, but I hope you won't try anything like that again."

I had no such plans. Once was enough.

***

That evening we told our story to the Tribe. It was a tale of success and failure, ups and downs, good and bad.

Hearing about Columbo's injury caused great distress. We all feared that he might die. Felicity suggested asking Mr. Pegasus to check on him, and Mariah agreed to do so.

Pepito, it turned out, had appeared with his flock and tried to make their mission clear.

When Mariah finally figured out what they wanted, although not what they wanted it for, she broke off some aloe leaves for them. The little green parakeets flew off, holding fat juicy leaves in their beaks.

Maybe they really would be able to help Columbo!

***

It was getting late. I was exhausted. While the others crowded around Felicity and asked a lot of questions about what happened at the puppy mill, I went outside.

Stretching out under the oak tree, I thought I'd sleep for a while.

Suddenly, THUD! Something warm and furry landed on my head.

"Get off me, you little creep!" I yelled.

Oliver laughed and tumbled to the ground. "What's the big idea of running off and leaving me behind again?" he cried, shaking a grey paw at me in mock anger. "I could've helped. Like I did at the dogfight place."

"Yeah, right, Super Cat. No way could you have helped. Go away. I'm trying to sleep."

He gave me a fake hiss and slunk off, like the little criminal he is.

But sleep didn't come. Too much stuff swirling around in my head. I guess Jodi would be surprised at how much goes on in there.

I think I've mentioned how sometimes she stares into my eyes and says, "Puppins, there's nothing in that big head of yours, is there. You have no brain!"

Harsh. But I know she loves me, because she pets me a lot, rubs my belly and slips me those red licorice ropes. That's got to be love.

Then, in the midst of this muddled meditation,

Felicity appeared.

"Alright to join you?" she asked.

"Sure."

We were quiet for a while. Then she asked, "What did you think about Ruby and Bill leaving the way they did?"

Aargh. Did she have to bring that up?

"It made me angry," I muttered. "It was so rude."

She nodded. "How do you feel about Ruby now?" she asked.

Why is Felicity always so direct? It's unnatural. I didn't answer. I knew her bright eyes could probably see right through me anyway, and it was embarrassing.

She sighed. "Well, she is very beautiful. And she has many good qualities."

I tried to think about Ruby's good qualities. She was strong, smart, sometimes playful. Independent, fearless, fit. All good. But something definitely was missing.

"I don't know. Sometimes it seems like being attracted to someone doesn't make much sense," I mumbled.

"I know," she agreed. "It's hard to figure out why that happens."

"Yeah. Why can't you look at someone and see fabulous roman candles go off, without getting all crazy and stupid over them?"

She laughed. "I'm not an expert, but I think it's possible to be friends with someone and have respect for them, and still see those fireworks. But when you are caught up in a dream, it can be hard to see what's real."

I thought about that. Maybe that's all it was with Ruby. A dream. But if so, why couldn't I wake up?

Some words dog-paddled (excuse the pun) around in my brain: *It does not do to dwell on dreams and forget to live.* Sigh. So true.

40

Kristin came home, none the wiser. I felt guilty(ish) about my disobedience. But in my mind, going to help Felicity was a noble thing to do, and probably made up for breaking one of Kristin's rules.

A few days later, as I dozed in the Carriage House with the Tribe, the pet door flew open.

In bounded a huge black Rottweiler. The menacing monster who, with those hoodlums from the dogfights, caused Loofah's homeless owner to have a heart attack.

The fearsome dog we'd left behind when we raided the fight ring.

"Tolliver Yar!" Loofah screamed. She ran and hid behind Mariah, as Tolliver's awful eyes scanned the room, stopping on Oliver, then on me.

I quaked. He recognized us, for sure. If my knees hadn't turned to mashed potatoes, I would've run to hide behind Mariah too.

The cats, including Oliver and Jade, bristled and hissed at Tolliver. Easy for them to be brave; high up on their shelves, they were well out of reach.

At that moment, Pasadena Fats popped out of his hole like an oversized cork shooting out of a bottle.

Scampering around the room on his nightly quest for spilled kibble, Fats came face-to-face with Tolliver.

He slammed on the brakes. "Flaccid! Get me out of here!" he cried, streaking back to his hole.

Mariah stood up tall and looked the enormous dog straight in the eye.

"Who are you?" she demanded.

"Tolliver Yar, like that little dog said. Don't know where she knows me from ..."

He paused, then glared first at me, then at Oliver.

"I know these two, all right," he growled harshly. "They let most of the fight dogs out, but not me."

Fear shot around my brain like popcorn in Dora's old stovetop popper. Was he out to get revenge?

Mariah stared coldly at him. "Then how did you get away? And why are you here?"

"I'll tell you, but make those cats stop hissing at me. I'm not going to attack anyone."

Mariah signaled the cats to be quiet, then turned back to the Rottweiler.

"Well?"

Tolliver, sending daggers with his eyes to Oliver and me, told what happened after we released the other dogs.

"The cops came in and saw it was a dogfight place," he said, "and they called Animal Control."

He paused, giving me a burning look. "Why didn't you let me out of my cage?" he demanded.

I seemed to have lost my voice. But Loofah had not.

"Because you killed Odette!" she burst out.

He stared at her. "What are you talking about?"

Made brave by anger, Loofah flashed her teeth at him. "Odette! You and those two awful men in Donut Alley! You scared her to death!"

Tolliver squinted his eyes at her like he was trying to remember. "Donut Alley? Wait. The old lady? I didn't know she kicked off."

Loofah wailed. "She's the only person who ever cared about me, and it's your fault she's dead!"

Mariah broke in. "Go on with your story," she said

curtly to Tolliver.

"Well, Animal Control showed up. They opened my cage to get me, but I bolted and ran past them and through the door. The cops tried to catch me and they pulled out their guns, but I jumped over the fence and got away."

He stopped for a moment, then continued. "I never stopped running all night and the next day. I got to where there's a bridge over a big cement ditch."

I was well acquainted with that place: the Los Angeles River, which is only a river when it rains. And the Old Bridge, where I almost died.

Tolliver went on. "I stopped there to hide out. Nobody was around, no people, no animals. When it got dark, I was scared. I never been alone like that before."

Ha. Tolliver Yar scared? No way. Loofah and I snorted.

Ignoring us, he continued. "I tried to sleep, but I kept hearing strange sounds. I lay there all night, shaking and wondering how I was going to take care of myself. At the fight ring I was a star, and they fed me and took care of me."

Toby, an orange tabby, hissed loudly. "Disgusting. How could you kill another dog for no reason?"

"I had a reason," Tolliver answered. "Just one of us in the ring was going to get out alive, and I wanted it to be me."

Silence. He went on. "Everything at the fights was bad. I hated the jerks who came to watch. They jeered and whistled at us. They bet on us. They just wanted to see blood and death."

"What about Donut Alley?" Mariah asked. "Why did those dogfight men take you there?"

"Stites and Onions got paid to round up new dogs, and they used me to help," he replied.

"That's terrible!" Loofah cried. "And why did they go after poor homeless people like Odette?"

He shook his massive head. "They're bullies. Maybe they learned to be mean when they were small. Like me. My first owner trained me that way, then sold me to the ring for a lot of money."

"But why are you here?" Mariah demanded again.

"I'm getting there," he said. "At first, I thought I'd look for another fight ring. I heard there's lots of them in L.A. But then I started thinking. Did I really want to fight again? Maybe I could live on the streets and take care of myself. Be another kind of survivor, not a killer."

"You're lying!" Loofah jumped up, snarling. "You're trying to fool us!"

Mariah pulled the little dog down next to her, then told Tolliver tersely to go on.

"I tried to find garbage at night when no one would see me," he said. "Then one night I couldn't find anything. When I came back to the bridge, three dogs showed up. They had some food, and they shared it with me. I couldn't believe it -- dogs sharing their food!"

He shook his head, then continued. "I hung out with them for a while, and finally I told them I'd been in the fights but wanted to change. One of them told me about a greyhound that might help me. That's you, isn't it?" he asked Mariah. She nodded.

"What did the dog look like?" I asked. "The one that told you about Mariah."

"Small. Brown. Kind of ugly. Bad leg. Her name's Felicity."

Just as I thought.

"Who were the other dogs?" asked Mariah.

"A black and white dog named Winter, and Mr. Pegasus, an old greyhound. He showed me how to get here. He said he and Felicity were on the team that freed the other fighting dogs."

Loofah snarled at him in her tiny voice. "What about Odette? Don't say you're sorry, because I don't believe you. And even if you are, it doesn't bring her back!"

"I know it doesn't. But I am sorry. Can you forgive me?" He peered at her with pleading eyes.

"No! I'll never forgive you!" Loofah cried.

She ran to a corner and caved into a whimpering heap. I crept over and tried to comfort her.

Mariah turned to Tolliver.

"We'll think about what you've told us. And whether we can help you change your life, if you really want to," she said. "But we are not ready to welcome you to the Tribal Base."

That was an understatement.

Tolliver hung his head, turned around and left.

***

All of us were shook up over the encounter. While Loofah and I huddled together in the corner, Mariah started talking to the others about forgiving.

"It's hard to do," she said. "Sometimes it takes a long time. But it's the right thing to do. And if you can do it, you will feel better."

Loofah covered her ears with her little round paws. I knew she would not be forgiving Tolliver anytime soon.

Me neither.

41

Things settled down. Mr. Pegasus agreed to check on Columbo, and we waited nervously for his report.

Then Tolliver Yar turned up again, and Mariah said he could come in for a short visit. She told us that if we got to know him, we'd find out whether or not he was on the level about changing his ways.

Loofah was dead set against allowing him in the Carriage House. I was not thrilled about it myself, and I don't think any of the others were either. But we went along with it because we respect Mariah's judgment, even when we don't agree with her.

This day, no sooner had Tolliver come in than Kristin appeared in the doorway.

"How many for dinner?" she asked cheerfully. Then she spotted Tolliver. Startled, she stepped back toward the door.

"Oh my! Where did you come from?" she gasped.

Mariah trotted over and licked Tolliver's muzzle to show he was invited.

Kristin relaxed. "Well, okay! These big black dogs -- you just never know about them. Right, Puppins?" She winked at me as she headed out the door.

She returned with dinner, set the food on the floor and left. We crowded around the bowls, allowing Tolliver plenty of space. Loofah, balled up in her corner, didn't eat.

After dinner, Mariah told Tolliver to leave. Then she gathered us in a circle, with Loofah next to her.

Turning to the little dog, she said, "Loofah, you have good reason to fear and hate Tolliver. But he says he is sorry and wants to change. Do you think you could accept that?"

"No! I hate him!" Loofah cried. "I hate all Rottweilers. They are cruel!"

"Not all Rottweilers are cruel," Mariah replied. "But they are a strong and protective breed, and sometimes people train them to attack. That's what happened with Tolliver. And at the dogfights, he had to be vicious to survive."

Was Mariah saying that humans are to blame if a dog is mean? I guess I'm fine with that, now that I know there are bad people out there who deserve to be blamed.

Mariah went on. "Tolliver was taught to be brutal, but I believe he can be untaught. It would take a lot of time, patience and love, but I think it would be worth a try."

"I don't believe he's ever going to change," Loofah insisted. "Some dogs are just bad. Odette told me about that. She didn't trust Rottweilers. Or pit bulls or chows. Or Dobermans. And I don't either."

"But don't you think it's unfair to bunch all dogs of a kind together? It's like saying all small dogs are yappy and nippy. Do you believe that's true?"

"No. Well, some little dogs are, but not all. I'm not."

Oliver and a couple of other cats made snickering sounds. Mariah gave them a look, then continued.

"That's right, Loofah. Little dogs should be judged as individuals. And what about dogs like Puppins?"

"What about them?" Loofah asked suspiciously.

"Labradors are usually sweet-tempered. But I've

seen a lot of people be afraid of them, and other dogs too, just because they were big and black."

What Mariah said was true. Kristin made that joking remark about big black dogs because her mailman was afraid of me. And Ruby told me it's common knowledge on the streets that black dogs have a hard time getting adopted at shelters, so they are put to death more often than most other dogs.

Mariah asked us to think about whether Tolliver deserved a second chance. We looked at each other but said nothing. Loofah slunk back to her corner.

I think I've mentioned that Mariah learned a lot about different breeds from listening to the trainers talk at the racetrack. Now she told us what she'd picked up about Rottweilers. They used to be cattle dogs, but now they mostly work as police dogs or to help disabled people.

They also are really good at dog sports competitions, she said, and that got my attention. Maybe, if Kristin got us a deflated ball, Tolliver could play touch basketball with me!

Tolliver became a regular at the Tribal Base, spending his time with Mariah. He would tell her about his life at the dogfights and say, over and over, how sorry he was for what he'd done.

Mariah told him that instead of just beating himself up over his bad past, he should start thinking about what he could do to make up for it.

"There's no way I can take back killing all those dogs," he replied, "or scaring Loofah's owner to death."

"True. But you can do better in the future," she said.

"How? I don't have a clue about being good."

"Just do little things. Be kind to the dogs and cats here, and find ways to help anyone who needs it."

"I'll try," he said, shaking his big head doubtfully.

42

One evening when Kristin came to the Carriage House with our dinner, she went over to Loofah and picked her up.

"I think I've found a home for you, sweetie," she said, rubbing Loofah's ears.

Loofah stiffened as Kristin continued. "The family is coming tomorrow to meet you. I'm pretty sure you'll be happy with them." She filled our bowls and left.

None of us could eat. We gathered around Loofah and tried to cheer her up, but she could not be comforted.

"I don't want to leave here! This is my home!" she cried, her round eyes glistening with tears. "What if that family has children who pull my tail and ears, and ride me like a horse, and only do it when no grownups are around? I've heard all about that from dogs who ran away from home."

"I don't think Kristin would put you in a family with wild children," Mariah said.

"Well, then they'll probably have a cat, and it will hiss at me and claw my nose."

"Hey!" cried Oliver. "Why do you assume a cat would be mean to you?"

"Cats hate dogs. Everyone knows that," she declared.

"What about us Tribal cats?" Oliver replied. "We don't hate you, and we don't claw you. We put up with all you dogs, even though dogs are dense. And as you know, Puppins is my best buddy."

That was still true, despite his despicable habit of pranking me by dropping on my head.

He went on. "Mama doesn't hate dogs, even though she is afraid of them. Dogs are more likely to be mean to cats than the other way around."

Kudos, the ancient gentleman cat, harrumphed. "I've known plenty of mean cats in my day, and some mean dogs, too. I've also known cats and dogs that were the best of friends, like Puppins and Oliver."

"Si, Loofaaah," said Jade, Oliver's girlfriend, who talks half like Pepito and half like the rest of us. "Te queremos todos, Loofaaah. We all luff you. If el gatos in nuevo casa, why they not luff you too?"

"I'd be invading their territory," Loofah replied. "If cats or other dogs already live there, they won't want me getting a lot of attention because I'm so adorable. They won't want me playing with their toys, or sleeping in their special spot."

She had a point. Some of us knew what it was like to have a real home, and some didn't. But we all knew about the territorial instinct.

Even here in the shelter, where we have to be nice to each other, we stake out little islands for ourselves, a certain rug or a particular shelf. But we aren't supposed to put up a fuss if someone comes in and takes over our favorite place.

It's a rule, like the one against fighting. Mariah sets the rules because she is the Tribe's alpha. You have to follow them or you can't be there. I'm not fond of rules, of course, but apparently you have to have them when you don't live by yourself.

***

The rest of us finally ate our kibble, but Loofah just crawled back to her corner. I knew there would be little sleep for her that night.

Things had been harsh for her lately. First, Tolliver Yar shows up and gets welcomed, even forgiven, by Mariah. Then she's told she has to leave the Tribe to be adopted by an unknown family. That's a lot for an anxious little dog to handle.

***

I woke up early the next morning. I sleep in Kristin's bedroom, the same upstairs room where, on a clear morning long before Kristin bought this place, Mariah took us to the window to show us the mountains.

This day, I trotted over to that same window. The San Gabriels were hidden, as usual, behind a shadowy haze.

If they had been out and painted pink by the sunrise, it would have been a good omen -- *flaming symbols of hope,* to use the words that bombed my brain that other time.

No such symbols this day, and I had to face reality. What if I never saw Loofah again? She aggravated me a lot with her worries, complaints and neediness, but she was my friend, almost like a little sister. I would miss her for sure.

And what if there *was* an aggressive pet in her new family? Or a mean kid? What if they didn't brush her white powderpuff fur like Kristin did, or forgot to put flea repellant on her?

Still, I was pretty sure Kristin would check out the family really well. This was one of her first adoptions, and she would want it to be good.

***

Later that morning, in the Carriage House, we told Loofah that if her new home was a bad scene, she should get word to us -- maybe through the wild parakeets, or Pasadena Fats and his mouse underground network. We would rescue her. After all, we were experienced

213

liberators.

As the day dragged by, Loofah swung between fits of crying, threats to seek sanctuary at Felicity's camp, and fantasies of running away to join the circus.

"Mariah said bichons are good circus dogs," she reminded us. "I can spin really fast, and I'll learn to do some other tricks. Maybe I'll wear a sparkly dress and ride on a pony or an elephant, and I'll be famous." She did some twirls to show us her skills.

We urged her to approach her adoptive home with positive thoughts, but positive thoughts about being adopted were not likely.

***

Toward late afternoon, the new owners still hadn't come.

"Maybe they changed their minds. Maybe they don't want a dog after all," Loofah said, her bright eyes full of hope.

"Maybe they heard what a pain you are, and decided to get a cat instead," teased Oliver.

"That's not funny!" cried Loofah, as the rest of us tried not to laugh.

Then it happened. Kristin came to the Carriage House, brushed Loofah's soft white coat and put a pink collar around her neck. She looked beautiful. We fussed over her, then touched her nose with ours to say goodbye.

"Your family will be here very soon," Kristin told her, then turned to me. "Come along, Puppins. I think you'll recognize who is coming for this sweet little dog."

I jumped up and followed her. Someone I knew? Who could it be?

***

They came into the living room, a couple with a little girl.

Wow. It was Lin Lu! I recognized her at once, even though I hadn't seen her since that time she appeared in The Cottage garden so long ago.

On that day, she and Kristin talked about leprechauns and made wishes. Kristin wished for a bigger house, while Lin Lu had two wishes: for a puppy, and to be Kristin's friend for her whole life.

Now, bubbling over with excitement, she ran up to me and gave me a big hug.

"Puppins! Do you remember me? Why didn't you come to my birthday party?" No sooner had that spilled out than she ran to Kristin and Loofah.

"Is this my new dog? Oh, Kristin, she is precious! I'll take such good care of her!"

Taking Loofah in her arms, she turned to her parents. "May I keep her, Mae? May I, Paw Paw? Please?"

Her parents glanced at each other and smiled. The mother took Loofah from Lin Lu and spoke softly to her in her language, stroking her curly white fur. The father touched her shyly on her black button nose.

Whew. I breathed a sigh of relief. It was going to be a loving, forever home for my *almost* little sister.

Loofah tried to be standoffish, but she melted under the attentions of her new family. I just had time to give her a farewell lick before they carried her out the door.

Dashing to the window, I watched as they got in the car and drove off. My heart hurt.

Kristin came over and gave me a hug. "Isn't it wonderful, Puppins? Lin Lu's dad helped me with some repairs last week and I remembered her wish. This will be perfect for our little bichon!"

Maybe it was perfect for Loofah. And for Lin Lu. But what about me? Now there was another big hole in my heart, right next to the one left by Dora.

43

Days passed. Tolliver spent most of his time at the Tribal Base with Mariah. The rest of us avoided him like spoiled meat, or -- like me -- got used to him and tried to be polite.

Mariah was training him to be the Tribe's Street Scout. His job was to look for animals who needed food and shelter, then lead them to the Carriage House.

Every day he went out on the streets, trying to keep a step ahead of Animal Control in his search for strays.

Approaching them was tricky: dogs and cats ran away or cowered in fear when the big Rottweiler came near. He was trying to learn to go slow, and not use his outdoor voice.

Tolliver seemed thrilled to have a job to do. But for me, it was not a happy time. I missed Loofah. And seeing Oliver and Jade together made me feel even lonelier.

The way they played games and whispered and nuzzled each other was bittersweet, reminding me of my one-way crush on Ruby.

It seemed like a curse. No matter how hard I tried, I couldn't stop thinking about her. Why was she the way she was, and not the way I wanted her to be? Couldn't I change her mind about me, if I just had one more chance?

Anyway, how could she prefer that ugly boxer over me, just because he's macho and bursts with boxer energy? My nose might be a little too large by show standards, but basically I think I'm a pretty good-looking guy.

After obsessing like that for a while, I'd yell at myself: Get over it! She doesn't want you hanging around, trying to latch onto her like a ravenous tick.

This mess of thoughts simmered in my brain for hours, like the beef stew Dora used to make. Sometimes I could push it to the back burner and think about something else, but before long that same old pot would boil up again.

***

One day, Mariah saw me moping under the camellias after I'd turned down Oliver and Jade's invitation to play chase. She came over and settled down next to me.

"You seem sad, Puppins. What's wrong?" she asked.

Yikes. Was it that obvious?

I didn't want to admit the major reason I was feeling down, so I told her the secondary one: "I miss Loofah."

"I miss her too," Mariah said. "She's so lovable. And she was special for you."

"Yeah. Even though sometimes she ... Anyway, I kind of wish she hadn't been adopted."

"Sometimes I wish that too. But Loofah is not suited to be a shelter dog. Or a street dog, even though she lived on the streets with Odette for most of her life."

"I know," I said. "It must have been really hard for both of them, especially when it rained. Why do those homeless people choose to be on the streets?"

"Most don't really choose it, Puppins. It's a very difficult life, especially for old women like Odette. I think most homeless humans, like most street animals, aren't there because they want to be."

"But ... but some really seem to prefer it."

She gave me a look with her piercing eyes. "You're talking about Ruby, aren't you?"

I didn't answer.

Mariah went on. "I know you probably still think about her a lot. Maybe it's hard for you to give up hope that she'll change, and that it might still work out for you."

"There's always hope, isn't there? Isn't that what you say, Mariah?" I countered.

She smiled. "Yes, that's what I say. But sometimes you have to take a closer look at what you hope for."

"What do you mean?"

"It's fine to hope that Ruby will change. But it's not a good idea to plan your life around it, because it might not happen. And if it doesn't, then you have to decide if you can accept her the way she is."

I thought about that.

"I don't know," I said finally. "We don't seem to want the same things. But I guess that if she's not going to change, I could change myself to be what she wants."

"Didn't you already try that?"

Ouch. I sighed. "Yeah. It didn't work out so well."

I searched my sorry brain, trying to come up with an explanation for all of this.

"Kristin says I'm a teenager in human years, so maybe that's why I'm so screwed up," I offered.

She smiled. "I think obsessions can happen to anyone. I've had them myself, but that's a story for another day."

"Well, Oliver says I just have an epic crush on Ruby but it will go away. But how do you erase something from your brain, once it's been tattooed there?"

She laughed. "Tattoos are permanent. Attractions, not so much. It may take a while, but you can do it, if you really want to."

"But how?"

"You probably already know," she replied. "What do you think would help?"

I wished she would just tell me, so I wouldn't have to poke around that pile of poop in my head, hunting for a good answer.

"Well," I said finally, "I could try thinking about something else, or is that too simple?"

"It's a good idea, but not so simple. Maybe it would help to have something ready to plug in when you find yourself thinking about her. Think about someone else. A friend. Someone you admire."

I had quite a few friends now, with the shelter dogs and cats. But ... someone I especially admired?

Well, there was Felicity, and she was a friend for sure, and I admired her. But she was nowhere near as cool or exciting or gorgeous as Ruby.

"Uh, yeah," I muttered. "Okay. Cool. Well, what's another thing I can do?"

"Get involved in something. You can't go out on the street like Tolliver, but maybe you could help with the animals who come to the shelter."

"Nah. I don't have any talent for anything like that. Or any training."

"You could be a Listener," she responded. "It doesn't take much training, just patience."

"Listener? What the heck is that?"

"Well, most street animals have no friends, no one they can trust. Just listening to them talk about their fears and worries does them a lot of good. That's what you did with Loofah, you know."

"Loofah? Worrying was just her thing. She talked about it all the time to whoever was around. I don't think I helped her at all."

"You helped her more than you know. And you could do the same for others."

"I don't know," I said doubtfully. "I'll think about it. But isn't there anything *else* I can do to get Ruby out of my mind?"

"It sounds strange," Mariah replied, "but it might help to think about her on purpose. Think about what attracts you to her. Is it her free spirit? How beautiful she is?"

Guilty as charged, on both counts.

Mariah went on. "Try to think about whether those things are enough to make a good relationship."

"I guess I don't know what it takes for that," I admitted.

"Well, to me it takes really trusting and respecting each other. Supporting each other. Being able to talk about things and share your feelings."

Wow. I didn't have any of that with Ruby. It was all pretty one-sided.

Mariah continued: "You've been obsessed with her for quite a while. But obsessions do die out, you know."

"Do they?"

"Yes," she replied. "I've noticed that eventually they burn themselves out, like those roman candles you've talked about."

Had I told Mariah about the roman candles? Embarrassing.

Anyway, their dying out did not seem likely. I probably was doomed to be scorched by Ruby forever.

44

After thinking it over, I agreed to become a Listener, which means I'm supposed to sit quietly and listen to animals that have some kind of problem and want to talk about it.

Being a Listener was the first step in helping street dogs and cats, Mariah said. (She took care of the second step: working with them to figure out solutions.)

According to her, really listening to someone is like a school for the heart. When she said that, some words flashed through my brain: *It is only with the heart that one can see rightly.* So I guess making my heart go to school would be good for it.

To be a Listener, I'm not supposed to yawn or doze off. That's hard, because some of these dudes and dudettes, especially the cats, drone on and on, saying the same thing over and over. I don't want to be rude, so I pretend that I'm interested.

Mariah says that after a while, it will become easier to focus on what they are really trying to tell me, and I won't have to fake it.

There's another hard thing about the job: You have to know when to be a Listener and when to be a Storyteller.

In other words, I'm not supposed to interrupt with some tale of my own, even when my experience is way more awesome than theirs.

For example: If a mutt starts talking about some

lame event that he thought was scary, I could top it by telling about the time I almost fell to my death on the Old Bridge. (I'd leave out the part about being rescued by a girl, of course.)

Also, Listeners are not supposed to give advice. It's tempting, but Mariah says it's a no-no.

It is okay, however, to say something helpful, like I did recently during a session with Duncan.

Duncan is one of Pasadena Fats' horde of tiny rodent cousins. He told me he was afraid to go to the park with Fats because he thought he'd be eaten by an owl.

To help him get over his fear, I informed him that owls are extinct in Los Angeles. He was so relieved that he ran right out to play in the park. I hope I was right about that.

***

One evening, after listening to a calico cat yowl endlessly about her two-timing Maine Coon boyfriend, I went out to the courtyard regain my sanity.

Usually it cools off in L.A. when the sun goes down. But that night, we had those winds that Kristin calls the Santa Anas.

Those hot, dry winds that blow in from the desert always make me feel crappy. I couldn't sleep. It was as hot as the kitchen got that time Kristin forgot to turn off the oven. I wished the sprinklers would come on, but we were in a drought and had to save water.

Felicity appeared. "Puppins, I have something to tell you," she said.

Uh oh. Maybe it was the Santa Anas, but I had an ominous feeling that it was bad news.

"What is it?" I asked.

"I'm going back to Puppy Haven," she stated firmly. "I wanted you to know."

Talk about bad news.

"Seriously? Why? You already freed a lot of those dogs. What's the point of going back?"

"I need to finish what I started. I want to shut that place down, once and for all."

Oh my god. The memory of her and Custard being shot at was still fresh in my mind. She was my friend, and I did not want her going back to that awful place.

She continued. "This time, I'm going alone. After what happened to Columbo, I can't take the chance of anyone else getting hurt."

Wow. I couldn't go, of course, but why not take one of the other dogs? Maybe Zeke, the tough German shepherd?

"Felicity, you almost got killed last time. Please don't go. Or at least ..."

"Don't try to talk me out of it, Puppins," she interrupted. "My mind is made up. This is my mission. I'm going, and I'm going by myself."

She got up and trotted back inside without another word, her limp reminding me of why she hated the puppy mill so much.

After that, she would not talk to me about her plan or say when she was going. I doubted if Mariah was in favor of it, but I didn't think that she, or anyone else, could talk Felicity out of it.

***

Jodi came over one evening. She slipped me a red licorice rope and let me sit on the sofa beside her. Kristin rolled her eyes.

They talked about guys for a while. Jodi wanted to fix her up with someone, and Kristin went into her usual rant about L.A. men and how unreliable they are.

Boring. Almost as bad as that calico cat. I'd heard Kristin complain too many times about her failed relationships. I dozed off.

When consciousness returned, Jodi was saying, "One of my coworkers is letting me use her time-share in Palm Springs this weekend. Why don't you come too? Maybe we could meet some 'reliable' males out there."

Kristin gave a snarky kind of laugh. "Ha! As if. Thanks, but Ken's given me an assignment that has to be in by Monday, and he'll go ballistic if I'm late. I endured one of his firestorms last week, and that's my quota for the month."

"Well, can't you just take your laptop and work by the pool in Palm Springs?"

"Don't tempt me. I could, but I've got a lot of other things to do. Not a good weekend for me, Jodi."

Darn. For a minute, I thought maybe she would go with Jodi, and – if the timing was right -- I could sneak out again. I still didn't know when Felicity was leaving, but I figured it would be soon.

**

Sure enough, in the Carriage House after dinner, Felicity announced that she was headed out that very evening. Zeke and two other burly dogs offered to go with her, but she turned them down.

A lot of us told her it was a bad idea. She just shook her little brown head and said she had to do it, but promised it would be her last attempt to free all the dogs.

"It's now or never," she said. "If I fail, that will be it."

We wished her good luck. She trotted out of the Carriage House without looking back.

I put my head down and closed my eyes, pretending to be asleep. I did not want to talk to anyone. My stomach was in a knot as hard as the tennis ball Kristin throws for me to fetch.

What if Felicity got hurt? Shouldn't I be there if she needed a backup? The whole thing sucked.

**

Kristin came and took me into La Casa Royale. I went to my corner of the kitchen while she multitasked, washing dishes and talking to Jodi on her cell.

She had the speakerphone on, like always, but I was not that interested. I had Puppy Haven on my mind.

Then my ears perked up.

"I'm thinking I might go with you after all," Kristin was saying. "I could call Ken and tell him I'm working at home. He'd give me a hard time, but what else is new?"

"Well, call me in the morning if you decide to go," Jodi replied. "Got to get an early start. I want to hit the pool before lunch."

"Alright, but don't count on it." Kristin said goodbye and hung up.

Wow -- maybe she'd really go away!

I trotted over and shot off a volley of loud barks right in her face. Maybe if I was obnoxious enough, she'd decide that leaving me for the weekend was a good option.

She just smiled, shook her finger at me and led me upstairs to bed.

***

In the morning, she got up early and put me outside. When I came back in, she was making breakfast for herself and Miss W.

Then I saw the small suitcase waiting by the front door. It was a go!

I quickly devised a strategy. After Kristin left, I'd speed up to Puppy Haven, make sure Felicity was alright, then hurry right back.

Miss Wisteria didn't miss me last time, and with her weak eyes and befuddled old brain, she wouldn't notice me gone this time either.

It was a good plan. Perfect. Maybe even genius.

45

Jodi arrived. Kristin took me to the Carriage House and told all of us to mind Miss W and be good while she was gone.

I tuned her out. Who was she to lecture me? Wasn't she abandoning me again?

I agonized over whether to tell Mariah about my plan. For sure, she would not like it. But if I didn't, she would notice me gone and go looking for me. I decided I had to clue her in.

"Puppins, that is not a good idea," she responded predictably. "I know you are worried about Felicity, but she is very capable on her own. And you would betray Kristin's trust once again."

Ouch. I didn't answer. I knew she was right, but I had to go. Felicity was such a good friend. And didn't she come to my rescue on the Old Bridge? I'd never forgive myself if she needed help and I wasn't there.

Anyway, I was a teenager, right? Something about breaking rules just seemed to attract me.

I said goodbye to Mariah, who shook her brindle head.

Trotting out through the doggy door, I lifted the gate latch with my nose and headed down the alley.

Despite my nervous excitement, I had eaten all of my breakfast so I'd have plenty of energy. Once on the street,

I broke into a run toward the foothills, aiming to arrive at Puppy Haven before the worst heat of the day.

I figured Felicity would take a lot of time to check things out and make her final plans, and then wait until dark to go in. She'd be so surprised to see me!

***

I trotted briskly on. The puppy mill started to seem much farther than I remembered, and when the sun got hot, I had to look for shade and rest for a while.

I hadn't been out on the streets by myself since Ruby dumped me. I'd forgotten how tough and lonely it was.

I trotted on. It got dark. There were only a few streetlights. I thought I knew the way, but everything seemed strange.

A fork in the road loomed up. Left, or right? Sniffing around, I tried to find Felicity's scent with my less-than-perfect nose. Nothing but skunk, squirrel, and USD (unidentified stray dog).

Collapsing under a spindly tree, I tried not to panic. Should I give up and go home? Did I even know the way back?

In the midst of this anxiety attack, SPLAT! A soft furry blob landed square on my head.

Oliver? What was he doing here!

"Hi, Puppins! I followed ya!" he crowed. "How come you're always running off? Chasing a girl again?"

"None of your business, stalker!" I replied angrily. "What are *you* doing here? And get off my head, you little pest!" I gave myself a violent shake that sent him flying.

"I heard you talking to Mariah about Felicity," he smirked, picking himself up. "Thought I was asleep, didn't ya! Ha! I guess you forgot your promise to take me along on your next adventure, lover boy."

"Did not! And this isn't an adventure, cat face. I'm

just making sure Felicity's alright. Now go back home."

"Well, I think you're lost. Admit it, big shot rescuer. And FYI, I know the way. I followed Felicity last night. So, you need me, right? Ha!"

Grrr. If he really did know the way, I actually *did* need him. "Okay, okay, blackmailer. Which way?"

He strutted to the left, chanting "Dogs drool, cats rule!"

Maddening. Led by a cat.

Anyway, I was glad he set a fast pace. At that rate, we should arrive at the mill in no time.

***

Sure enough, it wasn't long before we reached the creepy-looking house and sinister kennel building. Oliver surveyed the scene.

"Where do you think Felicity will be?" he asked.

"In those shrubs over there," I told him, pointing with my paw. "That's where we left Columbo and Sue and Custard. I wonder if they're still there?"

I signaled Oliver to stay where he was. I wanted to surprise Felicity. Trotting quickly, I headed to the shrubs. Deserted.

Oliver joined me. Thankfully, he did not clown around. "I guess Felicity is already inside," he said.

I nodded. We hunkered down, straining to hear any sound that might come from the mill, but all was silent.

The night air settled over us. Then, suddenly, the soft thud of paws running toward us reached our ears.

Felicity!

She saw us. "Puppins! Oliver! What are you doing here?" she cried.

I started to explain about Kristin leaving, but she broke in angrily: "Puppins, I can't believe you would do such a thing. What were you thinking?"

"I was worried about you. I just wanted to check ..."

She turned away and ran off without waiting for me to finish.

"Wow," Oliver ventured. "I've never seen Felicity get mad at any of us."

"Me neither," I choked. "Maybe ... maybe I shouldn't have come."

"No kidding, dork. Aren't you ever going to stop chasing females?"

I was too upset over Felicity's reaction to deal with him. I watched her as she paced back and forth a distance away, whispering fiercely to herself.

I couldn't hear what she was saying, but I doubt if it was anything complimentary about me.

"I guess we should go back home," I told Oliver with a sigh. "But first I want to tell Felicity I'm sorry I ran out on Kristin."

I crept meekly to where she was pacing. "Felicity, I guess I made a ... a bad choice ..." I began.

She turned around. She had tears in her eyes.

"Oh, Puppins, I shouldn't have yelled at you. You were wrong to sneak away from home, but I am glad to see you."

Whew! I let out my breath, which I didn't know I'd been holding.

She continued. "I don't know what to do, Puppins. My mission is ... it's hopeless."

"Why? What happened? Weren't you able to get in?"

"I got in, but it was hard. I thought it would be easier this time, because Master and Mistress aren't home. But they've put in outside lights that shine at the slightest movement. Of course my tunnels are all filled in and the electric fence turned on, and I had to be very careful while I dug a new outside tunnel ..."

She stopped, took a breath and went on. "I finally managed to get inside. I shut off the electric. But ..." she put her head down on her paws and sobbed.

"Felicity, what is it? What happened?" I asked.

She looked up at me and shook her head. "Oh Puppins, everyone thinks I'm this brave warrior, carrying out great missions. But ..."

I kept quiet, remembering my Listener lessons.

Finally she went on, her deep brown eyes spilling tears down her muzzle. "They have a lot of new dogs, even more than before. The new kennels are smaller, more cramped. Puppins, you wouldn't believe how many dogs are crammed into that revolting place!"

"Wow. That's ... that's terrible!" I cried.

"That's not all," she continued. "The dogs told me they get barely enough to eat, and not enough time outside. Their kennels and runs are filthy. It smells awful in there."

She paused and shook her head again. "They put stronger latches on the kennels and I couldn't get most of them open. I was only able to free two mothers and their pups."

Lying there on the prickly grass, she started sobbing again.

"I've failed, Puppins. I realize that I cannot keep ahead of Master and Mistress. I'll never be able to put them out of business!"

It broke my heart to see her that way. I lay down beside her, trying as best I could to comfort her.

Out of the corner of my eye, I saw Oliver creep up. He had heard what she said. Like the whole Tribe, he knew how much shutting down Puppy Haven meant to her. He didn't make any jokes. He just curled up on her other side, his furry little body next to hers.

***

As we lay there, I thought about what Felicity said. That she had failed. Some words bombed my brain:

Failure is not fatal. It is the courage to continue that counts. Without thinking, I blurted those words out loud.

She raised her head. "Puppins, is that what you think? It ... it sounds like something from a book."

Uh oh. I'd blown my cover as a closet nerd.

"I guess I heard it somewhere," I mumbled. "Not sure where."

"Well, I think ... I think it's right. But I don't know if I have the courage to continue. I just don't know if there's any way that I could succeed."

Was there a way? I tried to think. It takes me longer than the average dog to figure out what to do in a crisis, and this was a crisis, for sure.

Then I remembered our raid at the dogfight ring. We freed most of the dogs that were forced to fight against their will. But if the neighbors hadn't called the police, those evil men would just go out and get more dogs and start all over again.

Hard to admit, but maybe sometimes, no matter how heroic us animals are, we need people to help finish the job.

"Felicity," I ventured, "do you think that if the police knew about this place, they'd arrest Master and Mistress? And would they make sure all those poor dogs found good homes?"

"Well, I know that what they are doing is wrong," she answered, "and I'm pretty sure that if they were caught, they'd be put in jail and the dogs would be rescued."

I told her what I was thinking. That what we needed here, like at the dogfight place, was some human help.

"But how can we get people involved?" Felicity asked. "We have no way to ask for help."

Oliver broke in. "We do have one way, Felicity. We're good at getting attention. Isn't that what you guys did at the dogfights?"

"Yes, but ..." Felicity began.

"That's it!" I said excitedly. "We just need to get the attention of some people and lead them here, and they'll do the rest!"

"But no one lives around here," Felicity pointed out.

"There must be someone," I persisted, thinking as hard as I could. "Oliver, did we see any houses close by? Wait -- didn't we pass a ... a fire station not too far back?"

He jumped up, his whiskers quivering with excitement. "Yeah! I saw it, and I wondered if they had a Dalmatian, like at the fire station near the Carriage House. Sometimes I sneak in there. That Dalmatian is friendly and doesn't bark at me, even if I jump on the firetruck and take a nap on the driver's seat."

"Too much information, Oliver," I said, batting him on the head. "Anyway, I'll bet firefighters are helpful. If we go there and make a lot of noise, maybe they'll follow us to see why we are doing it."

Felicity was quiet. I felt like if she thought it was a stupid idea, it probably was.

"Well," she said finally, "I guess it's worth a try. But if they do follow us, what happens then? How will they know what's going on inside the kennels?"

"Oh yeah," Oliver said. "They'll think you guys have rabies and call Animal Control."

Yikes.

Then I had an idea. "Felicity, if you lead us to the new outer tunnel when we get back here with the firefighters, we can go inside and get the dogs barking up a storm, and the firefighters will break in to see what's wrong."

"Yeah!" Oliver exclaimed. "And they'll call the police, and when Master and Mistress come home, they'll get busted!"

"So many if's ..." Felicity said, shaking her head. "No. I can't agree to it. I don't want you two getting involved. Remember what happened to Columbo? I'll go to the station by myself, and maybe if I bark really loud the firefighters will follow me. It's my mission, and I'm doing it alone."

I'd heard her say that one time too many. I looked her straight in the eye. "Felicity. Read my lips. We're a team, got it? We're all in this together."

She stared at me. Then, she actually smiled. "Got it. We're a team. Fine."

"Yea!" meowed Oliver, running out to the road. "Come on, team! Move your shaggy butts!"

This time I was fine with being led by a cat.

***

We started down the road at a good clip and hadn't gone far when, suddenly, a wall of frightful screeches blasted our ears.

Pepito and his band of wild parakeets! Out at night again? Had they turned nocturnal?

Swooping down, they landed in feathery formation on the road in front of us.

"Puppeens! Que pasa?" squawked Pepito.

"Uh ... nada. Que pasa for you?" I managed lamely.

Oliver looked disgusted. "Puppins, is that the best you can do?"

"I suppose you can do better, bird brain," I shot back, hoping Pepito didn't catch the phrase.

"Actually, I can," Oliver answered smugly.

Turning to Pepito, he began chattering in parakeet and Pepito chattered back!

Felicity and I stared at each other. What was going on?

I broke into their dialogue. "Oliver! You know how to talk to Pepito?"

"Si. I mean sure. They talk the same as Jade, and she's been teaching me."

Jade. Oliver's white-furred, green-eyed girlfriend. I'd seen them off by themselves, but thought it was just love stuff. I had no idea he was taking foreign language lessons.

"Uh, well, what are you and Pepito saying?"

"I asked him why they were up at night. He said they've become a rap group. Pepito and the Peeps. They had a gig up here at a club called Birdland. It's for owls and bats."

Wait. Pepito and the Peeps? Those squawkers give rap concerts?

Inconceivable.

Oliver went on. "Pepito asked me if someone got hurt again and needed more healing plants. I said no, that we are trying to shut down an evil puppy mill, and we're going to get some firefighters to help us."

Pepito and his backup rappers screeched something to Oliver, and he translated. "They want to help. Pepito says if it's noise we need, they have the right stuff. Anyway, they are too buzzed from their gig to sleep."

"Well, why not?" I answered. Somehow, it made perfect sense.

Some words bombed my brain. The same words as when we freed those dogs at the fight ring: *When spiderwebs unite, they can tie up a lion.*

There were a lot more of us web-spinners now. But we had to tie up Master and Mistress, and they had guns.

A lion might be easier.

46

"Vamonos!" shrieked Pepito. We followed down the road as they flew low over our heads. When we got within sight of the fire station, they landed in a tree and Pepito squawked something to Oliver.

"He says they'll circle over us and screech as loud as they can when I give the signal," Oliver reported. "That's sure to get the firefighters' attention."

"Tell them okay," I said.

"Esta bien!" Oliver called out to Pepito.

We crept closer and surveyed the scene. In front of us was the station, with two shiny firetrucks parked inside the big open garage doors. No Dalmatians in sight, which probably was just as well.

The firefighters sat around the doorway, eating chips and drinking soda.

"Wow, that must have been exciting!" one of them, a young woman, was saying. "Nothing's happened up here since I joined, not even a false alarm. Just a stupid cat stuck up in a tree."

I gave Oliver a nudge with my paw and stifled a laugh. He ignored me.

Another firefighter spoke up. "Just wait 'til the dry season kicks in. That's when things get hot around here, if you'll pardon the pun."

An old-looking guy chimed in: "Yeah. In a bad season, there's brush fires almost every day. You won't think it's so much fun when there's an out-of-control inferno up here."

They fell silent for a moment, and we gave each other a look. Game on!

Felicity and I rushed forward, barking our heads off. As we raced toward the station, Oliver leaped on my back.

"Owww! Get off me!" I yelped.

He dug his claws in deeper. "Giddyup, Puppins! Whooeee!" he shouted in his loudest cat wail.

We made a ton of noise, for sure. As for the birds, you never heard such screeching! In a truly awful way, it was beautiful.

The firefighters jumped out of their chairs. One of them yelled, "What the hell! What's going on?"

"Dogs? A cat? And ...and look at those birds! What is this!?" the old guy croaked.

"Maybe they're shooting a movie up here!" exclaimed the young woman. "But where's the cameras?"

We slammed to a stop just before reaching the station so they could tell we weren't trying to attack. Then we turned and ran back the other way, keeping up an unbelievable barrage of noise. We stopped, turned, and stared back at them. Repeat. Repeat. Repeat.

They stood staring at us with their mouths open. "I think they want us to follow them!" one cried. "You know, like in those old 'Lassie' movies. Should we?"

"The rest of you go ahead," the old one said. "I'll hold down the fort. Call if you need me to come with the truck."

"Okay, Chief. Hey! At last, some action!" the young woman said.

We ran down the road, Oliver clinging tight to my back, the birds overhead and the two firefighters not far behind. As Puppy Haven loomed up on the hillside, we put on a final burst of speed and reached the outer fence.

Oliver shouted to the birds to keep circling and squawking, while Felicity, digging wildly under a pile of dry brush, uncovered the new tunnel's opening.

"Make sure you don't touch the fence," she warned breathlessly. "I think I got it turned off, but don't take any chances."

I had a sudden thought. "Wait. Shouldn't one of us stay outside to keep the firefighters interested?" They agreed. And as much as I wanted to go in with them, I volunteered to stay behind.

"Thank you, Puppins," Felicity replied quickly, and she and Oliver dived into the tunnel.

I raced back to the road where the parakeets, still screeching, swirled like a flying whirlpool over the firefighters' heads.

"What's going on?" shouted the female. "What is this place?"

"And what are these danged green birds doing?" the other fireman cried.

I ran up to them and barked like crazy in my best pit bull imitation.

"Whatcha tryin' to tell us, boy?" asked the guy. I ran a little way and then came back, barking without stopping.

"Okay, okay, we'll follow you!" he said.

I ran to the tunnel and, with the firefighters right on my tail, nosed furiously at the opening.

Just then, from inside the kennels, came an incredible eruption of sound. It was awesome.

***

The rest is kind of a blur. Basically, the firefighters took charge. They banged on the door of the house, got no answer, then called their chief to see if they should break into the kennel building.

237

I guess the chief told them to wait for the police, who arrived shortly with Animal Control.

As they tried to figure out how to get into the kennels, Master and Mistress got home. They were ordered to unlock the building. And as soon as the door opened, Felicity and Oliver streaked out into the darkness.

In the chaos, the three of us ran, unseen, out to the road, where Oliver told Pepito and the Peeps they could go home. "Gracias!" we shouted to them as they took off.

"Adios, equipo!" they screeched back. "Hasta luego!"

Felicity, Oliver and I watched from under the shrubs as the Animal Control people, helped by the police and firefighters, brought out dog after dog, large and small, and put them in the truck.

One of the officers led Mistress inside the house. When they came out again, the officer held a little white dog in her arms -- the current favorite of Mistress.

She showed it to the others. "Isn't she sweet? Maybe I'll adopt her," she said. "But what a dreadful place this is! Just wait 'til the news gets out. People will be lining up to adopt these poor things."

Master and Mistress got put in handcuffs, with Mistress screaming that it was all a big mistake and they had a breeders' license. The cop told her to save it for the judge.

***

The three of us straggled back to the Carriage House just as the sun peeked up behind us. As we pushed in through the doggy door, Mariah bounded over.

"Thank goodness you're back," she exclaimed. "I was so worried, especially when Oliver turned up missing too."

Oliver took a flying leap up to the shelf where Jade was sleeping. "Buenas noches, my querida!" he purred, licking her nose.

Opening one eye, she gave him a look. He buried his head deep in her fur and promptly fell asleep. Sweet.

Felicity and I fell down on our rugs like dead dogs, telling Mariah we'd fill her in later. But she was not about to let me off the hook.

"Puppins, Miss Wisteria noticed you were gone when she brought our dinner last night. She is more on top of things than you believed."

Ouch. "What did she do?" I asked. "Did she call Kristin?"

"No. She called someone else and told them she thought you'd gone for a walk with Felicity. She said if you weren't here for breakfast, he should come over and help look for you."

"Phew. Made it back just in time," I mumbled sheepishly.

"Puppins, you know it was wrong to leave the Tribal Base," Mariah said severely. "You've gotten away with it twice, but that doesn't make it right."

"I know, Mariah. I won't ..."

Felicity raised her head and broke in. "Mariah, I told Puppins he should not have come. But as it turned out ... well, we'll tell you about it after we rest. But Puppy Haven is finally shut down. And without Puppins – and Oliver and the parakeets and some helpful humans – it would not have happened."

I closed my eyes. "We were a ... a team," I managed. "Spiderwebs. ... You know, lots of ... of spiderwebs."

***

When Miss Wisteria brought our breakfast, she shook a gnarled finger at me, petted me, and left. Felicity, Oliver and I ate our kibble, then went back to our rugs and slept all day.

***

At dinner time, Miss W brought out a bag of bacon treats along with our food. I wondered if she knew that Kristin would not approve.

That night we had a big celebration. Everyone was stoked that the puppy mill was history. We made an awful uproar -- it's a good thing Miss Wisteria can't hear too well.

After a while, Pasadena Fats popped out of his hole and joined in the fun. "Totally turgid, Puppins!" he squeaked. "You did it, my man, even though you're not the sharpest cheese in the pantry! Ha ha! Now pass those bacon treats!"

Oliver told our tale several times, strutting around with his chest puffed out and playing the hero.

That little nuisance does not know the meaning of humility. However, he does know how to talk parakeet, and for that I am pretty grateful.

***

Miss W, not taking any chances on me disappearing again, brought me in the house for the night.

Lying on the floor in the upstairs hall, I felt all alone. I missed the Tribe, and I missed Kristin.

Then I noticed that Miss W's door was open a crack, so I stuck my head in. She was in her big chair, wearing a robe and reading a large book with her magnifying glass.

Curled up on her lap was Harriet, while Victoria slept at her feet. Harriet hissed at the sight of me, then streaked under the bed with Victoria fast on her tail.

Miss W looked up and smiled.

"Puppins, come in. I was so happy to see you in the Carriage House this morning."

I trotted over and hung my head to show I felt guilty(ish).

Miss Wisteria, in her quavery voice, went on. "When I couldn't find you last night, I was very worried. I'll have to tell Kristin about it, of course, but all's well that ends well."

Wait. Tell Kristin? Yikes. Would I get grounded?

Come to think of it, I was already grounded, at least in theory. But if Kristin got really mad at me, I could end up serving time in Dog Detention again.

Miss Wisteria patted me. "You can stay in here tonight if you wish. Harriet and Victoria will survive."

Good. I did not want to be alone. I sat next to her chair and surveyed the room. Books piled everywhere, posters of butterflies on the walls. She was a lepi ... lepi ... butterfly scientist, now too old to go on expeditions.

She returned to her book. It looked like it might have a good scent, so I put my nose on the open page and sniffed. Sadly, it smelled like paper, not like butterflies or flowers.

Noticing my interest, Miss W turned the book around so I could see the pictures better.

"These are butterflies that live in the Amazon jungle," she told me. Wow. They were huge, and a lot more colorful than the ones I chase in our courtyard.

Seeing how intently I stared at the pictures, Miss W smiled at me. "Puppins, I think you are a very intelligent dog. I don't know why Jodi says you have no brain."

I guess Mariah was right. Miss W *is* much sharper than I thought. Apparently it's possible to be old and still be on the ball. Who knew?

I settled down at her feet, noting with satisfaction that Harriet and Victoria were silently raging at me from under the bed.

Tough. They might not like me, but now I had a new friend. Maybe, despite being ancient, Miss Wisteria could help fill up those holes in my heart.

47

I did get grounded. First, I had to endure a lecture. Then Kristin told me no more overnights in the Carriage House for the next eon. Sigh.

In the meantime, Tolliver Yar, our Street Scout, was doing a good job of directing strays our way, so Kristin had a lot of new refugees on her hands.

Here's the process: When new animals arrive, Kristin calls a vet who comes out for free, checks them out, gives them shots, and takes them in for medical care if needed.

They also get spayed or neutered. Ouch. I got that done in Seattle; thankfully, I don't remember the event.

Anyway, according to Kristin, it's a good thing. "There are too many homeless animals on the streets of L.A. already," she says, and I know that's a true fact.

The lost and abandoned dogs and cats who come here need food, care, and a safe place to be. A lot of them also need comforting and understanding. And as I said, my job as a Listener helps with that. The Tribe pitches in too, welcoming newcomers with friendly sniffs and licks.

Toward Christmas time, I started noticing that more and more animals needed cheering up. Kristin claims the holidays are a joyful time for most people, so I was puzzled.

"Isn't this a happy time for street animals?" I asked Mariah.

"Not always," she said. "If they used to be in families, they might remember how nice the holidays were, and feel sad that those days are gone."

Mariah said we should try extra hard during this season to make newcomers feel welcome. But really, she wants us to do that all the time.

"You should always welcome strangers," she says. "They might be angels, without you even knowing it."

Wait. Did she mean that some scruffy, stinky mutt might actually be an angel? That was hard to swallow.

Then some words popped up in my brain: *All God's angels come to us disguised.* I shared that with Mariah, and she liked it. However, I still had significant doubts.

"Are you saying that *Oliver* might be an angel dressed in a gray cat suit?" I asked her.

"No reason why not," she replied with a smile.

I could think of a hundred reasons why not. Mariah and Felicity might be angels in disguise, but Oliver? Give me a break.

***

Christmas in Los Angeles is different than in other places, according to Jodi. Since there aren't any chimneys for Santa to come down, apparently he shows up at the mall wearing red surfer shorts, flip flops and sunglasses, has a nice tan under his white beard, and drives a convertible instead of a sleigh.

It was different in other ways, too. Usually Kristin and Jodi went to the beach with friends on Christmas Day, played volleyball, rode on standup paddleboards, and roasted crabs and corn in a sand pit. (I had to stay home because that beach allowed fires but no dogs. Go figure.)

Anyway, Kristin wanted to start some new holiday traditions. "This is my first Christmas here," she said, "and I want it to be spectacular."

First, she and Jodi strung little golden lights everywhere -- all around the doors and windows of La Casa Royale and the Carriage House, and on all the trees and shrubs in the yard.

Next, they did a whole day of baking. Kristin does not believe in sugar, but Jodi is a believer and talked her into it. (BTW, as you probably know, I'm a believer too.) Decorating cookies turned out to be a messy business; to help, I got under the table and licked up the spilled sprinkles.

When Kristin saw my blue muzzle, she sent me outside. Harsh. Hadn't I cleaned up the floor for her?

Then one day they dragged a humongous, shaggy tree into the living room. I wondered why they brought a tree in the house, and why they scolded me for trying to mark it.

Turns out it was a special tree for Christmas. It cost a fortune, Kristin said, because Christmas trees have to be trucked in from up north. But it was worth it, she said.

A bunch of friends came over to help decorate it, and they brought cool stuff to hang on the branches: stars of different shapes, old-time bubble lights, fake birds with real feathers, and wooden dogs and cats. Jodi hung a black Lab near the angel at the top, which made me feel proud. Then Kristin plugged in the bubble lights and everyone cheered. I thought the tree was awesome, but staring at those bubbles made me dizzy.

Jodi brought out the sugar cookies, and one of the guests slipped me a red pony that went down in a single gulp. Again, to be helpful, I sucked up all the crumbs that people dropped. It was a tough job, but someone had to do it.

Then the doorbell rang. A latecomer. I ran over and barked, which is another one of my jobs.

Kristin opened the door and in came a young man. He was wearing a black suit with a white collar, and he looked and smelled familiar.

Then I remembered. It was the Father who shared his church picnic with me and my friends!

Kristin introduced him to everyone. "This is Father Nicholas, the priest from Church of the Angel," she said. "I met him when Puppins went missing and I was combing the streets for him. I've asked Father Nicholas to do a Blessing of the Animals here on Christmas Eve, so please come back then and bring your pets."

She smiled at the priest, then rubbed my ears. "Nicholas, this is Puppins. Maybe you've already met?"

He patted my head. "Ah, the prodigal dog. I'm pretty sure he was in that little pack that stopped by our picnic. I thought they were just ordinary wayfarers since none wore a collar. But when you came by and asked about a black Lab, I put two and two together."

Kristin sighed. "I don't know what happened to his collar. He was wearing it when he disappeared."

Aargh. My collar. The one that Ruby chewed off and tossed in a pond. The high point of our so-called relationship.

A wave of memories washed over me, sweet and sour, like that Chinese chicken Dora fixed sometimes. I slunk off to a corner to brood.

But after a while, thinking about Ruby made my skin itch. I decided to do what Mariah had suggested: focus my brain on someone else.

Felicity. She had been away, doing whatever she does at her camp by the Old Bridge. I guess she was my best friend now (along with Oliver), and I missed her.

Sigh. That made me feel sad.

Okay. Think about something else.

I started watching Kristin and the priest. They stood

awfully close together and looked at each other a lot, with kind of dopey expressions on their faces.

Kristin hadn't been on any dates since she adopted me. In addition to claiming that L.A. men could not be trusted, she said she was much too busy for love.

"Puppins is the only male I need in my life," she sometimes proclaimed. That was fine with me. I deserved her full attention, right?

So, what was going on with this guy in a Boston terrier suit? Was he trying to move in on my exclusive territory?

An ominous feeling crawled up my spine like an unpleasant spider.

But wait. Didn't he feed me and my pals when we were hungry?

Hmmm. I guess it was possible he wasn't all bad. Anyway, I had to admit that they looked good together. Her skin is the color of vanilla ice cream, while his is like caramel syrup. I tasted that combination at Double Rainbow Ice Cream once, when Dora let me lick out her bowl, and it was pretty darn good.

Anyway, I guess Jodi noticed something too. While the priest was talking to Miss W, she whispered to Kristin, "What's with you and Father Nicholas? Aren't priests supposed to be un-dateable?"

Kristin blushed bright red. Then she whispered back, "It's okay. He's Episcopal, not Catholic."

No clue what that meant. Spare me the details.

48

After the tree decorating party, the days went by in a blur. Then it was the day of Christmas Eve, when we would find out what a Blessing of the Animals was all about.

That morning was as crisp as a potato chip; the afternoon sweet and warm, like the cherry toaster tarts Dora used to share with me.

Okay, so my mind was on food. What else is new?

I trotted around the courtyard with Kristin to make sure all the shrubs and trees had tiny lights on them. As we circled the yard, she pointed out the tall red poinsettias, creamy white gardenias and pink camellias.

"They've all bloomed just in time for Christmas!" she exclaimed. "Don't they look like beautiful live ornaments?" They did.

The Tribal animals and I were all set for Christmas too. We were bathed and brushed, mostly against our will, and suffered patiently while red bows were tied on our collars. We didn't know what was going to happen, but we hoped that treats would be involved.

Anticipation hung in the air like a piñata that was waiting to be whacked. (I saw a piñata once at a birthday party in the park. I thought it was brilliant. You get to take out your frustrations by smashing it to bits, then it rewards you.)

***

Jodi arrived. She and Kristin were dressed up. Jodi wore a green and purple thing that was kind of like pajamas, only nicer. Kristin's unruly light hair was stifled by a sparkly headband, and her long blue dress matched her Australian shepherd eyes.

Wait. Wasn't that the dress I chewed on when I was in Dog Detention? I guess she got it fixed.

They set up a table and piled it with snacks. Then they brought the Tribe to a place by the fountain marked by red and green ribbons, and told everyone to "stay."

Ha. Good luck with that.

As the last bit of sunlight spilled pink and orange colors on the sky, people began filing in with their pets.

First were Mr. and Mrs. Quintero, who lived on one of our old walking routes. While I welcomed their cocker spaniels, Carmelita and Pablo, Mr. Quintero shook Kristin's hand enthusiastically.

"You buy old casa and fix up! Es bonita!" he exclaimed. "But you brave to stay in neighborhood. It no good no more."

Kristin laughed. "You've stayed too, Mr. Quintero. I'm happy about that."

Miss Wisteria came down from upstairs with Victoria and Harriet in a carrier. They hissed when they spotted me. Kristin says that getting blessed is a good thing for your soul, so I hoped it would improve their attitude.

The courtyard soon filled with people and dogs and cats. We in the Tribe greeted the visiting animals with friendly sniffs, then said our new motto: "Mi casa, su casa!" Jade taught it to us. I forget what it means, but it sounded nice.

A steel drum band that Jodi hired arrived. They set up their drums under a palm tree and began to play. I wagged my tail to the beat. The bonging sound those big drums made was really cool.

Suddenly, a blast of horrific screeching filled the air. The wild parakeets!

Kristin's guests held their ears. Most had never seen a parakeet that wasn't in a cage, and wondered where those squawkers came from.

Jodi had a theory: "I think they're an exotic species from Brazil, smuggled into L.A. and released just as the feds were closing in!" As good an explanation as any, I guess.

The flock dropped by a couple of days ago, and Mariah (who can talk to Pepito a little) exchanged a few words with him. I hardly had time to yell, "Adios!" before they zoomed off again.

This time, they landed with a green swirl onto the branches of our oak tree.

"Feliz Navidad!" they shrieked to us animals.

"Mi casa, su casa!" we barked and meowed back.

It turned out that Mariah had asked Pepito to spread the word about the Blessing. "And he did," she told us, "and so has Mr. Pegasus. Perhaps some friends we haven't seen for a while will join us today."

Felicity, I hoped. And who else? I could hardly wait to find out.

**

The first old friend to show up was Mr. Pegasus himself.

He rubbed noses with Mariah. "You are looking well, old friend," she told him.

"So are you, Mariah, so are you. Will you agree to a race after the festivities? After the festivities?"

"Yes," she replied, "I'll look forward to it!"

Those two ex-racing greyhounds loved to run. Even though they were getting kind of old, they still enjoyed a good face-off when they got together.

Just then, Oliver came scampering up, mewing excitedly. "Puppins, my sisters are here! Mama and I haven't seen them in ages!"

I looked over. Collette was stretched out on a low branch of the same oak tree harboring the parakeets. Her two wandering girls, Cleo and Patra, were grooming her, and Oliver leaped up to join them.

At that moment, Tollivar Yar arrived, trotting in with a ragged sheepdog and a nondescript mutt.

As he introduced us, Mariah whispered to me, "Our Street Scout is doing a fine job, don't you think?"

Before I could mumble a reply, a commotion by the back gate got my attention.

Oglala Sue, Custrd, and Columbo!

We had heard nothing from them since Columbo's horrible accident at Puppy Haven. All of us ran to the gate.

"Welcome back! How are you, Columbo?" we all yelled.

Grinning his familiar toothy grin, the big bloodhound broke into a couple of feeble steps of his signature tap dance.

Sue scolded him. "Columbo, stop. You know you shouldn't overdo."

He took a bow and gave her a kiss. She just shook her head and sighed.

"How are *you*?" Mariah asked her.

"Alright, I guess," the borzoi replied, "and Columbo does seem a lot better. The juice from those plants the parakeets brought really helped with his pain. I put it on his nose, and he was able to sleep much better. Thank you, Mariah."

"We sent a lot of good thoughts and prayers for him as well," Mariah said. "And for you. How have you managed?"

"Custard is such a help, and she keeps our spirits up," Sue answered, nuzzling the furry little dog fondly. .

Columbo heard Sue's comment. "We've adopted her!" he announced proudly. "She's going to be part of our tracking team when I go back to work."

Sue shook her head at him again. "If you go back to work, you'll have to be a sight hound like me. That burn on your nose ..."

"My nose is *almost* as good as ever," he protested. "I'll still be able to out-track you any day!"

All of us laughed. The Battle of the Senses, just like old times.

***

More people and pets arrived. Then I heard Kristin call out, "Mr. and Mrs. Bunnag! Lin Lu! And ..."

"Puppins!" Loofah squealed, tumbling out of Lin Lu's arms and running to me, her black eyes sparkling.

She wore a red and green coat, and perched on her curly white topknot was a tiny green bow.

"Guess what!" she cried. "I've got my own bed, a little basket with a pink cushion. And a pink food bowl with my name on it. And look at this tag on my collar: it tells who my owner is if I get lost. I have lots of chew toys, and ..."

"Loofah, it's great to see you!" I interrupted her. "We didn't get any messages that you needed help, so you're alright?"

"Oh, Puppins – yes! I'm treated like a princess," she exclaimed. "Lin Lu is so much fun. We go looking for leprechauns in the garden, and ..."

She got interrupted again, this time by an excited cry from another familiar voice: Dora!

Jumping out of a taxi up front, she ran into the courtyard as fast as her plump little legs could go, her shar-pei wrinkles shaking with joy.

I raced to meet her, leaped up and put my front paws on her shoulders. Against the rules, of course, but I couldn't help it.

"Puppins!" she cried, wrapping me in a hug, kissing me repeatedly on the head like a woodpecker on its favorite tree.

Kristin hurried up. "Dora! I'm so glad you could make the trip!"

"I just had to come," Dora told her. "I was thrilled when you called me about the party."

She hugged Kristin, then hugged me again. It was way too long since I'd been smothered in Dora's soft hugs.

She chattered on, nonstop. "I miss you so much, Puppins! Will you come live with me? I'm sorry, Kristin, he's your dog, of course. And you've got this big house now, with lots of room and a safe yard. Anyway, I have a dog. Sam. An Australian shepherd. I didn't want to own another dog, remember? But I'm glad I do. He's a bit active for me, but he's very sweet. Like Puppins."

She stopped gushing long enough to hug me once again. Then she reached into her oversized purse and pulled out a package.

"Open this, Puppins -- it's your Christmas present. I hope it fits. You've lost so much weight!"

It was my first-ever wrapped gift. I pulled the glittery ribbon off with my teeth and tore open the paper.

Something fell out. Wow -- an L.A. Lakers muscle shirt! Gold and purple, just like they wear on TV. We used to watch the games together, and she had promised me a shirt someday.

Slipping it over my head, Dora pushed my front legs into the arm holes. It drooped around my chest because she had thought I was still fat; otherwise it was perfect.

Dora admired me in the shirt, then patted my head.

"I'm going to get something to eat, Puppins. I'm starved! They just gave me a tiny bag of pretzels on the plane. I'll bring you some food. You are way too thin!" She hurried off with Kristin toward the snack table.

Loofah ran over to see my shirt. She didn't know who the Lakers were, but she said it made me look buff.

Oliver, up in the tree, had a sour expression on his fuzzy little face as he looked at me. I'm pretty sure he was jealous.

Just then, a tough-looking dog with a squared-off muzzle came up to me. Bill. Bill the boxer. Alone.

Sue, Columbo and Custard saw him and trotted over. Remembering how he and Ruby ghosted us at Puppy Haven, we stared coldly at him.

"Where's Ruby?" Sue asked abruptly.

He didn't answer her question. Hanging his head, he mumbled, "I owe ya all an apology. Ya saved me from the fight ring, and then I just ... just ..."

"It's okay," I said, even though it really wasn't. "What's going on?"

"It didn't work out with Ruby. She run off. She told me I was boring."

Wait. You mean I'm not the only one to get ditched by Ruby? I found that strangely comforting.

Loofah piped up. "I'm not surprised," she said smugly. "That dog doesn't think of anyone but herself."

"She's a loner, for sure. But she don't pretend to be nothing else," Bill muttered, coming to Ruby's defense. "There's nothing wrong with that, I guess."

Unless you have a Velcro heart and it stupidly gets stuck on her, I thought with a sigh.

While the steel drums bonged out another tune. I crept off by myself. This was a new development in the never-ending drama of Ruby, and I needed to process it.

I just got settled under the poinsettias when Mariah

appeared.

"Puppins, there's someone arriving that I think you'll be glad to see," she said.

I looked up. A little brown dog with a twisted leg trotted through the gate and rubbed noses with Loofah.

Then, as Mariah faded into the crowd, she made her way over to me.

"Hello, Puppins. It's good to see you," she said, looking at me with her steady gaze.

"You too, Felicity. Why haven't you come around lately?" I blurted it out kind of rudely.

"I've been really busy," she answered. "And, I wanted to give you time."

"Time? For what?"

She laughed a sweet little laugh. "Oh, you know. Time to get over Ruby. Have you?"

Yikes. I'd forgotten how direct Felicity is. But wait. Why did she ask me that question? Does she ... does she like me in a ... a special way? I did not see that coming.

Totally flustered, I didn't answer. She turned and limped away.

Aargh. I think I blew it, whatever "it" was.

As I tried to figure out what was going on with Felicity, Kristin walked up with the priest.

They were holding hands. Ugh. Why was everything suddenly so complicated?

Father Nicholas saw my Lakers shirt.

"Puppins, I'm a Lakers fan too," he said cheerfully. "Maybe we can watch a game together sometime."

He gave Kristin a mushy smile, and she smiled mushily back. Double ugh.

Then he reached into his coat pocket and pulled out a sugar cookie, slipping it to me without Kristin noticing.

A bribe, no doubt. But it went down well. I guess priests know the way to a dog's heart.

49

The people took to their chairs and a hush fell over the courtyard. The night was soft and dark, with no lights except the "little fires" that Jodi was lighting.

"It's an old Spanish custom called luminarias," she explained to everyone. "On Christmas Eve, you put sand in small paper bags, stick candles in the sand, then light them outdoors. They are to help show the way through the desert."

I didn't have a clue what that was all about. Then she read a story to explain it. The story told how, long ago, a huge star appeared in the sky. Three smart kings and some shepherds saw it. They knew it was special, so they decided to follow it.

The star led them across the desert to a small town, where they found a young couple named Mary and Joseph and their newborn baby, Jesus. He was born in a stable because all the rooms in town were booked.

The story raised some new questions in my mind. But just then, Kristin flipped a switch. And suddenly, a billion stars fell out of the sky and landed in our courtyard.

Wow!

Oooohs and ahhhhhs echoed from all the people. Lin Lu and the other kids clapped their hands. The cats mewed; we dogs barked and yipped.

The parakeets (who had promised Mariah they would keep quiet during the Blessing) could not resist a chorus of awestruck twitters.

As the steel drums bonged softly in the background, Father Nicholas stood up.

"This is what it must have been like on the first Christmas Eve," he said. "Bethlehem has palm trees like these, and our weather is similar to theirs.

"And tonight, we welcome animals into our midst, just as Mary and Joseph did at the manger."

I didn't know what a manger was, but I was glad the baby's parents loved animals. That meant they were good people.

Father Nicholas went on. "These twinkling lights remind us of the star that lit the way for the shepherds and Wise Men. These lights remind us of Jesus, and the special light he brought to us: the light of love.

"And they remind us that each of us can shine a light for others, when their night is dark."

I glanced at Felicity, whose soft brown eyes glowed. She was a light for the Tribe, for sure.

Then Father Nicholas told about the blessing of animals. He said the tradition was started a long time ago by a man named Saint Francis.

"He loved all animals, especially the birds," said Father Nicholas.

The parakeets twittered proudly when they heard that, but a look from Mariah shut them down. The priest continued.

"To show his gratitude for the animals, Saint Francis called all kinds of creatures together, and he asked God to protect them all."

Father Nicholas ended with a prayer for us: "Bless and protect these beloved friends, dear God. May we always treasure them as the sacred gifts they are."

Amen.

***

The first blessing Father Nicholas gave was for Pepito and his Peeps up in the oak tree.

While this was going on, Lin Lu helped Kristin and Jodi line up us animals. (Getting the cats under control was a problem, but what else is new?)

As each animal filed past the priest, by itself or with its owner, he put his hand on its head and said the blessing.

When it was my turn, I didn't understand all of the special words. But they gave my insides a really good feeling. Like a bowl of warm broth on a chilly night.

Felicity took her turn after me, followed by Loofah, Oliver and his family, Mariah, the rest of the Tribe, and the visiting pets.

Miss W presented Victoria and Harriet in their carrier. I knew it was a longshot, but I hoped Father Nicholas's words would take the anti-dog hostility out of their hissy little souls.

At the very end, Pasadena Fats waddled up, hiding behind a fluffy dog so people wouldn't see him and scream. (BTW, why are humans so scared of such a tiny thing? I don't get it.)

Father Nicholas, not blinking an eye, touched Fats' forehead with his finger and spoke the blessing in a whisper.

When it was done, Fats scampered over to me.

"My man, that was totally turgid!" he proclaimed. "Totally turgid! Now bring on the snacks!"

***

Kristin and Jodi did just that. While people helped themselves to cookies, frozen red grapes and other stuff, Kristin passed out treats for us animals, and Jodi put seeds in a bowl for the parakeets.

She included some carobs for old times' sake, and Pepito and his crew pecked and squawked and noisily shared their feast with Fats.

Afterwards, Pepito asked Mariah if the birds could do a rap number to show their appreciation.

"Rap is not appropriate for Christmas," she pointed out kindly. "But please come back another time and do a performance for the Tribe."

***

During the snacks, Kristin took Miss Wisteria around and introduced her to everyone. She was dressed up and looked very nice. She has dark skin, kind of like chocolate, which is a really good thing, is it not?

As Miss W told people how happy she was to share La Casa Royale with Kristin and me, her face glowed in the mellow light. Some words swam to the top of my brain and I said them out loud to Mariah: *As a white candle in a holy place, so is the beauty of an aged face.*

"That's lovely!" Mariah said. "Where did you hear that, Puppins?"

As usual, I had no clue.

Kristin and Miss W drifted off. Then Felicity appeared, settling down next to Mariah and me.

"This is such a wonderful evening," she said. "It feels like so many good things have come together."

Whew. I guess she wasn't mad at me, which was a relief. I probably hurt her feelings earlier when I didn't answer that question she asked.

Anyway, what she just said was true. It was an evening of good things and good friends. It seemed like everyone I loved most was there, at least for a while.

***

While Kristin's guests sang holiday songs accompanied by the steel drums, Mariah gathered the Tribe around her.

"Remember how fearsome Tolliver Yar used to be?" she asked. "He said he wanted to change, and he's been trying really hard. I think this would be a good time to celebrate that."

We gave a few half-hearted barks and meows for Tolliver, and the huge Rottweiler ducked his head in embarrassment.

Loofah didn't join in the tribute. Later, when she and I were alone, I asked her if she had forgiven Tolliver yet.

"I have tried, Puppins," she told me, "and I feel like my heart has gotten a little softer. Mariah told me that no one ever loved Tolliver, and that's what made him mean. But I still feel angry when I remember what he and those hideous men did to Odette in Donut Alley."

I got it. But then some words pushed their way up in my brain, and I said them out loud to Loofah: *Every day you don't forgive, it's like eating tiny bits of poison.*

"Oh, Puppins!" she cried. "Do you think I'm poisoning myself?"

"I don't know," I told her. "It's really hard to forgive something so bad. But maybe after a while, if holding onto it is hurting you inside, you should let it go."

She ran off, her usual response to the subject. I felt bad for her. It seems like forgiveness is so easy to say but so hard to do.

Just then Felicity showed up.

"Puppins, look who's here," she said, pointing her paw toward the back gate.

My heart did a flip flop.

Ruby. Just as gorgeous as ever. Gulp.

"We should invite her in," Felicity said.

"No way!" I yelped.

"Why not?"

I couldn't answer. My feelings swirled around inside me like that chicken and rice mess Kristin makes in the blender when my stomach is upset.

"I think we should ask her to join us," Felicity persisted. "It's Christmas Eve. Maybe she is lonely."

Ha. Not likely. Probably just wants to mock me. Or snag some food. Or see Bill.

Felicity didn't wait for a response. She limped over to the gate and said something to the red-haired stunner, who tossed her head and said something back.

Felicity returned. "She won't come in, but she wants to talk to you."

Yikes. I dragged myself over. Ruby stared at me with those eyes, and the usual fireworks went off in my brain.

"Hi. How've you been?" I said lamely.

"Fine," she replied, her voice as sweet as honey. "Listen, I'm headed up the hill to the L.A. Zoo. I know how to sneak in at night. No humans around, and we can tease the bears and lions."

She paused, then went on. "There's a great view of the city lights from up there. Want to come? Maybe we could ..."

Pausing again, her eyes burned into mine. In them was a world of possibilities, all of them incredibly awesome.

Of *course* I wanted to come. Not to tease the lions and bears -- that would be mean. But just to be with her one more time. One more chance to make her like me.

A plan flashed through my brain. With all the commotion in the courtyard, no one would notice me gone. I could be back before bedtime, no harm done.

My heart thumped a familiar rap: Me. Ruby. Together again. Me. Ruby. Together again. Me. Ruby ...

Then it hit me. Did I really want to run out on Kristin again? Not for anything noble, like shutting down a puppy mill, but just to take another ride on Ruby's crazy rollercoaster?

I shook my head. "No thanks."

A flicker of surprise appeared in her glittering eyes; then a mask of indifference fell over her face. She turned away, her long, regal nose in the air.

I swallowed. "You're welcome to come in and join the party," I told her bravely. "Jodi is here. I bet she'd love to see you again ..."

Oops. Bad suggestion. Jodi tried to tame Ruby once, remember? It did not go well.

She didn't answer. She just strode out the gate and down the alley, the plume of her tail held high like a red flag of independence.

Ruby was gone. Again. This time, though, it felt like a huge sack of butcher bones just rolled off my shoulders.

I trotted over to Felicity, who had questions written all over her furry brown face. "Ruby tries not to show that she cares about anyone, but I wonder ..."

I did not want Felicity speculating on whether Ruby might or might not care about me, so I sidestepped.

"She's always going somewhere," I said. "But I can never figure out where. I wonder what she's looking for?"

"I think she tries to make herself happy by being free," Felicity said thoughtfully. "For me, when I try to make myself happy, it doesn't work. But when I try to make someone else happy, it makes me feel happy too. That's strange, isn't it?"

It was one of those things Felicity says that take a while to sink in, and I was way too overwhelmed by the events of the night to figure out anything so deep.

I bumped her nose with mine. "Come on, Felicity -- let's see if we can find some abandoned cookies on the ground."

She laughed, and off we went.

50

Kristin's guests began to drift away. The band packed up its steel drums. Pepito and his flock took off in a green cloud, screeching, "Vaya con Dios!" as they disappeared over the rooftops. They were on their way to a Christmas Eve gig at Birdland, according to Oliver.

Lin Lu, leaving with her parents, held Loofah down so I could rub noses with her and tell her goodbye. Then she asked Kristin if I could come over sometime for a play date, and Kristin said yes.

That was great news. I wanted to see Loofah again, of course, and Lin Lu, and play with Loofah's new toys.

Then it was time for Dora to go. Wrapped in a wooly yellow coat that was way too warm for L.A., she hugged me one last time. She tried to be upbeat, but I saw tears in her eyes.

"Puppins, you'd love Sam. He likes to play basketball, like you used to with Oliver. Maybe Kristin will let you visit someday. I'll make you a banana cream pie. You are much too skinny!"

As she petted me, I sniffed her gloriously wrinkled face to preserve her memory. I had missed her awfully, and not just for the food.

Dora opened her pudgy fist and gave me a sticky date bar she'd been clutching. I chewed it slowly, wanting the treat -- and the moment -- to last. But before

I had finished choking it down, she got in her taxi and was gone.

These goodbyes were killing me.

***

Father Nicholas helped carry things inside, then patted me and said he hoped he'd see me again soon.

He and Kristin were still glowing. Right there in front of me, he took her hand and pulled her up close. I made a gagging sound and shut my eyes. If he was going to kiss her, I didn't want to be a witness. Triple ugh.

I wondered if she knew about all those kids he has — the ones that called him "Father" at the church picnic. That could be a deal-breaker, right?

***

As soon as the priest drove off, Kristin and Jodi blew out the "little fires" and turned off the twinkling golden lights, then led us animals inside the Carriage House.

Surprise!

There, hanging from the ceiling, was a piñata!

But wait. It was in the shape of a mailman. We dogs gave each other a look. We did not want to smash a mailperson.

No canine I know hates mail people. In fact, most of us like them a lot because they spice up our day. Barking at them is just a game we play when we are bored.

"Let's call it Master -- you know, Master at Puppy Haven!" bellowed Columbo.

"Or Stites or Onions at the dogfight ring!" Tolliver Yar growled.

"Or all three of those jerks!" yelled Oliver, and barks and mews rang out from everyone.

Jodi had a plastic baseball bat and showed us dogs how to hold it in our mouths and swing at the piñata.

Then she took hold of a rope that let her raise and lower the piñata so dogs of all sizes could have a turn.

We battered and bashed and smashed that thing to shreds. At last it burst open, raining toys and treats down on our heads.

The cats joined us as we scrabbled for the loot. Kristin and Jodi, watching at a safe distance, laughed themselves silly.

***

After they left, we were too keyed up to sleep, so we got on our rugs and relived the epic events of Christmas Eve. (Thankfully, no one – not even Oliver -- mentioned Ruby.)

After a while, I saw that Custard was fast asleep, and so were Oliver and the other cats. I pulled my rug next to Columbo and Sue, with Felicity and Mariah on my other side.

Felicity, her voice soft so as not to wake up the sleepers, turned to Sue. "You used to tell us about the Oglala Sioux Reservation where you lived with your owner," she said to the borzoi. "Do you think you'll ever be able to go back there again?"

"Someday, I hope with all my heart," Sue replied. "But it's a long, long journey. Maybe when Columbo is back to his old self, we'll find a way. I want him to be there too. Once you've lived on the rez, it's always a part of you, no matter where you go."

"What did you like about it?" I asked.

"Running free. Wide-open spaces, where coyotes howl just over the ridge. Red-tailed hawks circling in skies that seem to go on forever."

She stopped and thought, then went on. "I loved the clean air. The scent of parched corn and dry bones in the summertime, and rolling in fresh snow in the winter. Hunting. And camping at night under millions of stars."

Wow. Hearing her describe it made me want to go there too.

She continued. "I miss the Sioux people. They are very poor and have lots of problems, but their families are close. And I like what they believe: that animals are their brothers and sisters, and that people and animals and the land are all connected. It made me feel like I belonged. And it made me understand that what I do can affect everything and everyone else."

We all were quiet. Maybe, like me, the others were thinking about being connected. For sure, I felt connected to La Casa Royale and the Tribal Base, and to my special people and animal friends.

Some words popped up in my brain: *Only connect!* Then a bunch of other words crowded in: *by the coming of your fearless and complete love, all big wickedly worlds of world disappear.*

Whew. That was a bigger-than-usual brain bomb, and kind of a mashup. I guess it meant that being connected to friends and a loving home makes the world a less scary place.

I don't often say these bombs out loud, but this time I did, and Oliver woke up long enough to hear.

"Puppins, you are such a geek!" he mewed rudely.

Wrong. I am not a geek. I am a nerd, and I am getting to be proud of it.

"Where did you hear those words?" Mariah asked.

"I don't know. Just another Puppins mystery," I joked.

Mariah cocked her head thoughtfully. "That makes me wonder. What's next for you, Puppins?"

"What do you mean?" I asked suspiciously.

"Well, aren't you ready for another quest?"

I was horrified. "Quest? Like at the dogfight ring? No thanks. And Puppy Haven wasn't my quest, it was Felicity's. Anyway, I've had enough adventures to last forever. If I've learned anything at all about myself, it's that I'm a home-loving dog."

Mariah smiled. "I know. But you do have some unfinished business."

"What are you talking about, Mariah?"

Felicity answered for her. "Those sayings you share with us once in a while. Don't you want to know where they come from? Don't you want to discover who you were, before that car hit you?"

I didn't reply. Of course I wanted to know about that. I guess most anyone who's been adopted wants to solve the mysteries of their past.

On the other hand, why not let sleeping dogs lie, so to speak? I did not need to pursue another quest. Anyway, I told myself, I would never run away from Kristin again -- and this time I meant it.

But wait. What if I hadn't run off like I did? I'd still be overweight and spoiled. I wouldn't have met Mariah and Felicity and Loofah, and the Tribe.

And I'd never have found out what I was capable of: Flying over tall fences! Surviving life on the streets! Defying death on a dangerous old bridge! Helping shut down a vicious dogfight ring! Putting an evil puppy mill out of business!

Wow. Pretty amazing, right?

Mariah interrupted my orgy of self-admiration.

"Maybe there's a way to uncover your past without hurting Kristin or breaking the rules," she suggested.

I shook my head. There was no way. After all, my past was in Seattle, and I was in Los Angeles. End of discussion. I closed my eyes.

As I said, let sleeping dogs lie.

51

Sometime later, a nudge sent a surprising tingle down my spine. *What was that?!*

I opened my eyes and looked straight into Felicity's.

Wait. Those tiny stars sparkling in there. I never noticed them before. Or how smooth and soft her brown fur is.

Some words shot through my brain: *Her dark hair is like the wing of a bird.*

As I stared at Felicity, I felt my insides melt like butter on those apple pancakes Dora used to make. I was so dazed that I almost missed what she was saying.

"Puppins, if the rest of us can help with searching for your past, just let us know. You'll have a lot of explorers to call into action."

Columbo raised his big head. "That's right," he wheezed sleepily. "The great tracking team of ... Columbo ... Oglala Sue and ... and Custard ... will ... be at your service ..." His eyes closed again.

Aargh. They were ganging up on me. Was this some kind of conspiracy?

***

Later, when I was pretty sure Felicity and the others were asleep, I got up and shuffled out the pet door. My bombed-out brain needed a hit of fresh air.

Crumpling down by the fountain, I tried to sort out all of the things I'd been dealing with.

First, Ruby: Apparently I made a bad choice when I

fell for her. But after all, aren't I a teenager? Don't bad choices come with the territory? Aren't they just speed bumps on the road to becoming a fully functioning adult dog?

Unfortunately, that raised a new question. Were there a lot more bad choices lurking just around the corner? Aargh.

Then I had a genius thought. As soon as my next birthday rolled around, BOOM! I'd instantly be seven years older, no longer in my teens. Problem solved!

Next: That quest thing. Why was everyone hounding me (excuse the expression) about it? Hadn't I already paid my dues?

Maybe if I laid low, which comes naturally to me, the Tribe's compulsion to send me off on another adventure (or near-death episode) would blow over.

Worth a try. Okay. Quest problem practically solved. On to the hard one: Felicity. Why was she suddenly so ... And why did I get those tingles ...

I didn't want to go there. Too confusing. Maybe it was part of the overall *Teenage Effect*. If so, when my birthday came around it would automatically resolve itself.

Uh oh. I had no idea when my birthday was. I guess the only way I'd know was if I suddenly felt mature.

***

Sorting out the stuff in my brain was a messy business. Kind of like trying to separate the meatballs out of a plateful of spaghetti before wolfing it down.

I needed help. I gazed up through the leaves of the fig tree. Were there any stars up there that I could call on?

Kristin says there's always billions of stars in the night sky, but L.A. city lights make them hard to see. This night, there was only one: the super-bright star she calls Venus.

Actually, according to her, Venus is not a star at all. It's a planet, whatever that is. Still, if it's the only thing in sight when she comes out with me at bedtime, she makes a wish on it.

First, she says the magic words: "I wish I may, I wish I might, have the wish I wish tonight." Then she screws up her face, which I guess means she's concentrating, and makes a wish. She never says the wish out loud, because apparently that's like a curse and the wish won't come true.

I was ready to try it. I wrinkled up my muzzle, squinted my eyes at Venus, said the magic words and made my wish: "I wish I knew what's next for me. I wish I could just stay here and be an ordinary black Lab, and not get mixed up in another so-called quest. Or, in any inscrutable love stuff. Thank you. Have a good evening."

Hmmm. Maybe it was too long, too complicated. But at least I didn't say it out loud.

I wondered what Venus was thinking about it. "Hey, Venus!" I ventured. "Will my wish come true?"

Venus, a.k.a. the Wishing Star, did not answer. After a while, I closed my eyes and went to sleep.

***

Sometime later, PLOP! A ball of fur dropped on my head from the tree above.

Guess who.

"What do you think you're doing, bozo!" I snapped, giving my head a violent shake that sent him flying.

He was not fazed.

"Puppins! I heard what they were saying in there," he called out, bounding back to me. "Hoooeee! I just want to make sure ..." he paused dramatically.

"Of what, cat face?" I growled.

"That when you go on that adventure, you'll take me

along! Without me, you'd probably get lost. By the way, you aren't going to chase any females this time, are you?"

"Go back inside, you little monster!" I howled.

Felicity laughed. She'd come outside and was trotting toward us.

"Shh," she said to me. "You'll wake up the others. Oliver, it's late. Go inside and go to sleep. I want to talk to Puppins."

"Oh, all right," he grumbled. He sauntered back to the Carriage House as slow as he possibly could. So maddening. (He's still my best buddy, though.)

Felicity settled down under the tree. We were quiet for a while. Then she said, "Puppins, you don't need to answer that question I asked you earlier, about whether you are over Ruby. I think maybe you are, since you didn't go off with her tonight. Anyway, if you are, I'm really glad."

Oh my god. She was way too direct for me, as usual. Are boys always more dense than girls about this stuff?

I managed to stutter a reply of sorts: "Yeah ... I mean no ... I mean ... you know what I mean."

She laughed again. "Yes, I think I do. And Puppins, there's something else. About that quest. If you ever do figure out a way to uncover your past, I'll help you. I said that before, but I just want you to know that I really mean it."

"It's not going to happen, Felicity," I said, "but if it ever did, well, I ... I'd want you along for the ride."

Clumsy, but the best I could do.

She snuggled up close, and that tingling thing went through me again. Wow. Ruby made my skin itch; this was so much better.

***

We listened to the night wind rattling the palm fronds. It was an L.A. kind of lullaby, but I could not go to sleep.

What was happening with me and Felicity? She was just a friend, wasn't she? And who was she, really?

Suddenly, my brain's inner big screen went into hi-def and some new words showed up: *She rides the blue sapphire mountains, wearing moonstones for slippers.*

That's Felicity, I thought. Riding the deep blue mountains. Well, anyway, trudging up the foothills with her crippled leg, like she did on the way to Puppy Haven. Maybe she only wore sprinkler drops on her paws, not moonstones, but she really was kind of beautiful.

Wait. Was I on the verge of another epic crush, or what?

I thought about how Jodi says I have a Velcro heart. I know about Velcro because it's the way my collar stays on. But for the first time, I realized that it takes two parts to work, not just one.

Obviously, I had the "attacher" piece. Did Felicity have an "attachee" part, while Ruby did not?

Aargh. Once again, I was in over my head. It probably was going to take a while to figure out the Velcro thing.

Still, Felicity and I did have a history. We took on the dogfight ring and the puppy mill together, didn't we? Could we be a real team someday, like Sue and Columbo?

If so, and if I ever could find a way to go on that quest, maybe she really would help me discover who I used to be. Before I was me, Puppins.

***

Kristin and Jodi came to get me. I said goodnight to Felicity and gave her a quick nuzzle on the nose.

Was this the new me? Cool.

Kristin and I walked Jodi to her car. The winter moon made a golden trail over the dark San Gabriels; all was silent, all was calm, all was bright. Just like in that Christmas song the guests sang earlier.

"Isn't this a gorgeous night?" Kristin asked dreamily.

Jodi laughed. "It is. And you sound like someone in love."

Too dark to see if Kristin blushed. But she didn't deny what Jodi said, and I wondered: Was she in love? Was this priest guy going to stir up our lives? If so, would it be in a good way, or would I be forced to go into my dormant protective mode?

While Kristin was still gazing at the moon, Jodi held out a white frosted reindeer with a red-hot candy nose and little silver balls for a harness. I admired it for a nano-second, then gulped it down.

Jodi took my head in her hands and peered into my eyes. "Puppins, there's nothing in that big head of yours, is there? You have no brain. But never mind. We love you anyway."

"Yes," Kristin said fondly, stroking my ears. "We love you, Puppins, just the way you are."

Harsh. They still thought I had no brain. But that's okay. I licked their faces and wagged my tail to show that I loved them too, despite their multiple imperfections.

Then it dawned on me. It didn't really matter who my first owners were. I had a real family now. Kristin was my mom, Jodi my aunt, and the Tribe my sibs.

Wait. What about a father figure? Father Nicholas? Aargh. I'm not going there. Anyway, the rest of us had adopted each other, flaws and all, and it was good.

I even had a grandma -- Miss W. What more could anyone want?

EPILOGUE

Well, that's my story, so far. I hope Mariah thinks I've done okay as a newbie storyteller.

But wait. Doesn't she say that a good story should have a moral? Yikes -- I don't have a clue what the moral of my story is, or even if it has one.

Hold on. Some words are rising to the top of my brain: *Everything's got a moral, if only you can find it.*

If only.

Suddenly a bunch of new words flash on and off in my brain, like that sign at Yin's Donut: *What is it you plan to do with your one wild and precious life?*

Whoa. That's a really big question. It's going to take an awfully long time to answer that.

In the meantime, things will be cool with Kristin in La Casa Royale, and I'll have a ball with my pack in the Carriage House. And maybe, when I'm no longer grounded, I'll ask Felicity out on a date.

We'll revisit some of the classier garbage cans we frequented when we were on the streets. Maybe I'll get really brave and kiss her on the mouth, like people do in those movies Kristin watches.

Whew. It makes me sweat just to think about it. Anyway, I can hardly wait to see what comes next.

Wait. Another bomb is going off in my brain: *We'll live and pray and sing, and tell old tales, and laugh at gilded butterflies, and take upon us the mystery of things, as if we were God's spies.*

Spies? Oh yeah. Oliver's going to love that one.

THE END

POSTSCRIPT: Fact and Fiction

Once upon a time in Los Angeles, there really was a rescued black Labrador retriever named Puppins, who had a crush on a real Irish setter named Ruby, who truly was untamed. Oliver and his feral cat family actually lived under a vintage house known as The Cottage; and a band of roving green parakeets did, in fact, raid the front-yard carob tree every afternoon.

All remaining events and characters (human and otherwise) portrayed in **Gone Dog** are entirely fictional. As for the backyard shelter Kristin runs, such open-door neighborhood shelters probably don't exist in real life, but perhaps they should.

It's a fact that dogfight rings are common in some areas of the United States, and puppy mills are a problem nationwide. And, as barbaric as it seems, kill shelters are still the norm throughout our country.

A few states, including California, outlaw sales of puppy mill dogs to pet stores, requiring such stores to sell only rescued animals. Many individuals and organizations work tirelessly to shut down puppy mills and dogfight operations; to establish no-kill shelters; and to find new forever homes for lost and abandoned pets. **Gone Dog** is dedicated to all of them, as well as to the countless skilled veterinarians who help animals every day – including the author's daughter, Dr. Bonny Westlake, who saved the life of the real Puppins. This book is also dedicated to Helen Westlake, the author's first reader and most valued critic.

PUPPINS' BRAIN BOMB CITATIONS

Part One

Title Page
"We tell ourselves stories in order to live." – Joan Didion, *Collected Nonfiction* (Everyman's Library 2006)

"Things are not untrue just because they never happened." -- Dennis Hamley, *Hare's Choice* (Delacorte 1988)

"There's no one thing that's true. It's all true." – Ernest Hemingway, *For Whom the Bell Tolls* (Charles Scribner's Sons 1968)

Chapter 1
(Call me Puppins): "Call me Ishmael." – Herman Melville, *Moby Dick* (Wordsworth Editions Ltd. 1999)

Chapter 3
"The only people for me are the mad ones, the ones who are mad to live, mad to talk, mad to be saved, desirous of everything at the same time, the ones who ... burn, burn, burn like fabulous yellow roman candles exploding like spiders across the stars." -- Jack Kerouac, *On the Road* (Penguin Great Books 1999)

Chapter 4
"Ruby, Don't Take Your Love to Town" – Mel Tillis (1967)

"Born Free, As Free as the Wind Blows" – Don Black (1966)

"Neither have they hearts to stay, nor wit enough to run away." -- Samuel Butler, *Hudibras* (Palala Press 2016)

Chapter 7
"I, a stranger and afraid, in a world I never made ..." -- A.E. Housman, *Last Poems, No. 12* (Henry Holt & Co. 1940)

"Love, nightmare-like, lies heavy on my chest, and weaves itself into my midnight slumbers." -- William S. Gilbert, *Iolanthe* (G. Schirmer 1986)

Chapter 8
"Happiness to a dog is what lies on the other side of a door." -- Charlton Ogburn Jr. (izquotes.com)

Chapter 9
"My version of a triathlon is a donut, a pizza, and a hot fudge sundae." -- Charles Schultz, *Snoopy; Peanuts Treasury* (MetroBooks 2000)

"She walks in beauty like the night." -- Lord Byron, *The Golden Treasury* (Francis T. Palgrave, ed. 1875)

Chapter 11
"Bare feet allowed. Dogs and cats allowed. The sun, the stars, and the evening wind allowed." (author unknown)

"Heaven is a house with porch lights." -- Ray Bradbury, *Switch on the Light* (Pantheon Books 1955)

Chapter 12
"All happiness depends on a leisurely breakfast." -- John Gunther (goodreads.com)

Chapter 13
"let's touch the sky with a great (and a gay and a steep) deep rush through amazing day" – e e cummings, *95 Poems, 'if up's the word'* (Liveright 2002)

"How sad and bad and mad it was, but then how it was sweet." -- Robert Browning, *On Pauline: A Fragment of a Confession* (British Library 2010)

Chapter 14
"Everyone is a moon and has a dark side which he never shows to anybody." -- Mark Twain, *Following the Equator, Part III* (FQ Books 2010)

Chapter 15
"The heart has its reasons, which reason cannot know." -- Blaise Pascal, *Pensees, No. 326* (Penguin Classics 1995)

Chapter 16
"Safety is all well and good, but I prefer freedom." -- E.B. White, *The Trumpet of the Swan* (Harper Trophy 1973)

Chapter 17
"Oh, the house of denial has thick walls and very small windows, and whoever lives there, little by little, will turn to stone." -- Mary Oliver, *A Thousand Mornings, 'Hum Hum'* (Penguin Press 2012)

Chapter 18
"Numbing the pain for a while will make it worse when you finally feel it." -- J.K. Rowling, *Harry Potter and the Goblet of Fire* (Scholastic 2002)

Chapter 20
"To die will be an awfully big adventure." -- James M. Barrie, *Peter Pan* (Kingman Books 2016)

Chapter 21
"A cheerful heart is good medicine, but a crushed spirit dries up the bones." -- *Proverbs 17:22, New International Version Bible* (Tyndale House Publishers 2004)

"It's over, and it can't be helped, and that's one consolation, as they always say in Turkey when they chop the wrong man's head off." -- Charles Dickens, *The Pickwick Papers* (Wordsworth Classics 1998)

"The sun hung like a stone, time dripped away like a steaming river." -- Mary Oliver, *House of Lights, 'Indonesia'* (Beacon Press 1990)

"Love, passionate love, was his for the first time." -- Jack London, *The Call of the Wild* (Puffin Classics 2008)

Chapter 24
"To fear is one thing. To let fear grab you by the tail and swing you around is another." -- Katherine Paterson, *Jacob Have I Loved* (HarperCollins 2003)

Chapter 26
"around me surges a miracle of unceasing birth and glory and death and resurrection; over my sleeping self float flaming symbols of hope, & i wake to a perfect patience of mountains" – e e cummings, *95 Poems, 'i am a little church (no great cathedral)'* (Liveright 2002)

Chapter 29
"Life is either a daring adventure or nothing at all." -- Helen Keller, *The Open Door* (Doubleday 1957)

Chapter 30
"They also serve who only stand and wait." -- John Milton, *John Milton's Complete Works, 'On My Blindness'* (Everlasting Flames 2013)

Chapter 31
"It's such a secret place, the land of tears." -- Antoine de Saint-Exupery, *The Little Prince* (Harcourt, Brace & Co. 1982)

Chapter 32
"Bare feet allowed ..." -- op cit.

Chapter 33
"When spider webs unite, they can tie up a lion." – *Ethiopian Proverbs* (CreateSpace 2016)

Chapter 34
"It is one of the blessings of old friends that you can be stupid with them." -- Ralph Waldo Emerson, *The Journals of Ralph Waldo Emerson* (The Modern Library 1960)

"Heaven is a house with porch lights." -- Bradbury, op cit.

Part Two

Title Page
"This is the lesson: never give in, never give in, never, never, never, never – in nothing, great or small, except to convictions of honor and good sense." – Winston Churchill, *Harrow School Speech* (New York Times, Oct. 29, 1941)

"But ask the animals and they will teach you, or the birds and they will tell you..." – *Job 12:7, New International Version Bible* (Tyndale House Publishers 2004)

Chapter 35
"The fog comes in on little cat feet. It sits over harbor and city on silent haunches, then moves on." – Carl Sandburg, *Modern American Poetry, 'Chicago Poems'* (Louis Untermeyer, ed. 1919)

Chapter 35 (cont'd)
"But what in this world is perfect?" – Mary Oliver, *The Ponds, 'House of Light'* (Beacon Press 1990)

Chapter 38
"I want ... to cast aside the weight of facts, and maybe even to float a little above this difficult world." – Mary Oliver, *The Ponds, op cit.*

"In the arithmetic of love, one plus one equals everything, and two minus one equals nothing." -- Mignon McLaughlin, *The Second Neurotic's Notebook* (Bobbs Merrill 1966)

"I have always depended on the kindness of strangers." – Tennessee Williams, *Streetcar Named Desire* (New Directions 2004)

Chapter 39
"The only people for me are the mad ones ..." -- Kerouac, op cit.

"It does not do to dwell on dreams and forget to live." – J.K. Rowling, *Harry Potter and the Sorcerer's Stone* (Scholastic 1999)

Chapter 42
"around me surges a miracle ..." cummings, *95 Poems*, op cit.

Chapter 44
"It is only with the heart that one can see rightly; what is essential is invisible to the eye." – Antoine de Saint Exupery, *The Little Prince* (Harvest 1971)

Chapter 45
"Success is not final; failure is not fatal: it is the courage to continue that counts." – Winston Churchill, *Churchill By Himself* (Richard Longworth, ed. PublicAffairs 2011)

"When spider webs unite ..." -- Ethiopian Proverbs, op cit.

Chapter 47
"We should not forget to entertain strangers, lest we entertain angels unaware." -- *Hebrews 13:2, New International Version Bible* (Tyndale House Publishers 2004)

Chapter 47 (cont'd)
"All God's angels come to us disguised." -- James Russell Lowell, *The Complete Poetical Works of James Russell Lowell (Forgotten Books 2012)*

Chapter 49
"As a white candle in a holy place, so is the beauty of an aged face." – Joseph Campbell, *Modern British Poetry, 'The Old Woman'* (Louis Untermeyer, ed. 1920)

"Every day you don't forgive, it's as if you are ingesting tiny bits of poison." – Dr. Harold Bloomfield, *How to Survive the Loss of a Love* (Prelude Press 1993)

Chapter 50
"Only connect. Only connect ... and human love will be seen at its height. Live in fragments no longer." -- E. M. Forster, *Howards End* (Dover Publications 2002)

"by that miracle which is the coming of pure joyful your fearless and complete love, all safely small big wickedly worlds or world disappear." – e e cummings, *95 Poems,* op cit.

"Her dark hair is like the wing of a bird ..." – Mary Oliver, *House of Light, 'Singapore'* (Beacon Press 1990)

Chapter 51
"Riding the blue sapphire mountains, wearing moonstones for slippers..." -- Vinaya Chaitanya, *Songs for Siva: Vacanas of Akka Mahadevi (*HarperCollins India 2017)

"Everything's got a moral, if only you can find it." -- Lewis Carroll, *Alice's Adventures in Wonderland* (Penguin Classics, 2009)

"Tell me, what is it you plan to do with your one wild and precious life?" – Mary Oliver, *House of Light, 'The Summer Day'* (Beacon 1990)

"We'll live, and pray, and sing, and tell old tales, and laugh at gilded butterflies ... and take upon us the mystery of things, as if we were God's spies." -- William Shakespeare, *King Lear, Act V Scene 3* (Simon & Schuster 2004)

ABOUT THE AUTHOR

Carol Angel has raised a family, practiced law, worked as a journalist, handled communications for a hospice agency, and assisted in the front office of her daughter's veterinary clinic. She has walked dogs at Best Friends Animal Sanctuary in Utah; visited patients with her little dog Laddie at Hope Hospice in Florida; and volunteered at Marin Humane in the Bay Area, where she currently resides.

CONTACT INFORMATION

Website and Blog: carolaustinangel.com
Twitter: twitter.com/puppinsthelab

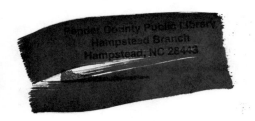

CPSIA information can be obtained
at www.ICGtesting.com
Printed in the USA
LVHW03s1444071018
592736LV00008B/258/P

9 780999 695203